THE DEVIL'S COLONY

MARIE LESTRANGE

This book is for entertainment purposes only.

Printed in Oliver Springs, Tennessee, United States of America

Description: Crimson Cult Media, 2025 | Audience. Adult. | Summary: The Lost Colony of Roanoke with Witches.

Ebook ISBN: 979-8-89467-026-3

Hardcover ISBN: 979-8-89467-024-9

Paperback ISBN: 979-8-89467-025-6

CONTENTS

I

WARNING

In high summer, 1587, English settlers arrived on an island of what is now known as coastal North Carolina. As the harsh winter came, John White, Governor of the new colony, travelled back to England for desperately needed provisions. Upon his return to the new world three years later, smoke wafted from the island trees, yet no trace of the colonists remained. Historians have searched for an explanation of the disappearance of the 117 men, women, and children of the Roanoke colony, yet none had an answer.

Until now.

The following journal entries were found among the scattered remains of the abandoned settlement. These excerpts of first-hand accounts from Roanoke Colony are quite graphic, and at times, disturbing. If subject matter pertaining to violence, witchcraft, or sexual content upsets you—heed this warning.

2

CROATOAN: THE END

ANANIAS DARE - AUGUST 1590

The prophet's words echoed in Ananias's mind, ringing loudly but not enough to drown out the hysterical screams of those left unburned.

"Son of man, I have made thee a watchman unto the house of Israel: therefore hear the word at my mouth, and give them warning from me. When I shall say unto the wicked, Thou shalt surely die, and thou givest not him warning, nor speakest to admonish the wicked of his wicked way, that he may live..."

He may live.

"...the same wicked man shall die in his iniquity: but his blood will I require at thine hand. Yet, if thou warn the wicked, and he turn not from his wickedness, nor from his wicked way, he shall die in his iniquity, but thou hast delivered thy soul."

Even to his last, he must not allow the knowledge of their disappearance to crumble in the ashes left behind. Those that return, whenever they do, must know the fate of the Roanoke Colony.

"Give them a warning..."

Somehow, he would tell them.

Ananias searched the surrounding woods, palms pressed together in prayer, blood trickling down his wrists. Surely, with the weight of his sins, God had abandoned him, neglected them all in their darkest of nights.

Yet, even in this final hour, Ananias prayed for a sliver of mercy upon his unworthy soul.

God, help him. Give him a way.

The scrap of paper, ripped from the Word not three nights ago still lingered in his pocket— but he had no quill.

What to use. How to write it. Ananias searched his person, desperate for an answer. He plunged his hand into the pocket concealed in his trousers and winced at the bite to his finger. Aye! He still had a knife, albeit small, often used for the skinning of rabbits and squirrels to provide for his family— but those days were gone. He'd forgotten it was there.

If only he had used it earlier.

Blood then? He could scrawl a word of warning on the scrap and pin it to the tree. Such abominable thoughts these were, to besmirch the words guided by the hand of God by writing on it with his own, but he must warn the others of their trials. The governor needed to know.

And yet, those that followed would have a better chance of reading it if he carved a warning into the tree.

Ananias turned, gathering what little strength survived in his body and limped to the gatepost, the forefront entry into their desolate colony. A colony that had become the ruins of hope for a new generation. Stabbing the tree, he set to carving.

God, giveth the time. Allow for him to atone for his sins, his mistakes, by leaving this message.

Shearing the bark proved a difficult task, the sticky sap mixing with his blood. The handle slipped from his grasp.

Damn this blade.

The effort pained his swollen fingers, but the crude letters were bold and legible once finished.

CROATOAN.

There was a chance this message would remain unseen. Governor White had all but abandoned them, as had England. But surely someone, someday, would find the bones of his fellow settlers, perhaps even his own, and make a connection as to what had happened here. He must carve as many as he could muster, further from the fire's spread on the large oak where his own family had rested on the Sabbath day when they first arrived. His heart jolted as bittersweet memories washed over him. His son's playful steps. The new babe, Virginia, first born in these lands, suckling at his wife's breast. Their daughter, Agnes, laughing and basking in the sun's warmth upon her face.

The blade faltered again, morality's weakness and pangs of sadness racking his soul as he desperately tried to prevail. How far they had fallen from those days.

With the last mark of the first "O" finished, he glanced behind at the smoke rising from the burning colony, the screams of his kindred still drifting in the wind.

Ananias turned back around... and her twisted face sneered at him from beside the tree.

He gasped, the knife slipping from his grasp, falling to the ground.

In this moment, staring into the eyes of hell itself, he stood still as stone.

God forgive him. Save him.

Hell hath no fury like the evil swirling in the black pits where once there had been a sparkling blue. He should run for safety, or fight back, but no power of God or man could move him from where he stood.

"Join me, Ananias," she purred.

3

THE NEW WORLD: THREE YEARS PRIOR

ANANIAS DARE - JULY 1587

"As nature doth persuade the leaves to change—a deepening of orange, yellow, and crimson red; so doth the wind extend her influence to rip each leaf from its home and carry it asunder. As leaves we cling to the branch. Hoping. Waiting. Changing. Yet when the wind begins her temptive whisper, growing in strength and wrenching us into the unknown, we must steady ourselves in the grace of God. For our sinful nature, and the wind that joins it, are similar to Lucifer's call. Temptation. We hold these truths tightly to the breast, for Lucifer's influence hath unfurled among our fellows that remain in England. God give us the morrow, that we might yet settle this land righteously within your vision, as the future of an English presence in the New World depends on it."

The rich, verdant shore crept closer to them now. Where once it was a pebble in the distance, moving about the horizon with each sway of the ship, the vast land of their new colony stretched before him as a promise. A promise for hope, freedom, and revival.

Ananias Dare surveyed their new home. Ahead, he caught a glimpse of the palisades, buried in the trees, their jagged shafts protecting the crude and abandoned colony homes of the previous settlement attempt from any and all manner of the ill-intentioned. England had tried in vain to tame these wildlands before, forming an outpost to intercept the Spaniards and their goods. But this journey was different. This colony was the beginning of a new world for the English.

Roanoke. Ananias smiled. He and his company were here to revive it.

It would be an arduous landing, evident from the late summer surf, but God desired that those upon the flagship Lyon of Chichester breathe life back into this colony. Their journey had been a fine one, starting with fair winds and weather for a time, and God had carried them through the more dangerous of times, against cross winds and many storms. As the cyprus and live oak trees clenched tightly to the soil, and the stones beckoned him to step earthward, Ananias drew breath and meditated on the goodness of God and his forgiveness.

This was his chance, an opportunity to right his wrongs and be the husband and father he achingly wanted to be. It was his moment to live up to the reputation that surrounded him, one he hadn't truly earned but desperately yearned for. Just as their intentions as a whole were to breathe life back into this forgotten colony, he could set himself upon a new path of righteousness, of servitude, placing God at the centre of their lives once again.

This small island covered in trees was not their beloved England beyond the sea. England could not serve as home anymore. His days as a bricklayer, comfortable but not steeped in the vanity of wealth, were behind him. T'was in England that sin ran unbridled and the Church of England did little to burn it out, hence the catalyst of their voyage. Truth be told, most back in England celebrated the journey, glad to be rid of those with pure intentions to live an untainted life in the eyes of God. They thought them simple. Unrefined. Buried beneath outdated and rigorous customs the Church of England had all but abandoned in their daily worship. There were those back across the great sea that believed their chances at survival were all but nill, but he, and the others, were destined to prove them wrong.

Those heretics didn't understand the calling placed upon them, but God had made known the truth of it to him. He and his fellow planters would enjoy the means of grace, of plentiful opportunity here– the pioneers of a new way of life on this distant shore. They would root in this land as the trees do, clinging to the soil, rising out of it, growing strong to produce the fruit of the spirit. The truth shall prevail, and as their kindred have often been plagued by the trials Satan hath raised against them, they shall now claim a victory for God upon these new lands.

They were on a journey towards Heaven.

He glanced at his beloved wife; the woman who showed him far more patience than he deserved. With one glance, she had stolen his heart nearly eighteen years prior. Eleanor White, known now as Eleanor Dare. She clutched a thread-bare, wool blanket around her shoulders, her dress scarcely concealing the bulge of her belly underneath. Two months they'd been at sea, and the closer they came to the New World, the more evident it was that soon they would be joined by a new life, a child, likely the first of their number born in this strange, new world.

They'd already decided upon the name. A name befitting a child born soon after their maiden voyage– Virginia.

Eleanor parted the blanket to cling to one of his cold arms. She was a good wife, a strong wife. Ananias knew within his bones that he deserved her not, but God help him, he tried. If he allowed himself to slip out of righteousness again, in a moment of poor judgement, he knew her patience would find its limit. She lived true as a mother and as a Christian, and suffered not a weakness in her faith– unlike him. He strived daily to conduct himself more similarly to her manner.

The sun's heat fought valiantly to warm them but did little against the whipping chill of the sea breeze. Giant masts creaked and groaned as the wind pushed the sails of their ship onward. If he looked behind them, he would only see the vast ocean that separated him from all that he knew. The heat of his wife pressed close against him kept the bitter cold at bay, and yet he wished that he could bring about the same fire in her heart. Ananias sighed, squeezing tight around her shoulders. He had snuffed that fire out himself.

But this journey was their new beginning. Their chance to reignite their love for one another. The strings of her bosom were loose, revealing the birthmark he knew well. It was small, and faint, but how often in the marriage bed had he stared at that natural necklace as he– *arrgh*! The ship jolted as they rushed into the shallow waters, wrenching him from his lustful thoughts.

How quickly he slipped into sin.

"Laaand HO!" their captain, George Raymond, called.

Eleanor clutched his hands, a rare moment of excitement flashing as a bolt of lightning across her weathered face. The wind whipped at her auburn curls, as she glanced at him with a small, forced smile. Together they gazed at the shore, ready to root within the soil and meet the New World with a fresh start. This would be the rise of Roanoke.

4
FOR I AM WEAK, BUT HE IS STRONG

Eleanor Dare - October 1587

"*A*s I look upon the dewy faces of the sweetest gifts one can ever receive, I am reminded of what blessings have been bestowed upon me. A new life. A fresh start. Plentiful land on which to build our fledgling farm, in the pursuit of a life grounded in scripture and far removed from the ills of our former home across the great sea. I try, God help me, I try to look forward; to be thankful and absent of all malice and deceit so that I, and my blessed family, might grow in salvation.

I know in my own heart that when faced with the difficulties of our corrupted, human nature, we are never tempted beyond what we can bear. But...God forgive me, I ask for your remission as I am wrought with sin in the form of resentment towards my husband. As we learn in the fifth chapter of Job, 'doubtlesse anger killeth the foolish, and enui slayeth the idiote'. And I try, Lord, to strengthen myself so that I might guide my husband back into your forgiving arms. I seek ye, my God, to wrap our hearts in your love. I seek your counsel. But I also know, and worry so, that those who commiteth an adulterous deed of the flesh shall not inherit the kingdom of God.

I worry for his soul, for mine own, and the souls of the children. We make our way back into the light, and in the face of this new land and its hardships. 'Blessed is ye man, that endureth temptation: for when he is tried, he shall *receive the crown of life, which the Lord hath promised to them that love him.' In Jesus' sweet name I pray, Amen."*

Eleanor surveyed the humble beginnings of the homestead, rebuilt of their own sweat and blood over the past two months to make a home for she, her husband, their teenaged Agnes, little Henry of four years, and their newest babe, Virginia. While some buildings remained from Governor Lane's prior attempt at settlement, the crooked clapboards and browning thatch of their home were in desperate need of repair. In 1585, two years ago, Sir Walter Raleigh had intended for this land to be the first English settlement of the new world, led by the pompous and ill-witted Governor Ralph Lane. Poor provisions and even poorer relations with the natives of this land led to their eventual failure and return to England. Unsurprising, really, as one among them had stirred their settlement into revenge over one missing cup, which they assumed the natives had stolen. In retribution, Lane's men had burned the native village to the ground, and this was only one of the atrocious things they'd been told. No, after Lane's barbarics, they were unlikely to receive any help this time.

God would provide. She must thank him for any roof over their unworthy heads, and for the protection provided by the fort walls.

Above her, rolling clouds of grey cast a dim, yet calm, shadow upon their small bit of overgrown land, squeezed between their fellow settlers both to the left and right. A distant rumble, one that reminded her of the ever-present misgivings uttered by their eldest daughter, Agnes Rose, spoke to her of a coming storm. The goats needed fresh bedding, the chickens must be fed, and the washing on the line flapped in the growing wind as if waving to her as a reminder of needed attention.

Beyond the line she stole a glimpse toward the Tilley family, whose homestead bordered theirs. Alice Tilley, their neighbour both in England

and here in the wilds, rushed about to herd her boys into their home before the storm.

Eleanor's own beloved son Henry, swayed about her skirts as he sang a song for the coming rain.

"Momma! Momma! I fink it's going to rain on us!"

She knew she shouldn't, but her eyes lingered as Alice sank into the arms of her husband and kissed him tenderly. They were two drops of rain melting into one.

Envy was a sin. She *must* tear her eyes away and not intrude, for further watching would allow for bitterness to crawl into her heart at the sight of their love.

Ananias had often kissed her like that, prior to...the betrayal.

She wondered if he had kissed his whore in that way, in the way he kissed her. She thought of his lips, his strong, rough hands. A barrage of unwanted images flashed in her mind. Did he caress her cheek? Did his plump lips kiss her upon the brow as he had so often kissed her? Did Ananias hold the woman about the waist as he had his way?

Consumed in her thoughts, Eleanor hardly noticed the small droplets of cold rain as they bit at her skin. These were the intrusive thoughts she had each time Ananias reached for her in the marriage bed, begging for an opportunity to make things "right". As if a renewed connection of a physical nature could wash away the stubborn stain of sin.

What would have happened had she not discovered she was with child before learning of his betrayal?

"Likewise let the wives be subject to their husbands, that even they which obey not the word, may without the word be won..."

"Momma!" Henry tugged at her skirts.

Torn from the visions, Eleanor turned her attention to the twinkling gaze of her dear son. These sweet eyes of pine forest green had seen so little of life, but in their journey had witnessed a great deal more than many back home. He had loved the adventure of coming to the new world, and it pained her heart that it was not gold and rich soil that greeted him here, but rather cold hardship and uncertainty.

Enough with such thoughts. God would see them through.

She wrapped little Henry into her outstretched arms, the warmth and love within his embrace melting the frost that had so quickly enfolded her heart. She must strengthen her resolve in prayers to their Lord. For Henry. For Agnes. For the new babe Virginia, born only weeks ago. God had blessed her beyond compare with the health and strong countenance possessed by their children. Ananias was a loving father...a good father, and had always led their family into the light and back into the Word in times of distress.

Little Henry's hugs were good for her soul. They calmed her. Soothed her. His unblemished love reminded her of what she had, in this moment, and to shed all envious thoughts of what she hadn't. His dough-like cheeks fit perfectly within her cupped hands, and she wrinkled her rain-slick nose against his.

She invited him to join her in bringing the linens in from the line. There'd be no sense in leaving them out to rewet in the rain. She made it a game, tossing the sheets on top of Henry in a large heap until he nearly fell over.

What joy did his laughter bring, sweeter than any honey and medicine for the soul.

She gathered the linens from him. "Time to go inside, sweet boy. We will catch a chill in this rain should we stay."

As she followed her fair-headed son through the doorway of their home, she saw the slender silhouette of Agnes Rose beside the fire, cradling their newly born Virginia in her arms. Sweet Agnes, always sure to complete her chores, but Eleanor knew this journey had been a hard one for her to make.

"Mother, I've set a venison stew upon the fire whilst Virginia was asleep. I thought we might make a fresh loaf of bread to pair with it." Agnes smiled, but as usual, Eleanor wasn't sure the tight-lipped grin met her eyes.

Thunder rumbled as the rain fell harder. Little Henry ran to her and clutched at her skirts once more.

"The funder scares me, Momma."

She crossed the room and pulled out a small bundle of sticks, tying it with a cord in the shape of a star.

"There, my little love." Eleanor placed the star in his soft, pudgy hands. "When the clouds clear, and the stars shine bright, we will thank the Lord for bringing peace to us in the storm." Henry grinned.

A small leak in the furthest corner dripped with a chime into the milk pail.

Milk.

The goats.

"Oh no! I've forgotten the goats and chickens..." Eleanor spun to race outside, yet Ananias entered.

He placed his hat on the spare nail beside the door. "No need, my love. I've done it."

There was a mischievous glint in his eyes, appropriately matched by the sly grin splashed across his whiskered face.

"No?" She raised her eyebrows.

From behind his back, Ananias produced a melon twice the size of Virginia; its orange flesh no doubt concealing a new treat inside.

"Father, what on earth?" Agnes Rose leapt to her feet, making her way across the room to examine their newest crop.

Ananias met her at the table, placing the melon down by the crooked stem on top. He chuckled.

"Remember the vines we discovered upon landing? That grew among the larger buildings near the edge of the fort? These aren't melons at all! I'm told they're called "pumpkins," a type of squash, they say."

In all her days in England, Eleanor had never seen such a squash, but was glad to see it now.

"Is it edible? Has someone confirmed the taste?" Some of the plants they'd come across on Roanoke Island were foreign to them, and consuming unknown foods was a dangerous game to play in the wilds– even as hungry as they usually were.

But it would be nice to prepare something other than stew and potatoes, for once.

Ananias cut around the stem, revealing a stringy flesh and plentifully seeded mixture inside.

"Why yes...yes it is edible. Mary Winthrop and her daughter even used one to bake into a pie!" The sparkle in his eyes softened her heart. This was the man she fell in love with all those years ago, the one who lived for surprises and sweet gestures, who carried her across the muddy street, and the one who warmed milk for her to soothe a sore throat. She cherished that man, the husband that hardly showed himself anymore, hidden behind the stern, serious presence that greeted them every day.

Ananias continued, carving and slicing with excitement. "We can roast the seeds and dry some for a future planting. The flesh can be used to make all sorts of things."

Eleanor lifted the sleeping Virginia from her eldest daughter's arms. "We must thank our Lord for this blessing."

Ananias smiled. His eyes met hers yet again. Come back to me, husband.

"Let us pray."

5

FOR THE ONE WHO DOUBTS

AGNES ROSE DARE - AUGUST 1587

"*Dearest Lord, I come to thee in fervent prayer for the misgivings and wicked thoughts that enter my heart. For I am of an awareness that you know all, but feel I must confess my sins and ask for a cleansing in which to make whole again. My thoughts have turned wicked, allowing resentment towards Mother and Father for bringing our family to this wild land. I have idled in my work, pausing often during tasks so as not to rush into the next one out of selfishness. I have yearned for the worldly pleasures I had grown accustomed to in England, and for pleasures unbecoming of one unmarried. I catch my thoughts turning to butter and plentiful sweet cakes, forgetting my thankfulness for your grace, as is my sinful nature. I know I am not worthy, and my sins only maketh my path to the hell-fire straighter, but I humbly beg for your correction in my ways. Lead me not into temptation, as I have lustful thoughts when meeting Jonathan at the gate, for he hath brought me a blooming flower yesterday. 'Twas a symbol of our blooming love, but this I have hidden away as a secret from Mother and Father. Deliver me from evil, as I worry about the whispers in the woods that Emme spoke of. Women of wicked intentions, she says, that the New World hides those we learn of in Exodus and Leviticus. For thine is the Kingdom, and the power, and the glory. Amen.*"

Spectral rays shone down from a full buck moon, anchoring it between a latticework of leaves and branches to rest upon the forest floor in front of her. Agnes trembled as the cool breeze licked at the nape of her exposed neck, and held the linen coif Jonathan had whisked from her hair just moments ago.

He trailed sweet kisses from her throat to the collar of her shift. A soft moan escaped her lips, but she was careful to keep quiet so none would hear them. Surely they wouldn't, as it was deep into the evening, and they had escaped far enough into the woods. She'd known this spot from gathering berries and chickweed earlier in the day.

Yet, even this deep within the woods, she heard no signs of animals at all– but that could be the ale they'd had earlier dulling her senses.

Fornication was a sin, but stolen whispers and soft kisses were hardly that... she hoped. Fornicators would have their place in the lake that burned with fire and brimstone, yet she wanted a taste of the treat without fully devouring it. Agnes placed her hands on either side of Jon's smooth, dimpled face, and looked up to stare into his grey eyes, to trace the line of his lower lip with her thumb. He leaned in, bringing his soft lips to hers, and she was instantly consumed.

They melted together, sinking further into lust with each quickened breath. He pulled her closer, and she happily obliged by pushing her hips upward into his.

They were dancing into dangerous territory now. Whispers of scripture and lectures on purity in the Reverend's voice echoed in the farthest corners of her mind, but at this moment she cared not. Jonathan loved her, and she him. Their hearts had grown inseparable since the soft, private conversations they had stolen with each other on the crossing from England.

She drank in the euphoric sensations of love and lust and sin. How could this be unnatural? Soon they would wed in the eyes of God and could begin their life together as one, so coming together in this way surely wasn't as grievous as they were told. Surely.

His strong hands felt good around her waist, one moving to shift her dress further down the shoulder, exposing her skin to the cool, night air. She leaned away, coaxing him to kiss her on the neck again, opened her eyes....and that was when she saw her.

A woman.

Standing among the shadows beyond, a pale face illuminated by the light of the moon, eyes black as night, a wicked sneer playing about the woman's snarled lips.

A witch.

Agnes sucked in a sharp breath, the ice of it hurting her lungs. She had no way of knowing what this was, but her friend Emme's words rang strong in her mind. *For rebellion is as the sin of witchcraft.* Agnes stepped away from Jonathan only to rush back and cling to him for safety. Was this their punishment? Were they to be used in a witch's potion, a work of devilry?

Surely God had nothing to do with this.

"What is it, beloved?" Jonathan's brow furrowed into deep creases as he frowned, his words cutting through the silent forest. "Have I fallen too far within lust?" His eyes were pleading, fearful of her sudden withdrawal.

The witch moved closer, slowly striding or gliding, but in the faint glow of night Agnes Rose could scarcely tell.

She wrenched him around to face what she saw. Jonathan started, then shielded her behind him with his arms.

"What say you!" He reached for a short, broken limb. "What manner of Devilry is this? Speak your name, watcher. You shall not claim us!"

There was no doubt this woman was not of God, or human form, as her soulless eyes were but two glassy orbs– like that of a raven.

"Our Father, who art in Heaven,

Hallowed be thy name."

Her whispered words did more to settle her frantically beating heart than actually cry for spiritual help. In the forest, in the dark of night and riddled with sin– God had forsaken them.

They were at the mercy of this witch.

Jonathan took one step closer, brandishing the broken branch in warning.

Her snarl warped into gritted teeth, long, crooked fingers bearing nails dipped in black and as gnarled as the branches in the trees. She was gliding closer... close enough that Jonathan pushed her on. "Run, Agnes! Flee from here and find safety in the trees!" She lifted her skirts and started to jog, the cold wind whipping past and blowing her hair. Jonathan was two steps behind, urging her onward in between prayers.

Suddenly, she stopped.

She was sure she had headed in the direction of the stream, the final marking point that let her know she would soon be free from the woods, but tonight, she had crested the small hill onto a clearing.

In the middle of the field, surrounded by a circle of erratically dancing women, stripped of all clothing, was a roaring bonfire. The flames stretched into the night sky, higher than the tallest tree she'd ever seen. Jonathan came to a halt beside her, panting. "I think we lost her." He glanced back to search for the one who chased them, but Agnes kept her eyes trained forward.

The bodies before them swirled and swayed in a ritual dance around the flames, their skin painted with unfamiliar black symbols, hair wild and free. Each woman looked of pristine beauty with perkish breasts and full, plump bodies. They had no wrinkles or white hair that Agnes could see. There was no doubt this was the work of the Devil.

But even as she watched the women dance and lustfully stroke each other, she was frightened further by the most obvious of mysteries— there was no sound.

A raven-haired woman with the same black eyes and ash smeared across her face beat her hands upon a drum made from pulled leather. Agnes wondered if the leather was human skin.

Lord, let that not be her fate this night.

They lifted their voices and arms to the moon, halting the dance and crying out in what she presumed to be an incantation– but still she couldn't hear it.

"Agnes, we *must* leave ..." Jonathan's words were stern, laced with fear.

As wicked and dangerous as she *knew* it was, something new and unbidden stirred within, pushing her footsteps closer.

The dance began again, but this time she could hear everything. The beat of the drum and guttural cries of the beautiful women invoked a primal awakening that shook Agnes to her bones.

This couldn't be evil. Something about this felt right.

A strong hand wrapped around her arm. "Agnes, enough. This is of the *Devil*!" His whispers were frantic now. "Please come away from this. Come home. Let us *GO!*"

Two women stood to the side, hoisting a white goat tied to a pole, bleating as it hung upside down. The witches circled and a blade appeared, as if out of nowhere, handed to the witch that had chased them through the trees.

With moaning and howling, the women crawled in a tight group, scrambling to kneel beneath the bleating goat. The witch with the blade stared straight into Agnes's eyes and in that moment... sliced the throat of their sacrifice.

The witches howled as one, drinking and showering in the blood of their kill, rubbing it across their skin, wiping crimson fingers on their faces, cupping the pouring blood and bringing it to their lips to drink it.

Agnes craved to taste the blood, to understand what these women knew.

But no. She couldn't. This wasn't right.

Unfamiliar but exhilarating temptation pushed Agnes further towards the bonfire, until she stepped into the ring of light cast by the flame, revealing herself.

The witches turned, their faces twisting sour and strange. The drumming stopped.

Stepping forward had been a mistake.

A low, singular hiss escaped from their lips as they crouched in their nakedness and chanted as they stepped closer. One woman threw a bowl full of the goat's blood onto the fire and with a sickening hiss, the flames turned black.

Screeching birds burst forth from the bonfire and flocked toward where she and Jonathan stood.

They had to get away. She clutched at his trembling hand as they ran, praying the witches weren't following. A bird swooped in from behind and violently pecked at them, screeching and pushing them onward.

As she had thought, *for the wages of sin is death*, God had abandoned them to die.

6

THE PLANTERS OF VIRGINIA

R oanoke Colonists' Appeal to John White

Late August, 1587

"May it please you, her Majesty's subjects of England, we your friends and country-men, the planters of Virginia, do by these presents let you and every one of you to understand, that for the present and speedy supply of certain our known and apparent lacks and needs, most requisite and necessary for the good and happie planting of us, or any other in this land of Virginia, wee all of one minde & consent, have most earnestly intreated, and incessantly requested John White, Governour of the planters in Virginia, to passe into England, for the better and more assured helpe, and setting forward of the aforesaid supplies: and knowing assuredly that he both can best, and will labour and take paines in that behalf for us all, and he not once, but often refusing it, for our sakes, and for the honour & maintenance of the action, hath at last, though much against his will, through our importunate, yielded to leave his government, and all his goods among us, and himself in all our behalves to pass into England, of whose knowledge and fidelity in handling this matter, as all others, we doe assure ourselves by these presents, and will you to give all credit thereunto, the 25 of August 1587."

The morning mist had all but cleared among the God-given sun this day. Fair weather, at least, for a journey which had come upon him so quickly. Governor White only hoped that God would part the waters with similar ease as the clouds opened up today. Upon the influence of fellow settlers of Roanoke Colony, it seemed there was a desperate need to exercise governance in making the crossing back to their former land across the sea.

He studied the worried faces of those surrounding the tattered map sprawled across their makeshift table. They had positioned themselves outside of the largest sundry house left behind by Ralph Lane's garrison one year prior.

"With little food, and questionable relations with the Roanoke Natives, we have no choice but to ask you to go." Ananias Dare crossed his arms, authority laced within his tone. John took notice of this small, but telling, act; to have demands be made of him by his son-in-law.

Eleanor whispered into Ananias's ear, placing a hand upon his arm as if to settle him. "We've none to blame but Lane for the diminished opportunities with the natives, for he was the one who murdered Wingina in his desperate attempt to exercise control over them." She turned to him with pleading eyes. "Father, I beg of you, consider the cost of staying the winter with what little provisions we brought with us. Think of your newest granddaughter, and see this as the opportune moment to do what is right by her." She wrapped his cold hands within hers. "For the sake of the colony."

Governor White sighed, his shoulders slumping further with each word, the weight of the world settling upon him. His daughter showed courage this day, of that he had no doubts. But, perhaps, did she speak with wisdom as well?

"Eleanor," he answered, "I cannot possibly sail back to England with the knowledge that I have left your family...nay, *my* family to the unknowns of the wilds alone." The few chickens they had managed to keep alive during their initial crossing pecked and clucked just a few feet away. They, too, expressed their piece about his returning to England.

He looked to Simon Fernandez, the Portuguese guide familiar with the area, hired by Sir Walter Raleigh to escort them to this new world filled with untold wonders and riches galore.

But it hadn't been riches and wonders they were met with after landing, only this Godforsaken land upon which they stood.

"You should stay, Simon…" Even as he uttered the words, lifting them with false persuasion in the hopes that he would protest a return entirely, he knew them not to be true.

Simon scoffed and collected the map with one grandiose swoop of his hand.

"Nonsense. We sail for England, to bring word of the Roanoke Island conditions and request back-up and supplies." He faced the governor with furrowed brows, their noses would be only inches apart but Simon was just a few hairs shorter. "Respectfully, *Governor,* you must do your duty to our Majesty Queen Elizabeth, and see to it that this attempt at settlement is a success."

Success.

Curious words from a privateer by trade, John thought. The demise of the fifteen men left behind before didn't seem to deter him in his quest to tame the wild beast that was the new world. His intentions rang with ire, chomping at the bit to resume the hunt for Spanish shipping vessels, with Roanoke as his port.

Eleanor spoke again. "Fear not, Father." She gestured to the Indian chief whom he had befriended during his stay in Britain. "We have Manteo with us. He will work to ease relations with the surrounding native tribes. They will help us in our time of need." She smiled at him. "Upon your return you shall find us a thriving colony, utterly grateful but hopefully without need for the provisions you will bring."

Such positive aspirations she had. Nonsensical, perhaps.

Manteo placed one fist upon his heart, the other opened the table. "This, I will do." Manteo met his gaze with fire in his eyes. "Go, now, Governor White. Fear not for your people and we will look for your return soon."

Two months to shore, then two months back again, this leaving the time it would take to gather provisions and new colonists to return with him. When word first reached him of the coming desire for him to sail again, he had demanded the settlers pen their request so that he might present the reasoning upon his arrival in England. He now had that request in hand. He'd only hoped, looking around at his daughter and her husband, that perhaps they would change their minds.

John sighed. "Look for me prior to the beginning of our newest year come March. I swear to thee, I will return."

"Aye, aye!" Fernandaz cheered. "Let us depart."

John knelt to little Henry, his grandson, presently clutching at his father Ananias's legs. He readied himself for one last embrace from all before he found himself again upon the sea. For even with planning, he hated the prospect of leaving them all behind.

Farewell to the new world. He would meet it again soon.

7
TO THRIVE

Jonathan Carver – September 1587

"The passing of time since the Governor and that Portuguese pirate set forth hath all but passed me by. I am unsure as to how long ago they left us, but God forgive me, I wish they had never gone. For on this day, and many days since the witching of the woods I witnessed with my beloved, I find myself seeking counsel again and fighting the urge to confess my sins to all that I have betrayed their trust. For they, my fellow settlers, most importantly the family whom I seek to join by marriage, think me a sinless man. A Godly man. But in my own heart I am troubled by the knowledge that this is farthest from the truth. As is our nature, and unceasingly known by all, we are as equals to Adam and Eve in our inescapable corruption and poisoned nature. But further beyond, I am unfaithful in my prayers and seek lustful intentions with my beloved, drawing her further away from the Lord as am I. They trust in me to help lead our begotten settlement, but how canst a man lead by example when, in secret, a man is tainted by the stains of sin? Upon returning to the Roanoke fort that night, my beloved Agnes and I conspired to keep the witches, which we knoweth to be true, a secret. And yet, I let our sworn Governor and guide sail away from us without a word of warning, in keeping my selfishness at the forefront, protecting mine own name, in the hopes that Ananias and Eleanor Dare would not learn of our lustful intentions within the wood. Have I endangered us all in keeping this secret? Doomed our colony to a fate unknown as we fight to survive? I tell myself that perhaps it had been *a dream, one which we somehow both had shared, but nay, I know in my own heart this can't be true. There is a wickedness within these woods, and I must seek forgiveness through self-examination and a strong effort to live a morally good life, that I might serve our Lord and bring us into his face once again. Look upon me, Lord. Know my sins. Punish me as thou wilt?, but I beg thee in thy unending grace to save the settlers from a similar fate."*

They could live here without provisions from England. Or at least, they would have to. A hard notion, but a truth that unceasingly presented itself in the passing days as settlers succumbed to scurvy and fevers in the night. Jonathan searched his home for the sugar cane fishing pole Mr. Dare had helped him make.

The rations of food would likely hold through the harshest of winters, looking forward to when Governor John White and Fernandez returned to the land. Jonathan surveyed the meagre portions bestowed to him. A hogshead of meal, a firkin of butter, six yards of cloth for the making and repairing of clothes. Most of the cattle survived, which allowed for equal shares between the families among us.

He thumbed the colourful wooden lure, brought along from England. The stained colouring was meant to look as if a minnow or crawdad swam just below the water's surface. He had spent much of the first few weeks on the island working with the other men to fortify and preserve the buildings left behind by Lane's men. Most of them were overgrown with melons by the time they had reached them, but the melons and strange orange squash provided many opportunities for variety in their diets. Squirrels, hogs, and deer roamed these parts, and with the proper hunt they would surely be able to cure enough meat for the winter to come. Strange, though, that Amandas and Barlowe had spoken of plentiful resources available to them in the new world, but failed to mention at what cost such resources came.

He gathered materials to form loop after loop, the longest of leaders attached to the fishing pole. Horsehair served as his line today, for it was known to be of the perfect density and stiffness to set about a strong fishing line.

If ever there would be a proper time to pass an offer of marriage to his beloved Agnes Rose, he would need a suitable home and plentiful resources with which to care for her and any future children they might have. Children could not be raised in the uncertain conditions at present, and he often wondered why Agnes's mother, Eleanor, had dared the trip—her being with child.

Agnes. Upon his decision to set out from his brother's home, breaking free from under his watchful eye, Jonathan had never expected to find himself taken within the heart so soon. He wanted to make a way for himself. A life. The New World's promises of riches and opportunity seemed too good an opportunity to pass up, and that promise lurked within him still. God forgive his selfish desires, but truly they, as a settlement, were here performing God's work. Coming to the new world meant an escape from the unbridled scourge allowed by the Church of England; providing them with a place to settle as God would have it.

Yet God had seen his sins. His lie. His lustfulness. His lack in daily prayer and devotion. If Jonathan were to see this settlement through, to step up and take the lead in providing nourishment and protection, he could humble himself and reclaim the path that led to the life of a righteous man.

He must renew his vigilance. Reclaim the strength in feelings he had when first departing from England. For Agnes. For the colony.

For God.

8

THE SPIRIT IS WILLING, BUT THE FLESH IS WEAK

Alice Tilley - Winter 1587

"*God forgive me, for on more than one occasion in the mind I have longed for a familiar connection with mine own married neighbour. It is that which my heart fervently desires, a salve for the open wound of the soul since my own husband has succumbed to the wilds. I am alone and with two boys who have yet to come of the age of assistance. To be a widow in the new world is a harsh fate, one I never expected when crossing the great sea, but alas, a fate I am owed for the sins of the heart and mind. I wish I could say that these envious thoughts were not of a frequent nature, forgive me, but even on more than one occasion during the great journey did I look to the crossness of Eleanor Dare, and envy her so. For she seemed unappreciative of Ananias's touch, or so said the distance she kept between them.*"

Alice peered from within her tiny sundry, settled next door to the home of Ananias and Eleanor Dare. Ananias's muscular arms tightened and released with each swing of the axe, chopping wood for her and the boys. Sweat ran down his brow, even with the chill outside. How kind he had been, how thoughtful, to take on the task of additional chores in order to help her survive. He swung the axe once more, tightly gripping the handle as he cleaved the wood in two. Even with both hands wrapped around his arm, she knew her fingers wouldn't touch.

She wanted him inside of her.

Ananias dropped the axe, exhaling a warm cloud of fog into the chilly winter morning. She brandished a water skin, offering to quench his thirst but secretly hoping to quench her own. The boys were still asleep, as the sun had hardly risen. She had only woken upon hearing his presence outside. His slow footsteps sounded upon the cold, hard ground. She shivered.

"Alice, I saw you watching me work again."

"Aye." She said, nearly breathless as he moved nearer.

"To what would thou look upon other than a lowly man chopping wood for the fire?" He reached for the water skin, the apple of his throat bobbing with each swallow.

"I see a great man in need of warmth, Ananias Dare." She closed the gap between them. She felt it. He must feel it too.

Ananias grunted. "I am no man of greatness." He wiped the water from his lips with the back of his strong hand. "I am sinful...and I am weak."

Dear God. He wanted her, too. "Suffer you a weakness of the flesh, Mr. Dare?"

As he bent slowly toward her, coming closer to her lips with his breath, his long whiskers tickled her face. She tingled. She could smell the sweat upon him and feel the warmth of each breath. He studied her, his brown eyes deciding.

Just as he reached her lips, he pinched his own. Ananias turned his face away and muttered, "Alice, I cannot."

She reached for his cheek and slowly turned it back towards her. The sun peeked over the horizon now, casting a soft orange glow upon them. If she stood on her tiptoes, she could barely reach him.

"Let me warm you, Ananias. Allow me to shower you with the tight, perkish gifts that a younger woman can offer." She clutched his hand in her own, guiding it down to the delicacies between her skirts. Even over cloth, the pressure from his strong hand excited her, thrilled her. She felt a slickness between her thighs.

Ananias groaned, temptation overtaking him. He sucked in a breath and smashed his whiskered face to hers. He parted her lips with his tongue, hungrily, forcibly pulling her closer to him.

It was just as she had thought it would be. Heated. Primal.

Perfect.

They stood in the doorway, hands making their way up and down each other's bodies, lips only parting to take a much needed breath.

Ananias started. "We must not be seen." He took her by the hand and, as she tingled down below, led her to the barn for goats and cattle. "If we shall do this. If we sip from the cup of temptative adulterous acts, we will not do so in the marriage bed. We lie among the goats upon the hay as the animals that we are." He turned to her. "Have your boys awoken?"

She smiled at him. "They have not. And yours?"

"None but Henry rises with the sun. But he is fine. I will hurry to him...after." He wrapped his arms about her waist. Ananias stared at her.

The thought of his shaft inside of her dulled any protest she could have made. She didn't care where he took her or how– only that he did.

"Take me, Ananias Dare."

He kissed her once more, his hands cradling the back of her neck, drawing her to him. It was as if he had a thirst to be quenched, and she was the only water. He lay within the hay, straddling her on top of him.

Ananias untied the simple cord that closed the top of her nightclothes, revealing her breasts to the cold morning air. She was pleased they remained supple and firm, fitting perfectly within his hands. She bent to kiss him, thrusting her delicacies on top of him, feeling the confirmation of his desire in his firmness.

He was ready for her.

She unbuttoned his trousers, licking the sweat from just above his member as she did so.

Salty. Full of sin.

He moved aside her thin nightgown and gently lifted her, sliding her wetness across his shaft. Ananias bounced her upon him, the wait and anticipation making her tingle even more.

She softly moaned, thankful for the bleat of the goats to cover their sounds.

"Ananias..."

His brown eyes stared straight into her soul. "Alice."

With her name, he pulled on her hips, sliding her on top of him. She enveloped him fully, noticing how much larger he was than her former husband.

Of course he was. He was Ananias Dare.

She rocked back and forth, guided by his firm hands on top of her hips. With each thrust, she could feel his member pulse inside of her. Soon he would be ready to release his seed.

She gasped. Inside of her?

Maybe she could carry his child.

Nearly forgotten trembles crawled along her legs now. She tightened her toes, gasping at each thrust as he forced himself further inside of her. God, this man was good.

"Don't release yet," he said.

But it was too late. As much as she enjoyed the thought of doing anything he said in this moment, his gravelled voice brought her to the crux of her passion. She slammed upon him, tightened and shaking in a euphoric bliss she'd wanted for so long.

Ananias rolled on top of her, hay clinging to his sweat-slick back. Further he pushed, back and forth inside her juices, preparing himself.

He plunged inside of her, deeply penetrating and twitching as he spilled his seed.

He softly kissed her lips. She never wanted this to end.

Still inside, Ananias relaxed, slowly pulling out of her to where she could feel their mixed wetness.

No doubt the guilt would consume her later, but in this moment, in the apotheosis of their coupling, she knew they would do it again.

9

NIGHTMARES NO MORE

ANANIAS DARE - WINTER 1587

"*FATHER!*" He heard her in the distance.

Ananias raced to refasten his trousers, stretching and straining to remove pieces of hay from his back. The smell of sweat, sin, and mistakes remained upon him. There was nothing he could do about that, now.

"*FATHER, Come quickly!*"

He bent down and kissed Alice Tilley on top of the head. He wouldn't let temptation take hold of him again.

"I must go."

Alice stretched her arms and wrapped them around her bent knees. "Will we meet again, soon?"

The last word hardly escaped through her lips, as a whisper of wind among the trees. He should end this before it began in earnest.

"Alice....I– "

The footsteps drew nearer, earth crunching underfoot bringing their discovery ever closer.

"FATHER!" Agnes Rose was almost upon them as she sprinted towards the barn. She must not see Alice.

"Go!" He hissed. He moved closer to the cattle, busying himself among them. He would pretend he was tending to their hay.

Just as Alice swept away through the back door of the barn, Agnes burst through the front.

"Father!" Agnes heaved and choked on her own word, tears streaming down her face. "It's little Henry. I found him face down, frozen– he's not breathing."

Dearest Lord.

God hath smote him for his adulterous actions this day.

He ran with Agnes to the stream beside their home. The bitter cold wrapped all around them, wind whipping at the blonde wisps of hair playing about Henry's ghostly white face as he lay upon the ground. His lips a pale blue, the colour of the sea they had journeyed upon not long ago. His dulled eyes, no longer holding the sparkle he so loved, stared beyond.

His youngest son, only four years of age– gone.

Ananias doubled over to clutch his stomach. Shock and disbelief ripped through him as a creature through their prey. He collapsed to his knees, a root digging straight up into the flesh. His cry echoed among the trees, blackened crows scattering to escape the horrid sound as it ripped through the air. Eleanor ran quickly, their babe Virginia nestled in her arms.

"What is it, Ananias? What causes thou to cry out so?" she yelled.

Agnes rocked, tears falling down her cheeks as she wept, curled upon the frozen ground with her arms clenched tightly about her.

Eleanor spotted their son.

In the soft calm before the storm, the frozen moment in time as one tried to make sense of a horror before them, Eleanor's eyes opened wide, and she shook her head as if she couldn't believe what lay before her. "No...no," she whispered. He watched as her lips parted, stunned, as she gently handed Virginia over to Agnes and crumpled to the ground. The anguished cries of his wife ripped through his soul while she reached for Henry's small shoulders. She shook him, violently, desperately, beseeching him to rise from his cold stare and greet them again.

But when he didn't, she held his limp frame to her, gently stroking his soft hair, kissing his forehead, whispering things Ananias couldn't hear. He went to her, wrapping his arms around the both of them, and together they held him.

Rocking, shaking, clinging to their little boy. The torrential downpour of sorrow consumed his every thought, digging into the recesses of his soul.

Why would God take away one so young and faultless? How *could* He be so cruel?

Yet even among his grief, Ananias knew the answer. *"For the wages of sin is death…"*

Death because of sin.

Ananias fell back, landing upon the cold, hard land, yet Eleanor cradled the lifeless body of little Henry still as she wailed into the sky. He forced himself to breathe as he held his trembling wife.

Eleanor cried. "WHY…God? Why hast thou done this to me?"

Agnes scooted closer to them, weeping, with no care for the leaves in her hair. Her eyes flitted between him, and Eleanor, and Henry. His daughter bit so hard into her lips, Ananias was sure she could taste the blood.

He steeled himself. He must be strong.

He raised his hands to wipe the tears from his eyes. The stench of Alice upon them was a gut-wrenching reminder of what he'd done.

And what it had caused.

"We must draw closer to God, thanking him for the time we were given with little Henry, and praise that he is now in the arms of the angels in Heaven." Ananias tried hard to believe it, but could hardly utter the words. "Away from this cold, sin-stained world, hardened by the bitter poisons of humanity."

Eleanor turned to face him with a fury upon her face unlike any he had ever seen. Her eyes flashed with a burning flame. A look of hatred.

"He hath taken away my precious boy. My *only* son to carry on *your* name, Ananias Dare. No–" she rocked her only son, "God be damned."

Icy wind cut through his lungs now, slicing through him as a painful dagger to the ribs.

Eleanor, his faithful wife of eighteen years, had smited the Lord with her own tongue. Her words weren't of the truth, as she spoke solely out of anger and hurt.

Her punishment could be next, if she were not to turn her eyes back to the Lord.

My God, what had happened to them?

Ananias needed to tell his wife the truth, that he knew of little Henry's awakening and chose instead to chop wood for Alice and warm her skin in the most sinful of ways. His actions had led to this, and were further leading Eleanor from their Lord. He had thought surely Henry would stay inside, that someone else would wake and care for him.

He was wrong.

It was cold. It was winter. Henry hadn't dressed before coming outside. Of course he wouldn't; he was but a babe himself.

Unless he was trying to follow him out there.

Breathe caught in Ananias's throat, the acid taste of bile rising into his mouth. He couldn't think. Couldn't breathe. Perhaps this was a demon rising from within to escape. A demon intertwined within his thoughts.

Satan's hold upon him was strong, that was sure. But even the devil's minions could be cast out of the body with enough grace.

He must repent. Urgently. Renew his spirit in being a better husband to Eleanor and father to Agnes and Virginia.

The rooster crowed, signalling the beginning of a new day. While yet his world might be shattered in this moment, he must use it as a catalyst to right himself as a Christian man.

Agnes lifted Virginia up to him. A now silent Eleanor jumped as Agnes put an arm around them both...her mother and her cold little brother.

With the sleeping babe tucked in his arms, warm and snug within her blanket, Ananias sat beside his family.

They sat in silence for a time.

Silence can be the most deafening of sounds. Agnes shattered their peace with one spoken phrase.

"Mother..." She looked at him. "Father?"

He cupped her chin in his calloused hand. She was chilled and shaking.

"There's something I need to tell you. Something Jonathan and I witnessed the other night, and I fear it could be the cause of this."

10
WHISPERS

"*Children are on loan to us, For it is in God's Kingdom, and under his care, where upon death they return to. I know within my own heart that I must not quarrel, or beseech you, Father, for taking your own at the chosen day, but as you know my heart, you know that I am riddled with wickedness as is my nature. Forgive me, oh God, for as I am stricken with grief, I bind myself to the scripture in remembrance that one day we shall be reunited. But oh, how I struggle in my heart. I sit with his body, wrapped in his blanket of wool, face uncovered so that I might look upon it as the candlelight fades this night. The ink of this prayer is yet smudged by the tears of my earthly body, raining sorrow upon the page. Blessed Henry, whom you loaned to us for four wonderful years, one which I had hoped to share the new world with and see him settle it as his own. But now, the lease has ended, and he sings with the angels on the most high. Will I know him, my Lord? When perhaps soon, I cross the pearly gates and sing with the angels myself? Pray thee forgive my transgressions, for I know my sin is great, and my thoughts are at times unbecoming to the Lord, that I might cling to your presence in my heart and cast me not into the lake of fire eternal. Forgive my words, for they were spoken in grief. I might fast and seek your grace in prayer and good works and the Godly raising of my other children. Strengthen me against the whispers which dearest Agnes Rose hath stated call to her from the woods. We question if the evil of the woods hath taken our Henry, a work of the devil among us. Protect mine own from the evils that surround us, and consume us. Lift us out of the shadows and into your holy light.*

As Zimri in the word of our God 1 Kings, I, too, nourish a passing thought of setting a place on fire and burning within it, taking me home to wrap my arms around my Henry. Nay, I struggle to stand, to speak, to eat, but my earthly husband doth turn my thoughts again to the word, and to our unfinished work on this earth. He also entertains the belief that Satan's grip in the woods might have contributed to the loss of our Henry, but only thou might know it. I cannot fathom that the Lord, my God, would allow for such an evil to meddle within our lives, to shorten the life of one of your own, but yea as I walk through the valley of shadows, I am reminded that their power, Satan's poison, hath no might against an almighty God.

My heart pines, for I know that you hath promised life eternal, and thus I mustn't end the journey in premature manners, and so I gather and write words for the brier within which the early vessel of Henry will forever lie among the ground. Ananias has fashioned a box out of the felled oak tree beyond our land. Tomorrow, we bury him, offering written verse and laudatory messages by our fellow settlers. We've set aside a burial place, among those of us that hath already passed, and soon will carve his name upon the stone. 'For we know that every creature groaneth with us also, and travaileth in pain together unto this present. And not only the creature, but we also which have the first fruits of the Spirit, even we do sigh in ourselves, waiting for the adoption, even the redemption of our body.' Amen."

Eleanor placed the quill upon the table. She rose to take a breath outside, all too aware that the small, covered shape upon the table would never fill his lungs with the cold night air again. She hadn't started a fire in this room, preferring instead to light her writing by the candle and suffer the cold as Henry did. Reflections of light glinted from the water trough just outside the door, for they had chosen a building unused and in much need of repair in which to place him until the morn. She would stay with him this night, against the protests of Ananias, but she wanted to spend every last moment with her son until she no longer could.

The small bundle of sticks she had crudely fashioned into a star dug into her hand. 'Twas the same star she had given him when he was fearful of the night storm. She brought it to her lips, kissing it before placing it upon him. She would send it into the ground with him.

"When the clouds clear, and the stars shine bright, we will thank the Lord for bringing peace to us in the storm." She whispered the words to him, hopeful that from Heaven he could hear them.

The wind disturbed the trees just beyond the tattered fence line outside. The cool breeze stung her wet cheeks as it blew. The sprawling forest, dark and menacing, beckoned her forth as if it called to her. Whispered to her. She stepped outside and lifted her arms to the Almighty Father.

"Shelter me, oh Lord. Protect me from what I cannot see."

She prayed God would hear her plea, and wrap her in his arms of protection, but after her words from earlier, she worried his embrace may never come. God knew her thoughts. Her doubts. Her hardened, wicked heart.

But the fight against her nature was of this world. She was not perfect, of that she was sure.

Smoke billowed from the chimneys of the homes that surrounded her. Families inside. Warm. Together. Loved.

Men without wives were forced to house together, for lack of suitable shelter in this new world. They worked hard to erect new homes, but with provisions scarce, it made sense for them to come together. Just beyond one hundred strong they had arrived, and their numbers dwindled by the day. She should be blessed that the rest of her family had not fallen to such afflictions yet, and grateful for the time she had with Henry. Two children remained, both gifted with the blessing to one day multiply and make their own way with one of these unmarried men. God would provide for them to reach those days. Those in the village had done what they could to support them, comfort them. Even Alice from next door had managed to bring over warm meals.

Eleanor.

She heard it then. A faint whisper called to her from within the shadows of the frozen trees.

Her chest tightened, the billow of fog from her lips stopping short as she dared not to make a sound. Was this the evil Agnes told them of?

No. She turned away, turning her back to the evils unknown within the woods. She would not allow Satan to tighten his grip upon her. She fixed her gaze upon the flickers of light visible from the next home over. It wasn't real. God would protect her.

Eleanor.

One black chicken, somehow roused from its roost in the barn, pecked at the ground before her. Its innocent cluck now a deafening sound, cracking through the silence of night as she trained her ear towards the woods.

A soft wind, a small wind, tickled the edges of her ear. The voice was right behind her now.

Eleanor steeled her heart. "Be GONE with you, Satan!" The chicken shrieked, wings flapping and clawed feet racing. Swiftly it ran towards her now, claws digging into the dirt. She whirled to confront the evil...

...but saw no one.

The night air had addled her senses– that was it. No witches lived within these woods. Only chickens pecking in the night. God would keep her from this evil. She must return to Henry.

II

PAPA

ANANIAS DARE – FEBRUARY 1588

Ba-dum. Ba-dum. Ba-dum.

The crisp night wind whipped against his face as Ananias drew near to the wooden box that held his frozen child. Unrelenting against his best efforts, the ground had been too hard in these winter months to bury his son. But life at the colony had endured, stretching forward while his family remained frozen in time. Unsure of how to proceed, with no underground vaults to store those that passed in winter, they'd turned to the only solution they had– to dip his frail body in the river, over and over, until his soft blonde hair and blue lips were encased in a tomb of ice.

Henry was kept outside in the frigid cold as they waited for the ground to thaw and for the time they could lay him to rest. Annais visited daily, rising when the work was done to put on his boots and coat again to sit with him. Eleanor visited, too, and Ananias could sometimes hear as she gently spoke and sang to their lifeless boy. She conversed with the little wooden box more so than she'd ever spoken to him.

The little wooden box across the yard that served as a constant reminder of Ananias's sin.

The little wooden box... that now thumped with a heartbeat.

Against his better judgement, Ananias approached it, his thin linen nightshirt doing little to stave the bite of the night air. Somehow, the box seemed to breathe with every beat.

Ba-dum. Ba-dum. Ba-dum.

His bare feet squished in the cold mud as he walked. The heartbeat grew louder as he crept closer. It tugged at his heart. Thumped in his soul.

He reached for the box. Little Henry.

His fingers curled around the wooden edges of the lid, one hand on either side, but as soon as he lifted it, the heartbeat stopped, as did his own.

The box was empty.

Ananias gasped and dropped the lid, the clack of wood shocking his senses further. This can't be. He'd put Henry inside it himself.

God grant him mercy. What had happened to his son?

Ba-dum.

Ananias spun round, the faint flickers of light illuminating a spine-chilling sight. His vision blurred from the ale he'd partaken, yet he could still see the one who stood before him.

Henry.

He held in the scream that roiled within as his son stood beside him, staring blankly at the small wooden box. The boy was blue and shivering, each breath sending a puff of fog skyward.

Ananias was numb. Fatherly instinct overwhelmed terror and he reached for his boy. Henry stepped back, as though seeing his father for the very first time.

The boy opened and closed his mouth, popping his withered blue lips yet there was no sound. Ananias knew what he had said.

Papa.

The blood-curdling shriek ripped through Ananias as if it were straight from Hell. Henry leapt forward, reaching for him. He twitched and tensed unnaturally, grasping with black-tipped fingers. All the while, his lips kept popping, *"Papa...Papa."*

Ananias stumbled backwards, falling in the mud. A crushing, frigid weight crawled up to his chest. Now eye to eye, he could see the milky eyes of death as the boy opened his mouth far too wide. His once plump cheeks cracked and tore, tiny teeth bared in rage.

Ananias cringed and closed his eyes. God help him. Let this end.

The front door of his weathered home crashed open and Eleanor's voice rang out across their land. "Ananias! Why are you out in the night? You'll catch your death in this chill." Eleanor stepped outside. "Come in, husband. I'll stoke the fire."

He sat up, all at once aware that he was alone. No dead son lay upon his chest. The only footsteps in the mud were his own. Henry's box sat next to him, the lid tight. Unopened.

Ananias scrambled to his feet, his linen shirt caked in winter mire. "I'm coming Eleanor," he managed to rasp. "I thought I heard...a wolf or someone prowling."

He crossed the way back to the safety of his home. At the door, the hairs on the back of his neck stiffened again. He turned and saw his boy once more. Even from here, he could make out the words on the frozen child's lips.

"Papa's fault."

12
WHISPER TO ME

Ananias Dare - March 1, 1588

Ananias set about skinning the rabbit he had caught this brisk morning, in the hopes that rabbit stew might uplift his broken wife's spirits. He knew the loss of a child was a terrible burden to bear, one that also settled upon him like a stone placed upon the chest. He would fast this day, and the next, and try to seek forgiveness for his wrongdoing. Agnes blamed Henry's death upon whatever darkness lurked within the woods, but he knew this not to be true. There may yet be darkness, for even while on the hunt he had sensed a disturbance among the trees. But for this tragedy, the loss of his only son, there was no one to blame but himself. Eleanor didn't know of his transgression against her, nor sense it. She had given him no indication that she suspected either. Were she to know that on that darkened morn he knew another woman instead of looking after their son, she would surely never forgive him. She might even involve Reverend Winslow, and call for putting him in stocks or worse yet, his death.

Surely not, as Eleanor had weathered the foulness of his sin before, but that didn't make it right, or mean that she would look so kindly upon him this time.

He turned the knife's edge facing up, slicing from the rabbit's genitals up to the cut he had already made on the neck, taking care so as not to puncture the stomach and contaminate the meat.

As he had contaminated the holiness of his marriage.

Ananias dressed the animal behind the smokehouse, its ramshackle walls a shield from the crisp winter wind. Placing his fingers beneath its skin, he grasped firmly to pull the fur away. Still warm, he winced. Taking a life was never an effortless task, but so it must be in order to fulfill the much needed nourishment of their bodies. Eleanor would enjoy a rabbit stew. He must be good to her on this the day they bury their son, and for every day after. The ground had thawed enough by now. He had not opened the box again– and wouldn't.

As he worked quickly, finishing the task, a gentle touch pressed his shoulder. Hot breath reached the back of his neck, like the smoke rising from the smoldering coals beneath the smokehouse. Eleanor had come.

He spun to meet her.

The penetrating amber eyes of Alice Tilley stared back at him.

Dear God, not now.

She clutched at his arms, careful not to touch any of the rabbit's blood or blade. "Whisper to me, Ananias Dare."

He turned from her, shrugging his greatest temptation away. "I shall not." He tasted the bitterness of his words and could not raise an eye to look at her.

"Ananias. I yearn for you." This serpent, a temptation of the flesh, moved one step closer to him. He wiped his hands on the ripped cloth beside the rabbit. But the fault of their sin lay not only with her, but with him, as he had caught himself looking at her long before the barn. Envied the touch of her husband and she. Nay, the fault of their sin rested on his shoulders as well.

"Alice, I'm busy. Leave me be." The newly familiar scent of her washed over him, a reminder of how close she had once been.

Another step. "Let me warm you again."

Rose water. He knew it now. His stomach twisted with guilt. Remorse. To lie with her had been the act of a godless man, a further stain upon his marriage.

Those of the town thought him a righteous man. A man of good intentions.

His past transgressions proved they were wrong.

But even among his misgivings, he sensed the familiar whispers of desire bend a beckoning claw. The way she bit down on her lower lip, peering up at him through feathery lashes– it consumed him.

"I had a moment of weakness. Nothing more." As he scrubbed his hands, dipping the tattered cleaning cloth in a water pail, the icy water shocked his senses further. She slid behind him, pressing her body against him and trailed her hands up his chest, resting her head upon his back, pulling him close. He wondered if she had held her husband like this.

"We could be happy together, Ananias Dare." One soft hand moved down his chest, to his navel, sliding lower.

His chest rose and fell with each quickened breath. Beads of sweat collecting on his brow stung in the frigid breeze.

No. This was sin. For the wages of sin is death.

Dear God. Henry's services were today. The rabbit stew. How quickly he had let her get so close to him. The Devil's grip was strong.

"Alice!" He turned, newly restored in vigilance against his lustful thoughts. "I am a married man. Put these thoughts from your mind, as I shall not know you again."

He grabbed the bucket and stepped away, heading for the well. Crossing his small bit of land, he knew there was a chance that they could be seen. He and Alice. Together.

Alice rushed after him, coif falling from her chestnut brown hair, wisps of it playing about her rose-colored cheeks.

"Ananias–", she hissed, "you know as well as I that life must go on when a husband dies. I'm not asking you to put your wife away...merely to add another."

Ananias halted, standing at the well, the rock used for breaking frozen water digging into his palm. He intended to throw it into the well, but had half a mind to throw it at *her* now.

But he wouldn't.

Whether she did not understand his frustrations or mistook his silence as permission to speak further, Ananias didn't know.

"Lamech. Moses. King David. Solomon. All men who were described in the Word to have more than one wife."

He slammed the rock on the edge of the crumbling well. "Alice...*enough*."

"But you know it be true, Ananias Dare. A man can build a large family on this earth to replicate in heaven. I would rather have half of a husband that was happy, fulfilled, rather than spend my days alone. We could build a new life, you and I, and you can live between the two houses with two families to warm your heart."

Today was not the day to talk of love and happiness. He cursed himself for tolerating this sinful language at all.

"Tell me you've not looked over to my land with a soft eye. Brought us wood to keep warm. Shared your meat to keep our bellies full."

Ananias finished tying rope around the rock, dropping it in the well. "I might have, yes." The rock cracked open the ice, much like his strength with her every word.

Alice grabbed his hand, her skin softer than the rabbit's fur, especially against the rough calluses of his own.

"It cannot be," he whispered. He tipped the bucket down into the icy depths of the well. A sickening squelch replaced the water's splash that he expected.

Odd. Must be chunks of ice. Once the rope was heavy, he heaved the water to the surface.

"Ananias..."

"Alice, *enough*! I'll not hear another word of it. You come to me, on this the day I bury my beloved son, *knowing* the fault is our own? We cannot. I shall not. Speak of this no longer!"

Alice leaned her head on his shoulder and softly whispered. "I can give you another son."

The rope slid through his hands, scraping, burning, falling back to the bottom. Rage consumed his every thought as she dared insert herself into the loss of Henry. His boy. The child who wouldn't rest in his bed tonight, but rather the frozen ground.

"Be *gone* with you, serpent woman." He seethed, heartbeat pounding in his ears as he wrenched from her grasp. He hardly noticed the burn on his hands as he brought the bucket to the surface again.

Alice stepped back, tears brimming in her eyes. "I–I didn't mean...I'm sorry Ananias. I only wished to–"

"*Gone.*" He spat.

Alice gasped, eyes trained on the bucket he now held within his hands. He looked down, and the sight of it forced the air from his lungs.

Crimson liquid sloshed within the bucket. Suddenly, he realized someone was watching them. He lifted his eyes to the doorway of his thatched-roof home, and there stood the woman who had no doubt witnessed this advance...the woman he didn't deserve– Eleanor.

The smell of the bucket's contents gagged him. It was iron. Salt.

Blood.

13
OUR LADY DAY

AGNES DARE - MARCH 25, 1588

"*Dearest Lord, I come to thee in fervent prayer on this the Lady Day, celebrated by others, as the new year beginnith in earnest. Our community believes that they for whom all days are holy can have no holiday, so they do not celebrate it. Feast days are nothing more than Roman inventions, or so my parents say, yet my wicked heart yearns for the edges of celebration I once saw back in England. Resentment towards Mother and Father still breeds within me, as I hate that they have brought us here, to this wild land of an unforgiving nature. More of us die, even with what help Manteo manages for us with the local natives. I resent Ralph Lane, the leader of the first settlement attempt. His murder of the Chief Wingina soured relations beyond solid repair. The natives are one with the land, their clothing, food, and shelter brought about from Earth, and we, as transplants from England, haven't their ways. I am wicked within as I question the purpose of our settlement, the reasons for our ways. If you are a God of love and light as the Word tells us, then why take my brother from this earth? Why forsake us so? If it is atonement for the sins of our coming, I cannot help but wonder why I am among the faulted. But then I am reminded that my sins are many, too. I draw ever closer to Jonathan, whom I'd intend to marry if he'd have me so, and if it be your will, God. And then there are the whispers from the darkened woods. I saw them dancing with my own eyes. I told Mother and Father what I'd seen, but I did not tell them what I felt, what I still feel. Hardships are a test from God, which I know, but when they call to me...I wish to answer."*

Agnes settled on the cool grass in the forest clearing with her friends. They nestled just within the trees around a strange-looking stone perched right in the centre. There was an eerie feeling here, not unlike the same she felt that night with Jonathan in these woods. Best to put that out of mind, as today she was surrounded by her friends and together they would partake in what little merriment they could.

Winefrid Chevon, Ambrose Wythers, and Emme Mermoth.

All were dragged here in a similar fashion by their parents, and no word nor protest could have changed it. An unspoken promise lingered over their heads, the same as the branches that hung above them now—that they would all wed one of the single, unmarried men. Plucked from those that had also dared to journey across the sea.

One hundred and fifteen. Fools, most of them.

Not her friends, of course, but the men who came in search of "gold and riches beyond belief" as they'd been falsely informed. It was a way to escape the clutches of Catholicism, all with hopes for land and a "fresh start" as Mother said.

But Agnes knew better.

It was greed that brought them to these shores. Besides, the only "gold" she'd laid eyes on came off of a strange plant belonging to the natives. Tall, stalked, and leafy. They'd called it corn.

Emme laid the biscuits she'd snuck away from her table on a blanket placed over the rounded stone. Birds chirped in the trees, announcing they were home for spring. Agnes felt confident she even heard a raven's caw. She'd always liked ravens. They were different from the other birds, much the same as she felt distanced from her fellows.

"All right girls, let's have the rest then. What did we manage to bring to our Lady Day celebration?" Emme grinned, revealing a small slab of butter she had concealed under her travelling cloak.

Our Lady Day, the celebration of the incarnation of Christ, marked the day when the archangel Gabriel visited the Virgin Mary to tell her that she would be the mother of Christ. Agnes mulled the very thought of it. Mary was no doubt younger than she, and told she would bear God's son. No choice in the matter.

Surely, that was wrong.

No. She mustn't entertain thoughts such as these. It was a blessing for her.

Winnie twirled to the centre of their picnic circle. Dancing in the day-light, she had always been the most daring among them. "Cranberries and cheese, girls," she said, carefully placing them next to Emme's biscuits.

"I've got apple jam and pickled eggs," Ambrose said.

Agnes fought to conceal her frown. Pickled eggs? Surely the daughter of the treasurer could have done better than that.

She held out her own. "Girls, I've brought something Momma and I whipped up from those orange squashes that were growing in town." She placed the cakes neatly on their stone table, a slight breeze lifting their blanket tablecloth. "We sweetened them with honey. Momma calls them pumpkin cakes." Her friends eyed them with anticipation, licking their lips. Winefred removed her coif.

Agnes continued. "They're a bit hard, as we've kept them for a while, but they still taste as good as when we made them." How she pined for the custards and berry cakes back home in England, but here in the new world, these would have to do.

"Thank-you, Agnes." Winnie smiled, raven-black hair whipping across her face. "Now let's eat!"

Their miniature feast brought a small bit of joy to her heart on this their secret Lady Day. The sun made eyes at them from time to time from behind grey clouds that blanketed the sky. They were puffy, like a sheep's wool, and she wished to shear it away and enjoy the sun for once.

"I saw Roger Baily looking at you during prayer last week, Emme." Ambrose giggled and popped another cranberry in her mouth. She was a sly girl, though hardly beyond seventeen years. "Perhaps he's fond of you, after all...did you know it?"

Emme gasped, mouth agape as she playfully shoved Ambrose's shoulder to the side. "You did not. Because if you *did* then that means you yourself had open eyes during prayer!"

They fell to fits of laughter, Ambrose caught in her sin as she, too, had rosy cheeks. She shrugged. "How else am I to steal a glance at Martin?"

Agnes laughed. "Martin and Ambry, sittin' in a tree, K-I-S-S–"

"Shhh!" Emme warned. "Best not carry our voices too loud, lest we be heard!"

A small puff escaped from Winnie's lips. "What. Afraid the *witches* might hear us and tell?"

Agnes froze.

Emme believed, and had told her of these suspicions before, that witches awaited on Roanoke island. Her uncle had come on the voyage before theirs. He would softly mention the evils they faced, but would never discuss the matter further. "To speak of evil summons it into the home," he always said.

But Agnes hadn't yet shared with the girls what she and Jonathan had experienced in the woods.

"We ought not have such idle chatter, girls." She looked down, unable to meet their eyes. They would see her fear and question further.

"Aggy?" Winnie frowned. "What's gotten into you? You used to love to talk of witches and geks back home."

That was before she had seen proof of it.

"Oh please." Ambrose scoffed. "We all know that anyone unfortunate enough to have a snaggle-tooth or sunken cheek was accused of having the *'evil eye.'*"

Winefred joined her in eye rolling. "Such hare-brained ideas. Those were no witches."

Emme shifted her gaze to the swaying trees surrounding them. "The Bible talks of witches. And you know as well as I that it was made a capital offence nearly 20 year ago. We've seen the hangings and burnings ourselves!"

Agnes stuffed her mouth full of more bread. If only they knew.

If she told them, and one of them spoke with loose lips to another in the village, then they'd all be questioned– most of all she. Her parents would be ashamed. Alone, in the woods, *at night* with Jonathan. It wouldn't suit them at all.

But if the witches came for them...she couldn't bear the thought of it.

Best not let her friends dabble in things they ought not encounter.

But maybe they would have advice for her.

"Girls. I have to tell you something. But you must *swear* to keep these whispers to yourself. None can know."

Winnie straightened, as gossip of any nature was her favourite. "Ohhh. Tell us, Agnes. Is it Jonathan? Have you known him, yet?"

Emme's eyes were wide. A follower of the rules at heart, her friend did not settle well with secrets and such. It had taken days to convince her to come with them to the woods at all. "Tell us you've remained pure in this, Aggy."

Agnes smirked. "Yes of course. Well, sort of."

Ambrose clapped her hands and squealed in delight. "Do tell us! Tell us your news!"

Agnes settled her breath, focusing on the tart sweetness that lingered on her tongue from the cranberries. "Aye. I've met with Jonathan on one occasion or another," Emme raised her eyebrows, "but nothing more than soft kisses and sweet nothings whispered in my ear." She smiled, "his hands are mighty strong from fortifying our palisades." Her friends gasped and giggled at the news.

She went on. "But one night not long after we arrived at this wretched place–" she lowered her voice, "we came upon a group of women dancing naked in the woods."

The girls gasped, all colour draining from Emme's face. She was the daughter of Reverend George Winslow, their leader in faith, and as such this news would hit her the hardest– a confirmation of her fears.

"I knew it, Aggy! I knew it!" she cried. "But why have you kept this from us for so long. Our coming was at least eight months ago. You've held this secret from us that long?"

The heat of shame rose to her cheeks, but she knew within her it was for a good cause. "Girls. I know. Their presence troubles me so, but I didn't want to burden your lives further with this knowledge of evil in the woods."

They stopped, all looking around as if suddenly caught in a bear's trap among the very evil they spoke of.

"But Aggy..." Ambrose whispered, "your brother..."

The sharp pang of his death stabbed her heart once more. In time it had dulled, but ever still did it linger just beneath the surface. She suspected it too, that the witches had somehow taken him from them. Satan's price for their presence in his lands.

Agnes sighed. "Aye. I know it. But even so, in the times since then that Jonathan and I have discussed it, we wondered if we even saw it. It was late, and both of us were muted by the last dregs of ale that night. Maybe we didn't see it at all."

Ambrose stared at the stone where they sat. "But Aggy. Come on now. Witches in the woods?"

She clearly didn't believe it.

"What did your parents say?"

Agnes stared at her. "I shared a bit of it, but not the whole of the truth. For if I had, then they would know of my meetings with Jonathan–."

"Aye." Her friend nodded. "So the fear of your parents outweighed your fear of the devil himself?" Ambrose laughed, the sound of it sending a bird from a nearby branch into the sky.

Winfered stood, gathering her apron in both hands, and walked a circle around them. "But did you hear their spells, Aggy?" Faster and faster she skipped around them in the clearing. "Did you hear their greatest desires or consecrations with the devil?"

"Winnie, stop it!" Emme rose to her knees, the treats of Lady Day long forgotten.

Ambrose rose to join in. "Perhaps they called for men to please them!"

Both girls laughed and danced in a circle, neither believing real witches to be true.

And maybe they weren't, but God be merciful she was sure of what she'd seen, and what she'd run from.

With the death of Henry and a cold silence resting in her home, she wasn't really sure of what to believe anymore. Mother had long ago stopped her prayers, but Agnes still clung to the smallest bit of hope.

Winnie and Amby danced together in a circle, laughing and calling their pretend spells to the sky. Emme sat still on the ground, silent as a grave.

"Old Mother Witch
When she wanted more room
Would fly through the air
On a very fine broom
Mother Witch had a house;
It stood in the wood
Where an owl at the door
As sentinel stood!"

Emme covered her ears, tears filling her eyes. "Girls, *stop* it! *Stop!* You'll bring evil to us all!"

Winne and Ambry halted their dance, arms holding tight to each other as the grins fell from their faces. Winnie moved closer. "Oh Emme, we're sorry. We were just dancin' is all, nothing to cause a fright in ye." Ambry nodded. "Right. We just find it hard to believe there's actually witches crawling around in these woods.

Whooo hooo, whooo hooo.

A simple call that on a typical day would bring her no fear. But there, perched on a branch not far above them, a tawny brown owl sat with piercing eyes and a sharp beak trained upon them. Agnes' heart hammered in her chest. Why was this bird of the night watching them now during the day?

Emme followed her gaze. A scream escaped her friend's lips.

"An owl!"

"The sentinel!"

"Quick girls, to the village!"

With one swoop, Aggy gathered their feast in the blanket and ran back to the safety of home, her heartbeat pounding in her ears as fast as her footsteps carried her.

If ever a confirmation of evil was to be had, the sighting of a familiar was surely it.

14

A LYING TONGUE

ANANIAS DARE - MAY 1588

"*The Bible says, 'As the Lord our God doth hate these seven things, I cannot beseech his forgiveness as I am at fault of them. His soul abhorreth seuen: the hautie eyes, a lying tongue, hands that shed innocent blood, an heart that imagineth wicked enterprises, feet that be swift in running to mischief, a false witness that speaketh lyes, and him that rayseth contentions among brethren.' Temptation hath called to me again and again and so is my wicked nature, I sometimes answer it. I beg of thee to cleanse this wicked heart, bringing back some goodness to my name, even if it be the size of a dust speck on the ground. Give me the strength to be an honest man, a good man, putting aside a lying tongue and cold heart in my own house. God give us the morrow, that we might yet settle this land righteously within your vision, as the future of an English presence in the new world depends on it. I yearn for the fresh start that Eleanor and I so wishfully spoke of. Lord, help me to have it. Strengthen me. Lead me true in this world. In thy holiest of names I pray, Amen.*"

The fog of early morn still suffocated their surroundings, encasing them in biscuit clouds that rested upon the ground and damped their view. Dew drops still rested upon the grass, the cool morning breeze a shock to his skin. Day after day Ananias watched as his wife solemnly sat at their son's eternal resting place before she tackled each task in their daily chores. She rose with the rooster's crow, wordlessly leaving their home to perch at the foot of her son's grave as a mother hen watching over a lifeless egg. She spent her days mending their tattered clothes, cooking to keep their bellies full, and fulfilling all manner of duties bestowed upon a good and Godly wife. She never complained. Nor rejoiced. It was with a pained heart that Ananias watched her, and pitied her yet. The day their little boy died, her smile left the earth with her son, for he had not seen any expressions of joy since that fateful day.

The day of reckoning evil that he had brought about with his own sin.

Sickening guilt wretched within him, a caged beast in need of release, yet his cowardice and shame had kept him from clearing conscience with her. On but one occasion since the winter she had softened at his touch, a desperate attempt to stitch together what they had from long ago, but even then she only lay still upon the bed, gazing out the window until he had finished and she kissed him on the brow.

He drew closer to her and watched as she brought her hand to her lips before placing it on his marker. A kiss for her boy.

Their chickens clucked and pecked at the ground, moving closer to him as if they expected to be fed at such an early hour, but he had nothing for them. Worms would be their only breakfast.

With a jolt of the heart, he thought of the worms in the dirt surrounding Henry, wiggling between the wood to crawl up his arms, into his eyes.

He stopped. God have mercy and remove these poisoned thoughts.

Eleanor turned and looked at him, the smallest of frowns settling upon her lips.

Ananias gasped, for beyond Eleanor, just within the forest trees and nearly unseen due to the fog, stood the shadowy outline of his long-dead son.

A spectral vision, but still clear enough for him to see, Ananias stepped closer towards Eleanor, closing his mouth, trying with all his might not to frighten her. She needn't see Henry like this.

Henry's skin was that of rancid chicken meat, greyed and speckled with bruises. His precious pudgy fingers were black, as was the rotten skin around his closed lips, peeling back and dangling in small strips. Clumps of dirt and hair clung to his skull, with sunken eyes that swam with milk. The stench stifled him, even this far away, but he couldn't show it because then Eleanor would know.

Henry extended one small arm out, walking towards them as bones poked out of the flesh that had rotted away. Maggots dripped from his open mouth as a centipede slithered from a nostril.

Papa.

Ananias forced himself to look away, to stare at Eleanor, moving closer to her with each step. But behind her, Henry moved too.

Papa lies.

The raspy sound of it pierced his skull, as if the devil himself whispered in his ear.

Papa lies. Henry was just behind his Momma now. Ananias needed to get to her first.

Papa LIES!

Pushing his legs the final two steps, Ananias lunged to wrap his arms around Eleanor and protect her from this unholy version of their son.

But as he grabbed her, Henry was gone.

"Ananias Dare! What ails you, so?" The look of concern on Eleanor's face did little to soften the thunderous beating of his heart.

Exhaling the breath he'd been holding, he sank to the ground. "My wife–oh my wife."

Eleanor clutched his hands in hers. They were as cold as her demeanour of late. "How did we come to this place, Ananias? So far from what we once were." She spoke softly, to the ground, unwilling to meet his gaze. "Shame fills my heart as I fear my resentment hath brought this judgement upon us."

His shoulders dropped, the weight of his own sin a boulder upon them. "Eleanor...the fault of this lies not with you. You are a good wife. A Godly wife. You've kept your vows and stood by me yet."

Her eyes welled with tears. "But if I had known, had kept watch over Henry as he toddled outside those many months ago, I might have seen where he went and kept him from harm."

He braced, squeezing her hands, rubbing his thumbs over the back of them. He could not let Eleanor bear this burden any longer. "Eleanor. Hear me now. Henry's death was not your fault."

"But how?" she whispered, raising her head and peering at him through her wet lashes.

Ananias drew breath, settling himself. It was time.

"I was awake that morning. I heard him shuffle from his bed, yet I wrongly assumed someone else would care for him." Eleanor tilted her head at his words.

"What kept you from his care, husband?"

He knelt, resting his forehead on their hands. "I was with our neighbour, Alice Tilley, on that morning."

Eleanor pulled their joined hands up, looking straight into his eyes. "A wife cannot fault a man for chopping firewood for a neighbour in need."

"Aye. I chopped wood for her, that is true, but that is not all of the wicked needs I attended to."

She pulled her hands from his grasp, clutching at her apron. "Ananias...tell me there wasn't more."

"I'm sorry, Eleanor. I am!" He stared at the ground. "I beg your forgiveness as I have begged forgiveness from God Almighty every day since. I am not that man any longer."

She scoffed. "Spare me, husband. Those words I have heard before, long before our crossing to this new world." Fire burned within her eyes.

Hatred. Rage.

And it was well-deserved.

He reached for her again. "I knew it then and I know it still. I am a wicked man, Eleanor, a Godless man. You've done nothing to deserve such treatment from your husband and yet I have faltered time and time again."

"So you've lain with her since?"

Ananias halted. Best to tell the truth in its entirety. "Aye. I've known her since."

Eleanor cast his hands from her, clenching her fists to her sides, breaths coming fast now. His wife's eyes darted around him, searching for words, for reason. "Damn you, Ananias Dare," she whispered, her eyes blurred with tears, voice dripping with disappointment. She rose, backing away from him. "How can you speak of this as we sit upon our child's grave?" she seethed. "Our *only* son!" Her words rolled from the tongue as a thunderous warning before the storm. She advanced on him, moving with purpose, with anger.

Ananias leaned back, raising his hands, "Eleanor, I–"

"For *months* you've watched as I visited here, overcome with guilt that *I* had failed in his protection when you *knew* of this sin." She shoved him further back, spitting in his face. "You are not worthy to sit with him now, nor with me. God has punished us all for your actions!"

He raised a hand to wipe his face, heart thundering in his ears. "I know it. As true as I live. I promise to be fair, Eleanor." He clenched his hands before him, begging for another chance. "I swear it."

She narrowed her flaming eyes, boring a hole straight into where the kind, gentle heart of a good husband should have been. "An idle oath from a Godless man." Her eyes cut through him as a blade, though he knew them to be true. "You'll not warm my bed any longer." She clenched her fists, standing still before him. "If your heart yearns for her then I bid you go. *Go* to her and settle with your new family, as clearly the one you have brings not the satisfaction you desire."

"I'll not," he whispered.

Eleanor shoved him, again. "You will!" she hissed. "Daily I prayed, before, seeking guidance on how to move past my resentment towards you, yet still you broke your vows." She turned from him, her voice rising. Soon, it would wake their neighbours.

"Perhaps our Agnes is right, that witches and evil lie in wait, but now I wonder if evil resided with us all along!" She wiped a tear as it rolled down her cheek. "How can you pray? How can you lead? You have grossly abused my kindness, Ananias. Your name in the town suffers not a word of dishonour as I have kept it so. I have protected you. Honoured you. And still, yet, I'll not breathe a word of this." She turned, looking away to the wood. "But hear me now, Ananias Dare, you'll not warm my bed any longer. Stay, if you must, but know that you'll find no comfort in me. I am done with it all. With you."

"Eleanor, I will be true. I swear it. Find it in your heart to forgive a sinful man? To pray for my soul?"

She waited before answering, never turning from the wood. "My prayers ended long ago, as God has brought me to this barren land and taken my precious son from me, and now I know your part in it. It is not to me that you need to beg forgiveness from, Ananias, but to God."

15
THE PLAGUE

Jonathan Carver - June 1588

"And the river shall teem full of frogs, which shall go up and come into thine house, and in thy chamber, where thou sleepest, and upon they bed, and into the house of they servants, and upon thy people, and into thine own, and into thy kneading troughs. Yea, the frogges shall climbe up upon thee, and on thy people, and upon all they servants."

A loud croak roused Jonathan from his dreams.

He wiped the sleep from his eyes, the blurry room sharpening before him.

Something was there. It covered every inch of his surroundings.

As he leapt from bed surrounded by the croaking of such vile leaping creatures, Jonathan knew they were held in a time such as the biblical plagues of Egypt. But there were no pharaohs here, no rod, nor prayer of Moses to release them from their grip. The cause of their coming was unknown to him.

What troubles they've encountered in this new world, this wild land of an unforgiving nature. If it were only a few that plagued them, he could blame the land and the waters for housing such beings, but nay, an untold count of them covered his home. He wished it were the other men playing somewhat of a game with him, but deep within he knew that isn't from whence this came.

The witches sprang to mind.

No. It can't be. A plausible cause and solution exists for this.

He rushed outside, gingerly stepping between the frogs as they leapt about his small home, careful not to squash them. Crossing the threshold into the morning light, he was met with a sight that was surely the same of those plagued in Egypt. Frogs. Everywhere. As far as the eye could see and covering their village. The sound of their low-pitched bellow rang in his ears, their throats engorging and deflating with each call. Bennet Chappell and Walter Mill also stood outside their homes.

"What on God's green earth has caused this?" Bennet said, as he trudged through the sea of bullfrogs.

Walter joined him, moving to the meeting table. "We've damn near a plague, it seems!"

Jonathan grabbed the sacks he'd piled near his front door for catching fish. "Boys, grab a bag. Whatever the cause, we surely need to move them on." Each frog he reached for wiggled and leapt, working hard to remove themselves from his grasp– but they weren't stronger than he.

Christopher Loude came their way. "Jonathan, what say ye? Could the snakes have driven these frogs out of the swamps? Into town?"

Walter scoffed. "Chris, ye know better. There's too many upon us! It's Exodus, my good man. Clearly this curse has come from the devil upon our lands."

Jonathan shrugged. Whether God had sent another plague upon them, or the animals in these wilds were unlike any they'd seen before, something had to be done about it. Now.

"Let's gather the men," he yelled, a frog escaping from his sack. "We need every man to help settle this."

"We can't do this alone!" Walter was fighting to keep his frogs inside the bag.

"Which is *why*," he caught a frog as it attempted to leap from his sack, "we need more to help us. Gather them now, Christopher."

Bennet scooped his bag along a trough. "Do ye think the natives have called for this curse because of our coming?" One jumped from his grasp, splashing in the water.

"Aye. They've called for our end!"

Jonathan glared at them. "And perhaps they shall. We've entered their lands and taken it as our own. Sin runs unbridled within these walls. If it's sin we're accountin' for, we've none to blame but ourselves. Caste out those blameful thoughts and look instead upon yourself!"

"Aye. Yer right." Bennet nodded. "But these bullfrogs have got to get on."

Christopher ran between the houses, knocking on doors and calling the village to wake and help them. Their shouts and screams, no doubt at the discovery of being covered up by frogs, rang clear across their village. But just as Christopher roused them from their beds, on Jon's command, Reverend Winslow slipped behind, demanding for all to head to the church.

Jonathan couldn't believe it. "We need help, Reverend! We cannot rid the colony of these frogs on our own!"

Reverend Winslow rounded on him. "Aye, son, we need help. From God, through prayer. You and your friends can handle this outside. We will meet with the Lord as you do it."

Jonathan held his tongue as the reverend stomped away, squashing frogs without regard as he went.

Deep in the questioning corners of his soul, in the place where doubt and self-reflection lie, Jonathan thought of the women he and Agnes Rose had seen in the woods. Dancing. Naked. Shrieking round the fire. In his bones he could feel it. This wasn't the work of the natives or God, but rather, whatever devils that lurked in the surrounding wood.

Prayer was needed, indeed.

It is the belief of the whole that some actions and occurrences are of God, and those of opposition are of Lucifer. Jonathan knew that no man had caught and brought about this many bullfrogs to plague their village in a single night, as yesterday there were none. Something evil was afoot, and now was the time they needed to lift their voices and pray. A reckoning had come to the Roanoke Colony, but God would see them through. He had promised it.

Jonathan clutched at the wriggling bag containing as many frogs as it would hold, tying off the top to prevent their escape. The intermittent bulges from the bag as they leapt and fought to escape their prison brought an ill feeling to his stomach. He wanted to be done with it. If only Manteo was here, with his familiarity of the land, to assure them if this was an occurrence of nature for this strange land, or if they really were dealing with a plague of biblical meanings. But alas, he was with his people, away in an attempt to seek their help upon them. He crept closer to the meetinghouse, as many had now gathered there.

Those that had come here almost one year ago, and had so far survived the tests of the wilds, gathered in the chapel at the behest of his friend, Christopher Lowde. Their governor, John White, had left a council of men as the leadership in the village for the duration of his absence, along with Manteo. Christopher and he were but two among them that now led. Sharp eyes were needed in these troubled times; times of death, insatiable hunger settled deep within their bellies, and low morale. And, of course, a sharp mind to aid in the fight against the ever-present sinful nature burrowed deep within them all.

Loud croaks sounded around them where they stood.

"We are undone!" Goody Chapman stomped at the frogs surrounding her, squashing them dead, their insides bursting to cover the warped floor.

That was one way to deal with the frogs, he mused. To kill them.

"They're everywhere!"

"In the water! A plague has come upon us!"

Jonathan knew they must do something, and quick, for the village was taking to hysterics. He moved to the front to stand on the raised platform Reverend Winslow used for his sermons.

"Ladies and Gentleman. Calm yourselves." He raised his hands to call order. "As we can clearly see, the village is overrun–"

But they didn't hear him.

"God has smited us!"

"There's wickedness afoot!"

"The natives have done it, I know it!"

"Friends!" he called. "Hear me now. We are in a foreign land, and this be our first meeting with spring awakening." What could he say to stoke confidence within them? "This could be the nature of the wilds, nothing more." He spoke with confidence, but rattled inside.

Try as they might, his fellow villagers wrestled with the leaping frogs, trying to find a free spot to sit or stand. As they cleared a spot, only more pounced to fill each place.

He addressed them again. "We gather the frogs and take them to the farthest end of the island, past the trees."

"They'll come back for us!"

"There's too many!"

"The devil is near!"

He raised his voice, nearly shouting now. "Hear me! We do what we can to rid our buildings of them, protect our meats and crops and pray." A murmur sounded among them. "We must seek our Lord in this! Ask for a cleansing, fast, if we may, for God has brought us this far and will see this settlement flourish!"

"Perhaps we should eat them." A figure in the shadows stepped out from behind the door and into the light with a grin peeking out from between his beard.

Richard Cheven, Winnie's father. Of course it was. That whole family was wrought with questionable actions. He held one frog in each hand.

Christopher spoke. "You take to this with amusement, sir?"

"Aye. I'm of the belief it is as you said. It's the wilds showing their arse. Nothing more."

"Mr. Cheven! Such language!" Goody Warren clutched tight to her babes.

Richard Cheven laughed. "No devil hops among these bullfrogs. Quit seeking him where he ought not be found."

Jonathan could hardly hear him over the frogs.

"But there be witches in these woods!" Emme Merimoth stepped forward, Aggy's face draining of colour behind her. "You've seen it, Jonathan Carver! You *know* this, you know of the evil that surrounds us. And today they've brought about their reckoning!"

His mouth clamped shut, sweat beading on his brow. How could this admission be explained?

Aggy had told them.

Emme marched forward, a blazing fire in her eyes. One to be feared when coming from a zealot such as she. "I've heard you've seen it with your very own eyes!"

The crowd's murmerings grew louder, contesting the sounds of the frogs.

Witches in Roanoke!

The devil will have us all now!

"Jonathan Carver, is this true?" Reverend Winslow stepped forward, a frog perched on his shoulder, yet he paid it no mind. "Have you been consorting with witches in these very woods?"

Jonathan glanced at Aggy, her face full to blushing, one hand covering her mouth. Her eyes pleaded with him. What was he to do? Her father, Ananias Dare, stood beside her with a face that could shatter stone.

"Nay, sir. I've never consorted with witches, but I did stumble upon a strange sight in the woods one night."

"Go on, Mr. Carver."

He looked to Aggy, stretching his shirt collar away from his neck in order to breathe. The air and stares stifled him. Every eye was trained upon him now, swirling with accusations and questions, frogs jumping among them.

"There were women, sir, dancing in the forest 'round a fire. They were naked."

Piercing screams rose from the crowd. Goody Pierce fell to the floor, quickly covered in bullfrogs.

God save us! The witches, they've sent their familiars!

Jonathan moved forward to help her.

"Silence!" Reverend Winslow narrowed his eyes, boring holes into the crowd. "Who here danced naked in the woods? Consorted with the devil! Yer wickedness has brought this plague upon us!"

"I recognized none of the women, Sir." To stir up whispers of witchcraft and devilry among such a small village as this was a dangerous path to take. He remembered well the women and men who swung from the noose back home in England and didn't wish to see it here.

But even then, how could he not also suspect the same after what he'd seen?

"Mark my words, ye children of God, this village will *not* entertain the devil or his minions. You there–" he pointed to Christopher, Bennet, and those behind them, "gather these creatures and cast them out of our homes! The rest of you–" he paused, "will join me in prayer."

Jonathan moved to join the other men in gathering the frogs when Reverend Winslow caught his arm. "Not you. You will pray with us. Later we will discuss the reasons behind your concealment of this finding in the woods."

He nodded. "Yes, sir."

God, have mercy upon his soul.

16
SICKENED

"Dearest Lord I come to thee in fervent prayer, if it be your will, God, to save our people from this wretched plague upon us. Just this morning, I have been called to attend to the Wicker family, a father, God, and his wife and two children. I've heard it that they have fallen ill, in connection with this sickness, and I'm to sit at their bedside to offer comfort and blessings, a conduit of your healing hand. Wrap your arms around this family's trials, Lord, and guide me in shepherding them into a new stage of life, a healed one, as every member of this colony serves your purposes in founding a new and righteous land. Give me the words, God, that I might strengthen their hearts and lead them away from the temptations of the wild, seeking not their own understanding of such troubles but, rather, basking further in your Word and endless grace. We live to serve you, Lord, and ask humbly for a blessing this day. Remove this scourge from upon us and allow this settlement of Roanoke to thrive in thine own name. Forgive us our trespasses, as we forgive those who trespass against us. For thine is the kingdom, the power, and the glory forever. In your holiest of names I pray, Amen."

The wretched croaks scratched at his brain as the rats did, the neverending vision of leaping vermin a despicable intrusion upon their lands and in their homes. It sickened him, the very thought that whilst he attempted to sleep in his hard, understuffed bed, that they could bound about him in the night. He'd awoken just this morning with five around him, their slimy backs glistening in the morning light, or what little light could shine through his grimy windows. Bile rose again in his throat as he watched them, splashing in the water trough, kicked out of the way by his fellows, squashed and bagged and burned yet still they returned. He'd never seen anything like it. Exodus tells of the pharoah's plight with a plague of the very same, yet this was no Egypt and he was no pharoah. He liked to think of himself as a simple shepherd, herding and guiding his flock into the light as a reverend was called to do, and yet too many times he'd already failed them.

He'd told them *clearly* not to ingest the frogs, as their coming was clearly not of the normal world and thus they could not be trusted as sufficient sustenance, even as their hunger persists. The Wickers hadn't listened, blatantly ignoring his warnings, or so he'd been told, and thus they lay upon their beds this very morn sicker than any had seen. Taken with fevers, they were, both the parents and the children. They'd called for the doctor, and the doctor called for him.

He knew within his heart that when one was sick and Doc Bailey sent for him, the end was near.

Reverend Winslow made his way through the weathered homes of their Roanoke Colony, sad to see how many were still in desperate need of repair. They were trying, as a people, they really were, but as hunger settled deep within their bellies, with little meat to be hunted in the forest, the arms of the men slowly grew weaker, their strength dwindling by the day. His heart pined for the Wicker children, desperately hungry and blindly consuming the meal prepared by their parents just two nights ago.

Their front door lay ajar, no doubt a feeble attempt of Doc Bailey's to allow a cross breeze in the sweltering home. The heat was outstanding of late, even as close to the ocean as they were. He gently placed one hand upon the door, swinging it wide to view what awaited him inside.

It was worse than he thought.

In their front room, the largest of this simple house, lay all four of the Wickers on mats on the floor. The eldest child retched into the bucket beside him, his mother and father staring at the ceiling with great perspiration on the brow. The other child was tended to by Goody Smith, cleaning up the visible excrement that surrounded the child. He was suddenly aware of the stench of this home, the putrid smell of sickness, waste, and impending death. Their faces were yellowed, bloodshot eyes staring at him as he stepped through the door.

"God's blessings be upon you, dear ones." Reverend Winslow strained to smile, holding his breath so as not to further taste the smell of their woes. They were not long for this world, of that he was sure.

"Reverend Winslow," Doc Bailey sat in a chair at their heads, "I think it time we pray with the Wickers."

"My family!" John Wicker cried, "I've led them astray in asking them to eat of the frogs. Forgive me, Lord. Take me, if you will, but spare my children and my wife!" In response, his wife, the poor Goody Wicker, vomited on the floor between them. "You've damned us all, John Wicker. Damned us to die at the poison of these frogs!" To add to their misery, the frogs remained inside the home, Doc Bailey and Goody Smith doing what they could to swat them away from their dying kin.

"Now, now. Let us pray for God's healing upon you now." He spoke the words, but seeing their condition, the clear marks of dehydrated bodies not long for this world, he knew they were beyond God's healing. He wanted to believe, to beg for a miracle, and thus, he would try, but his heart wasn't in it. These people were soon to greet their Lord as a family at the pearly gates.

"Join me, kin, as we lay ourselves before the mighty hand of God." Doc Bailey and Goody Smith nodded, never moving from the Wickers's sides.

"Blessed Lord, we come to you today, asking for a healing upon the Wicker family. If it be your will, smite this sickness from their bodies, allowing them the strength to carry on." The little girl, Josephine, cried again as she retched into the bucket.

"Momma! Momma! My belly hurts, Momma. It hurts real bad. My throat–"

"There, there, child," Goody Wicker reached from her mat to rest one hand upon her child, doing what she could to comfort her as they died.

"Lord, I pray for their souls this day. Free them from this earthly pain and give them the confidence that absence from this earthly body is to be present with you. If you are to take them with you, Lord, welcome them with open arms, without pain, without suffering, preparing their hearts for a blissful eternity with you."

"God, save us." John Wicker whispered, his clothes stained with bile and waste as he tried to rise from his mat. He lifted his neck mere inches from the floor before it fell again. Not long, now.

"God, grant them a peaceful death," tears welled in his eyes as he spoke, "and ease their fears of going beyond. May they know, God, that those that trust in you, and believe in you, shall abide with you forever."

He turned to the youngest child, their little girl. "Do you know the Lord, Josephine? Are you ready to meet him with open arms? You've always been so good to say your prayers and walk in his light. He kneeled, stroking her sweat-covered forehead and she lay back on the mat and cried. "Yes, Reverend. I know him."

He turned to the boy. "And you, Jackson? Have you pledged your life in service to the Lord, keeping his commandments and praying each day with intent upon you?" The child nodded, more a twitch of his head than a nod, but the sentiment was clear.

"God, help these people. Take away their pain. Guide them with your hands. Forgive them of their sins and settle them in your grace."

Goody Wicker vomited again, only this time, she was unable to rise, causing her to choke on it. Goody Smith rushed to her side, turning her to allow the bile to spill out. The woman heaved, unable to truly catch her breath. Doc Bailey closed his eyes and whispered, "Amen."

Reverend Winslow sighed, drawing his knife. "Amen."

17
SOMETHING TO LIVE FOR

At the edge of the woods she stood alone, her thin linen night dress clinging to her skin as it was drenched in sweat. The night air made it cool. Damp. Uncomfortable. She could see every tree trunk, every branch as she walked further, deeper into its cold embrace. She hardly noticed as the rocks and broken twigs dug into the fleshiness of her bare feet. That pain didn't matter now. Areas untouched by the moon's slicing rays were shrouded in a blackness ten times black, with unknown creatures snapping twigs and rustling underbrush along with her. On any other night, this would have quickened her heartbeat and brought with it fear, but tonight she had little to lose, thus now they were of minuscule concern.

Perhaps one would strike out and claim her. A swift, effective end.

But nay. She'd decided this. Chosen this. If ever she were to make a decision for herself, it was now, and she had selected the copses beyond their lands.

The woods. Far enough away that only someone intent upon finding her would do so. No need to risk little eyes or little hearts taking in the sight of what she'd planned.

For months upon months since her beloved Henry's death, she had wrestled with hideous bouts of madness, losing her spirit... her will... her mind. It was almost a physical sensation as her hope departed from her, the strength to move on, her unending piousness poisoned by the trials of this world.

God didn't hear her. Not now. Maybe not ever.

Perhaps, dare she consider it, the God above wasn't like the God she knew of. After months of wailing and pleading and crying, the silence in return had darkened her heart. Her prayers for peace and comfort had gone unanswered. She fought at the thought that pinched at her each time she begged for a sign, anything that could assure her of his presence. Yet still, perhaps there wasn't a God at all.

And if there was, he surely didn't live among them here in the wilds, as their bleak settlement was long ago forgotten. Yet, she firmly believed there was life *after*. Their governor had clearly abandoned them, with no word of coming provisions or hope of his coming any longer. And now, it seemed, there were plagues upon them. More and more died each day.

And she would join them.

Her fingers, rough and calloused from many days of hard work in her life, clutch tighter around the blade she stole away from their tools. A blade often used for the skinning of rabbits and deer, now to serve as her final decision. Pursuing perfection in holiness was an exhausting task, one managed at the edge of anguish by the hope of a greater tomorrow. But how could she retain any hope when God himself has taken her only son from her? When even in the face of broken vows, her devotion to her earthly husband was yet in vain, as he continued to seek comfort outside of their marriage.

She could not, and would not, endure it any longer.

She knew, the moment she could not feel any spirit or movement of grace when she prayed, that clearly she was elected to damnation. Her sinful heart had won out, and as many believed, their fates had long been decided at the time of their creation. *His* will was inscrutable, they were told.

At first, she had feared it. She feared the thoughts alone would break her covenant with God, forged so long ago when she was still a young girl. They would be enough to condemn her if he did exist. If he did, and she had doubted him, this would be the greatest of sins, staining her soul with their mire.

Yet as the silence grew, so did the distance between she and these fears of damnation.

None controlled her. Decided for her. She would take this stand upon herself, exerting her own will upon the matter of life and death. As little Henry now crumbled to ashes and dust in the ground, so would she. Wherever he was for eternity, she would join him.

She halted in the darkness, just before a small clearing in the trees, bathed in the cool illumines of the moonlight. She would not venture there, for this deed should be done in darkness, away from any radiant glow.

But she needed to see, to accomplish her task.

Eleanor stepped into the clearing, the soft grass a welcomed comfort to her swollen feet, the last comfort she would feel. She thought of Henry, his small warm arms wrapped around her neck, brushing his nose upon her before he kissed her cheek, as he often did.

A tear slid down her face. Soon, my little love. Soon we will be together again.

She settled in the cool grass, crossing her legs beneath her. So final, this all was. But now was the time. Slowly, she traced the blade across her wrist, watching as the crimson stream ran down her arm. Aye, there was pain, but with it she felt her heart release from its prison of despair.

Odd, tall shapes moved within the trees past the clearing. Whatever it was, she didn't want to wait and find out. Quickly now.

She sliced the other wrist and with a trembling hand brought the blade to meet her neck. This would surely be the last, as she was already feeling the faintness of blood loss engulf her. She pressed it into her flesh, knowing this would be the end.

She thought of Ananias. The man whom she'd given her whole heart to, and he had smashed it upon the rocks like the waves that crashed upon the shore. Her flash of anger quickly replaced with an unsettling calm. How wondrous it was to punish him and take this small bit of revenge against him. What little she could do.

She started the final cut, but the pain. The searing, burning pain consumed every fibre of her being. With one final jerk, she sliced the knife to the other side of her throat. Her task complete.

Dear God.

What was she doing? Perhaps she should stay, for Agnes, for herself. She tried to gasp, but could utter only a choking sound, a gurgling of blood. She clutched her blood-slick hands to the gaping wound in her throat. *Virginia!*

God. No. She was the worst of mothers, thinking of her own selfish desires before them.

But no. There were others who would care for the little one now. Blood trickled down to her elbows, her dress covered in the crimson flow. To Hell with Ananias and his women. Agnes would look after the babe. Henry had no one, but now he would have his Momma.

As she sat still, the warmth of her blood was an odd sensation coupled with the cold that filled her body. She saw them moving toward her from the trees.

Women. Naked. Arms outstretched. They were rushing towards her.

It does not have to end this way.

We know it is revenge you seek. Let us help you.

With us, you will be restored.

You can dance with your babe and *seek revenge.*

An all-consuming scent of peppermint and lemon filled her nose as one of the women held something beneath her nose. The dark of night faded away as her vision swam with what could be. Running through the woods, laughing, with little Henry just ahead of her. The scene sprawled before her as if she were really there, in this moment. Sunlight glinted through the leaves, casting small shadows across his plump, rosy face that beamed with joy, with life, with hope. "Come get me, Momma!" he giggled as he waited for her, reaching out one soft and tiny hand that she so desperately wished to hold in hers again. She scooped him up in her arms, she could hug him, smell him, *feel* the life pulsing again through her little boy.

"My... Henry."

As she spoke, the scene changed. She watched as she gathered her children; Agnes, Henry, and a now older Virginia around a well-worn wooden table full to the edges with a delectable meal. She could smell the roasted pig as it crackled on the spit above the fire. Smoke. Smiles. Warmth. She drank in every sound and sight before her.

The vision changed again, with a soft voice whispering in her mind, "This is what we can give you, sister. But also, something more." Her fallen husband came into view, choking and spluttering his last of pleas on this earth. Desolate words, again. As the sparkle of life faded from his eyes, his body bloodied and broken, she knew what could be.

"Revenge," they whispered.

Blackness crept into her view once more, the cold of night and the pain of her earthly body at what she had already done. God would not look kindly upon her choice. Her mind raced, the light of this life slowly fading. Her former resolve had all but dwindled, and yet, it left behind a gaping hole in which her hope could be refilled.

But turning from him was the greatest of sins.

She knew these to be the witches. But they'd shown her peace. Love. Happiness.

If witches were of the devil, at this moment, she didn't care. They gave her something God had never shown her on this earth…something to cling to…to live for.

She reached out to them with her bloody arms.

Hope.

18

SHE WAS GONE

"*Dear God, I come to thee in fervent prayer. I am a wicked man. A desperate man. You know of my sinful nature more so than I know it myself, and yet I plead with you to spare the woman of my life from an unknown fate. My Eleanor is missing. Stolen away from our lands with no signs of where she hath gone. I fear the worst, and know I am, at the base of it, at fault. She is a Godly woman at heart. A woman true. She mothered our babes and simply fell out of prayer in mourning for Henry and disgust at my own actions. Let her not suffer the consequences of my sin, for my actions in both led her down the path of unrighteousness, a path I have so sinfully tread in these last years. Hear my plea, my cry for mercy, Lord. Bring her back to us and let all be well with her. I will be the husband she deserves. Forgive us this day, and lead us back into your light. I humbly pray. Amen.*"

She was gone.

When he'd awoken that morning, Ananias had but a passing thought that her absence from their home meant she had set to the daily chores early. Perhaps she was milking the goats, or feeding the few chickens they had left. Washing linens to hang on the line to dry. But no, when breakfast came and went and she was nowhere to be seen, they found themselves afraid. Agnes looked after young Virginia, feeding and changing her while he went out to call for his wife, but even after searching the village and scouring the outskirts of their lands, he couldn't find her.

Ananias feared the worst.

He was being punished. Again.

He stood just beyond the palisades, at the edge of the wood. The wind whipped at his whiskers, blazing hot sun burning his skin to a crisp, yet he didn't care. The hot, sticky air tasted of salt, as it so often did, with their settlement being this close to the sea. The woods just beyond their lands leaned in a colossal wave of green, trees swaying in the breeze as if beckoning him forward. With all the hope he could muster, Ananias told himself that together, he and his kinfolk would find his missing wife.

And yet, burrowing worry rats scratched and clawed at his mind. God holds the unrighteous for punishment on the day of judgement, especially true of those who follow the corrupt desire of the flesh. It was written clear as this day in the word, not to be construed in any other way.

God was surely punishing their family now, for the wages of his sin they had succumbed to on this barren rock of "riches and gold." Such lies they had been told. Encouraged to start anew, to bring life back into this failed settlement that was slowly wasting away yet again. Resentment. Greed. Lust. He was guilty of them all.

But for Eleanor, he feared her punishment came from the gravest sin of all–denial. When she spoke the words against God the night they had shared a harsh word, he prayed for forgiveness and mercy on her soul. And yet, with his own wicked doings, he wasn't even sure if his own prayers were heard anymore.

Goody Dare!

Eleanor!

Shouts from the woods beckoned him further. He had gathered a party to scale the trees and walk among the brush to search for any traces of his beloved wife. Those of the village were too good to him. They trusted him.

Believed him to be a righteous man, and yet he was too cowardly to correct them in their thoughts.

If they knew of his transgressions against her, against God as he broke his vows, he would surely be ruined.

Repentance was the only way forward, and while he repented in private, he knew it wasn't enough.

Eleanor!

His voice was hardly more than a rasp at this point, but still he must try.

To his left, the crack of snapping twigs and rustled underbrush sounded. "Ananias!" Jonathan Carver made his way toward him, dried leaves crunching underfoot with each step. He was out of breath, distressed. The young man's eyes wide as saucers. "We've found something you need to see."

Please, God. Don't let it be her body.

Racing faster than the beat of his heart, Ananias tore through the trees, briars and thorns scratching at his arms, following Jonathan to their discovery. Men of the village stood in a circle, just outside of the small clearing with the table rock. None wore a smile.

No. Please no.

Before them, crumpled on the ground before them as a linen ripped from the drying line, were Eleanor's nightclothes. He knew them to be white when she wore them, but now it might as well have been a red dress for they were drenched in blood.

He gasped. Her blood.

"Ananias–"

He stood before the dress, in the centre of the circle, unable to meet the eyes of any that gathered there.

"Perhaps an animal–"

His knees crashed into the ground, jagged rocks digging into his skin. This searing pain was surely nothing compared to what had befallen his beloved wife. He reached for her night clothes, slowly, trembling. If an animal had attacked her, this cloth would be shredded…but it wasn't.

"Nay," he whispered, "no markings lie upon this cloth. No animal could have done this."

"But–"

"Nay, I say!" Anger rose in his heart. Anger at himself for allowing this to happen. Anger at the men who stood here and looked upon her blood. Anger at God.

And as quick as it had flashed, his fury subsided. "How can this be so?"

Jonathan stepped forth, leaning down to place a comforting hand on his shoulder. "Mr. Dare, if Eleanor no longer lived, she, too, would rest with her bloody nightclothes. She might only be injured–"

Reverend Winslow chimed in. "Aye. She would have known that the smell of this amount of blood would attract a beast in the night, so she might have used it to clot the wound before moving on."

"But to *where*?" His mind raced. Eleanor injured. But maybe she was alive. His kinfolk assured him that though the new world may be vast, their little island of Roanoke was not, and thus the chances of finding her were in their favour. Their words gave him the strength needed in this desperate hour… something to shield his worried heart and stoke the fires of belief within him.

Hope.

"That's a lot of blood, though…"

He scowled at Charles Cotsmure, the wealthiest among them and never one to keep his thoughts to himself. "That does nothing to help in our cause. We must find her. If she's not yet dead, she soon will be, based on this blood loss."

Jonathan nodded in agreement. "The search continues." The man whom he admired looked around at those gathered. "With *haste*, gentlemen!"

Their village volunteers scattered, resuming their search, and Ananias rose, still clutching the bloody clothes. Some parts of it were still damp, his wife's blood transferring to his hands.

"We'll find her, Mr. Dare."

"Aye, Jonathan. I pray we do. I just hope that she's alive when we do."

19
MOMMA

ALICE TILLEY - AUGUST 1588

Nothing compares to the soft warmth of a nestled babe held tightly to the chest. Their musk mingled together, the babe's bottle long empty. Thankfully, she'd reached the age where she ate much more than her mother's milk to survive, but they still prepared warm milk at night for her. Alice stared into Virginia's earthy brown eyes, the colour of bark, much the same as the bark on the trees Ananias cut down to build her a chicken coop all those months ago. They cooed and nuzzled one another, alone in the Dare house as the sun settled for its slumber.

"Momma loves you," she whispered.

Virginia stared up at her, her little eyebrows pinching together.

"Say, Mah-ma. Momma." She pointed to her own chest. "Momma"

Virginia tilted her head. "Momma?"

Alice nodded and smiled. "Yes, little sweeting."

She held tightly to her, swaying back and forth. Her own boys had grown beyond the days of whispered lullabies and sweet snuggles and how she missed those tranquil times. Not that she didn't enjoy their rambunctious nature now, but rocking them gently to sleep was something she had taken for granted, and sorely missed.

She held Virginia's tiny fingers in her own, taking in her pale pink nails, her smooth chestnut hair. A small hint of rose colored her cheeks and perfect, button nose.

She gently squeezed her closer. Yes, she had missed this terribly.

"See the dreaming of a sweeting

One who finds it hard to rest

In your dreams, we will be meeting

A new family, wholly blessed"

Virginia's eyes closed, her heavy eyelids too much to bear with a belly full of milk and a soft word whispered in her ear. She was such a good baby. Easily fed. Easily changed. Never one to fight sleep or fuss about. Virginia was like the daughter she never had.

But now she did.

Suddenly, the hair on the nape of her neck prickled as if someone had blown cool air upon it. Alice looked at the window, straining to see what rested beyond in the dark.

A flash of white. She settled her senses, taking care not to move, not to breathe.

A pair of eyes were watching her.

Whooo hooo. She let out a slow breath, careful not to startle the child.

Nothing to worry about. Only an owl. She stared at the creature as it watched her, taking in its brown, speckled feathers and sharp beak. A magnificent creature, one she'd never seen this closely before. With a screech, her new friend spread its wings and took flight, and again the window held only the darkness outside.

Alice glanced at the sleeping Virginia in her arms. She was stepping in to help. That was all. This wasn't a ploy to make her way back into the bed of Ananias Dare and give him more children to help this settlement thrive. No. Eleanor had only been gone a mere month. Whatever the village may say, she wasn't sliding herself into his home as a serpent of lust. She was helping. Virginia needed her.

Or at least, that's what she kept telling herself.

They needed a motherly figure. She was a neighbour helping out in a time of need. Ananias and Agnes surely couldn't keep the farm going *and* care for Virginia all at once. A youngling merely one year and a half needed constant care. Love. Affection.

And she was the perfect person for it.

It only made sense, regardless of the slip into sin between her and Ananias before. She was without a husband. He, without a wife. These wilds were harsh, and their farms sat beside each other. It only made sense. Together they forged a new land, as God would have it and had charged their colony with.

Virginia stirred, snuggling closer into her arms, puckering her lips and furrowing her little brow. Perhaps she was dreaming. Dreaming of their new family. Her new Mommy.

No. At least not yet.

She must put these thoughts from her mind. She was helping. If Ananias bid it be so, then she would answer his call, but it was too soon. The pain from Eleanor's disappearance still lingered in the village—Goody Dare's presence swept from them as a mouse fallen to a bird of prey.

These things took time. Ananias would come around. God had blessed her with a second chance, and she ought not squander it away with premature ideas. Yes, time was all Ananias needed.

Agnes, on the other hand, was less than thrilled to have her around. She stirred the town with talk of witches. Evils in the woods. She'd frightened them all into a frenzy. But in the four weeks since Eleanor's disappearance, no other whispers of evil had come to light in the village. Life was returning to normal, as normal as it could be in a settlement of the wilds. Soon enough their whispers would die down, their eyes would close much the same as little Virginia's just did and they, too, would move on. There were no witches in these lands...only their own fears and sin. God would look kindly upon them now. He'd help them thrive. They'll see it. All they needed was time.

20

LICE

Vile little creatures, they were. Scratching, biting, itching, awful beasts that crawled through their scalps no matter how hard she tried to rid their home of the scourge. She sat on the kitchen chair with Robert, *Alice's* son, between her knees. She watched as the vermin crept between his hairs.

Head lice.

A common affliction back in England, yet some small part of her hoped that the fresh air and limited people of the wilds would lessen their presence. But no, here they were, and it seemed every head within the village was infested with them this time. She'd seen Emme and Ambry scratching at their heads before, praying the little beasts wouldn't make it to their home as well. Yet here they were. An infestation brought to them by none other than the Tilley boys.

She raked the comb, carved out of bone by her father, dipping it in scalding water after each pass, hoping the bugs would just *die* already. Each time she combed their little heads, even more seemed to take their place. Agnes cringed as her own scalp itched. Virginia seemed to be the only one among them that was spared from this torture, and thank God. At least the babe was safe from the torturous itch that consumed them all.

"Is it my turn, next?" Thomas asked. He was Alice's youngest, not yet ten years old but almost there.

"Yes, child. I'll do yours next." She sighed. Not that it would do any good. The wretched beasts would be back soon enough, of that she was sure.

She'd washed their linens, and father had replaced the straw in their beds at least three times by now, more so for his and Alice's bed.

Alice. She pressed her lips tight.

Only two months had passed since Mother had disappeared and how quickly she'd inserted herself into their home, as if that were the normal thing to do. Alice and her boys stayed in this house far more than their own now. Father had explained they were a "blenden" family, in order to survive, of course.

Pfft. Survive. Clouded words with a meaning that she could see through as clearly as the holes in their tattered linens. Father and Alice were being selfish. Godless. How could they use survival as an excuse for desires of the flesh? She'd seen the looks they exchanged, and try as she might, had heard them late into the night, as well. Her mother was not yet confirmed to be dead. Father was still bound by their marriage vows. Surely that was a sin.

Still, she grieved for Mother's absence, and surely somewhere deep inside Father did too. He had to. Her presence there was still all around them. Mother's stars she made with sticks, her apron, her dried flowers hanging from the ceiling, all reminders of the Mother they used to have.

But she'd seen it with her own eyes, how Father looked at Alice. How she brushed his arm when setting the table with yet another meal of stewed potatoes and stale bread and whatever Father could hunt in the forest. Thankfully, the crops had managed somewhat this season, yet even though they kept her belly full, every meal prepared by Alice left a bitter taste in Agnes' mouth. The whole of it was just plain foul.

A louse lept from Robert's head onto her arm. "Ahh!"

Robert blanched at her shout. "I'm sorry, Aggy." The poor child turned to her with wetness in his eyes, about to cry.

Her heart softened. These babes were of no fault in this. Their father gone, their mother a whore...they were not to be blamed in any of this.

She wrapped her arms around him. Might as well, as she was already inflicted with the crawling bugs herself. "Now, now, child. It was only a small fright. I'm intendin' to get rid of these crawlers soon enough. Now sit still, I believe we've just about got them all."

She should probably just shave all their heads by now, as Father had suggested, but how would Jonathan look upon her then? With little spikes of hair as coarse as a goat's coat. No, she'd suffer their biting, dousing her head in scalding water and combing until they were gone. They surely wouldn't stay forever. Perhaps the winter would encourage them to die.

Of course, the winter could encourage the lot of them to die, anyway, as there was still no word nor provisions from Governor White. She'd decided he'd all but abandoned them, that England left them on their own now. Relations with the natives soured still, and after all that happened with Ralph Lane's colony, the killing of their chief, she really couldn't blame them, not that she said it out loud anymore. Jonathan still suffered the repercussions of his words in the church when the bullfrogs had overtaken them.

When the witches were revealed.

She dunked the bone comb in the hot water again, swirling it round so that the mites she'd removed would move to the water and drown.

No. Best not to think on it. "Thomas. Come here, little one. It's your turn."

Thomas Tilley sat beside the window, playing with a wooden carving sweet Jonathan had made for him. A wolf, howling at the moon. Sometimes, when the moon was bright and shone through the window, Robert would hold it up and whoop to it himself, which brought a smile to her heart. These poor children. Raised among filth and death and hardship in an unknown land with damn witches in the woods. If they made it to adulthood at all, it would be a hard-won victory.

21

REBORN

ELEANOR DARE - OCTOBER 1588

"Carve the skin, break the bone

Those that harm us, let them atone

Beseech your ways, the winds blow in

Accept the power of Croatoan"

Tonight, she was to be reborn. She looked upon the faces of her new sisters, where once she saw twisted features and naked skin, now she beheld lush beauty and the unbelievable power of healing and restoration. Each gifted with the tools with which they could quench their personal thirst. Some knowledge, others power in healing, but for her...she sought revenge.

Their work was more than a miracle. They had led her back from the brink, given her a chance at a new life, at the cost of her old existence. Her sisters had surrounded her, placing their hands upon her wounds, mending the skin with their touch. It was painful, yes, but even her scars were hardly visible now.

She missed her daughters, it was true, but they were all she pined for. Her old life reeked of pain and anguish, hard labour and a loveless marriage to a cold, unfaithful man. Yet, she'd caught a glimpse of her daughters from afar and they fared well enough without her. She remembered Virginia nestled in Alice's arms and anger stirred within her. How quickly they'd replaced her, quick as a flame burning paper into ash. They were fine.

The full moon glistened against the blackened sky, shining down into their ritual clearing. Their table of stone rested in the centre. Death. Life. All a cycle, one that could be manipulated if you knew the proper way, and this is what they taught her. And, her sisters held true to their promises. If, tonight, she could complete the ritual required of her, she would become one with Croatoan and could cross the veil of life to meet again with the soul of her beloved son whenever she so chose, among other, less wholesome intentions.

Her sisters had not taken Henry from her. She knew that now. He'd simply fallen to the freezing cold outside of a watchful eye, the one her husband had trained on another.

And God himself had done nothing to stop it.

He was to blame. Unwilling to spare her innocent son as he walked alone near the waters. Tonight, once completely whole, she would grasp the power in order to do what needed to be done.

Their fire blazed, flames licking and spitting towards the sky, her sisters' chanting already beginning as they danced in a circle around her. Latsvna, their leader, sat before her. She was the oldest among them and possessed abilities beyond Eleanor's wildest of dreams. She had lived in this forest long before the others had joined her– the wife of the Secotan village chief. A native to this land.

Yet her love on this earth, Wingina, was slaughtered by Ralph Lane. He was beheaded over false ideals of betrayal, even though they had welcomed the white men to their shores.

She fed them, nurtured them, and had even washed their clothes. Once her people had taught them how to survive on the land, taking only what was needed and with reverence, they returned their thanks with the beheading of her husband.

Eleanor shuddered at the memory Latsvna had shared with her, a stake, planted in the centre of their village, with Wingina's dripping head upon it.

She looked into the eyes of her new guide. Latsvna, too, had suffered in that fight.

"I crawled to the forest, seeking to die in peace among the trees," she'd told her.

And it was then that the Fallen One found her, restored her– with an offer Latsvna couldn't refuse. Eleanor knew not who this Fallen One was, and readied herself to meet them tonight.

He gave Latsvna the strength to end Lane's colony, driving them back across the great sea. Her sisters, too, had heeded his call during Latsvna's siege of suffering on the settlement. For they were once among those men. All in search of their greatest desires, ambitions their former lives would never have allowed.

Dreams of power. Bloodlust. Revenge.

"There will be pain, sister–" Latsvna reached for her, cupping her cheek with care and concern, never having spoken a word, but intending her meaning through visions in the mind.

"--are you sure you want to do this? The choice is but yours to make."

Eleanor nodded, glancing at her sisters. Whatever was required, she was ready for it.

"You'll not be the same, either, dear. After he's finished." Latsvna raised her eyebrows.

Eleanor stiffened. "He?"

Latsvna nodded, grasping her hands once more. "Yes, child. Our gifts come with a price, as most things do. You must give yourself to him completely, willingly, or you cannot become one with the gifts of Croatoan."

Their chanting grew louder, screeching, piercing the night. She wondered how the village had never heard them before, but her sisters had assured her that they would remain unaware. Such was the nature of their ways.

"Listen to the forest, sister. Whispers in the wind carry the knowledge that you seek." Latsvna gripped her hands tighter, never parting her lips but imparting her words all the same. "But, as you know, we are fueled by the presence of the Fallen One."

So this was it, the moment she had agreed upon when rescued by her sisters. To forsake the one whom she'd previously lived for, for another.

God had forsaken her. This she knew.

"I'm not to convince you to join in our ways, only to share that once you choose this way there is no return. Do you understand?"

She nodded, her breath caught in her throat as she choked down the full meaning of what she was about to commit to.

Latsvna continued. "And are you willing to give yourself to him, body and mind, and invoke Croatoan?"

Eleanor closed her eyes, rubbing her cold, sweaty hands against her skin. In this moment, she knew there was no return. Forsake God, the very pillar of her former life, and awaken in the shadows of this world.

She nodded. "My children. Will I remember them?"

Latsvna smiled. "Every earthly memory will remain, viewed with a clear eye. Our ways will allow you to open the deepest, darkest doors of your nature, allowing you to accomplish that which you seek." The flames mirrored in her eyes.

Latsvna's voice filled her mind, more of a feeling than a string of words, but she understood their meaning. "Become one with his flesh. Unite your soul to our cause, grab hold of it, and allow yourself to be filled with his gift to you."

Latsvna peered into the shadows of the trees, fierce determination set upon her face. Eleanor followed her gaze.

Emerging from the shadows, the beast drew near. Larger than any human, its lipless mouth bared jagged teeth, hoofprints leaving a trail of blood behind it as it stepped into the light.

Dearest...no.

Her heart hammered in her chest, sweat trickling from her brow down across her cheek. She held back the tears that threatened to fall from her eyes, but as they welled, her vision blurred. She mustn't let them see her fear. Dear God. She couldn't do this. Not this way. Not now.

But Henry needed her.

Or rather, she needed him.

Latsvna led her to the stone table. "Lie on the rock, dear one." Eleanor trembled, but knew this must be done. The stone was coarse and rough on her naked back, tiny shards digging into her. So close to the fire, the heat seared her skin.

Latsvna guided her own hand down to her mound, pressing her fingers into her flesh. "Prepare yourself to take him."

The emaciated beast stepped closer, desiccated skin with tufts of matted fur stretched tautly over its bones. The stench of death and decay overwhelmed her senses, its breath a wheeze, eyes glowing red as the coals of the fire. Yellow claws clutched at her thighs, a rope-like tongue snaking out to lick at her nethers. At first she recoiled, burned by the touch of it, but soon felt a sizzling warmth instead of fire.

Blood thundered in her ears as she rose to meet its gaze, trembling as she spread her legs wider. She thought of her life. Her trials.

She couldn't do it. This was not of this world.

But she must.

The eyes of the beast– she'd seen them before. They were the same icy blue with grey flakes like her Henry's. She tried to close her eyes but couldn't. They were held open with a force beyond herself. She couldn't move, couldn't breathe. Her body trembled under his touch.

Her sister's chanted louder now.

"CROATOAN."

Their voices, echoing in her mind, grew louder into shrieks of pain and pleasure all swirled together in one.

"CROATOAN."

Eleanor threw her head back, releasing all of her fear and despair into the great void of life and death. She could feel the darkness reaching for her, its beckoning claw welcoming her in. It was warm, and comforting in a way she hadn't expected.

The beast kneeled before her, its spiked member coming closer to her opening. Her trembles ceased. She opened herself to him fully, his hot breath searing against her skin as did the fire.

Dearest God. The pain. The sin. She was giving her soul away to Hell itself. A single tear wet her cheek, yet as it did she clenched her jaw and grasped his fur in both hands, pulling him closer. Exquisite pain, coupled with unfathomable pleasure rocked her senses as he drove deeper in between her thighs. The coarse rock scratched against her back with each thrust, her breaths coming quickly now. The beast licked her face once more, sliding its tongue from chin to cheek, leaning forward to growl in her ear. This was pleasure in its purest form, rising, begging for release from within her.

Every ounce of pain, betrayal, and suffering ripped from within her as she cried, "CROATOAN!"

22

SATAN'S GRIP IS STRONG

REVEREND GEORGE WINSLOW – OCTOBER 1588

It is late October, this the year of our Lord 1588 and we have served as shepherds of a new life one year and three months now. We had a truer understanding of the Israelites in their wanderings of the wilderness for those forty years, and cling to the Word for hope and commandments of how to govern our fellow men. Sin trolloped unbridled in England, hence why we men and women of this settlement chose to start anew, and yet, it seems that our sinful natures are buried deeper than even we realised as sin yet runs rampant in this New World as well. God has seen fit to bring about his wrath, as evidenced by our trials, but yet we continue on, as those in the wilderness did, for God himself hath bid us to do so. Aye, even though we walk through these valleys of shadow and death, still yet we fear not the evils that lurk here. For I know in mine own heart that thou art with us eternally, sheltering us from greater evils even still. It is time for our people to come to a reckoning within themselves, seeking out the flame of sin and dousing it with the holiest of waters provided by faith.

Reverend Winslow slid his gaze at those surrounded, all within the village save for the ghastly Chevren man who'd put aside his prayers on more than one occasion. He would be dealt with swiftly, but for now, this flock of sheep for which he was the shepherd was in need of guidance, the type of guidance he was the only man fit to provide.

"Who here among ye believes the reaching arm of Satan could not bear to reach us here, in the New World?" He narrowed his eyes. "Did you think we would not be tested of our virtue? Forced up against the wall against unknown evils that lie not only outside these walls, but within our very hearts?"

Their eyes were wide, which was good. He needed them to listen.

"Hear me when I say that evil lives among us! Inside us! Our earthly flesh is riddled with lustful desires unnatural to God and unbecoming to his great work in this world. We must devote ourselves *entirely* to the thoughts of our sinful acts we have all committed, our transgressions against God and our neighbour, allowing it to swallow us whole in that we might truly experience the greatness of God as he cleanses us from it!"

He chuckled, wiping the sweat from his brow. "Aye, the signs are clear, my fellows. As in Exodus where the Lord had turned their water in blood, we, too, have seen the bloody waters of this new world."

Ananias Dare, sitting three rows back, nodded his head.

"And did we *not*," he looked at the gathered crowd, their breath still, hinged upon his every word, "experience a plague by the way of frogs?" Murmurs and whispers began among them. Now they will see it.

"And *Lice*! My kindred. Are we not plagued by the crawling vermin who bite and claw at our hairs, keeping us from restful sleep and comfort in our homes?"

They nodded. "Amen, Reverend!"

"And *what* does that tell us, settlers?" His voice croaked as it grew in volume now, stepping out from behind the pulpit, his faithful Bible clutched tightly in his hand.

"That Satan's grip is strong!"

"That we shall overcome!"

He shook his head, looking down at the floor, allowing silence to once again claim the room for maximum effect before speaking again.

"That *we* are as the Pharaoh of Egypt." Questioning looks and furrowed brows met him again. He looked to Goody Archard, her signal to begin in song.

"Blessed Spirit of the King,

Of grace and love the Author,"

"To quote the word, speak unto yourselves in Psalms, and hymns, and spiritual songs, singing and making melody to the Lord in your hearts."

He continued, raising his voice above their song. "It is God whom we answer to, who leadeth in this strange and unforgiving place, and yet...as we are not yet plentiful as a people, God reminds us of his correction." He wiped the spittle from his mouth.

"Work repentance deep within,

And bend me at Your altar."

"Don't you *see it*? Can't we *know* that God has used this opportunity to correct our ways and set us once again upon the path which we came here for? We are to serve as a *beacon*, my friends. A light onto the path of the unrighteous, to show them there is a better way, a purer way, than the idolatrous worship of the Church of England, following their own bidding and looking beyond God's will."

"Melt my heart with majesty,

Then show my ruined self to me;"

"And that is why *we* must do it! Follow God's will! Absorb ourselves in His grace, seeking repentance and moving forward cleansed by the blood of the lamb." Emotions were heightened now, just as he'd hoped they would be. This is how a shepherd reaches his flock. "Cast out your demons! Put aside your wicked thoughts! If thou be the ones who danced naked in the woods, come forward! This is a time to cleanse ourselves of our sins and seek forgiveness in his grace!"

"Teach me—"

"Father, witness me! I wish to cleanse my thoughts of the evils in the woods!" Emme Winslow rose from the very first bench, throwing herself to her knees, raising her hands to God.

"—Your might and will to save me"

Yes, my child, be the example as we've discussed.

Reverend Winslow raised his hands, heated emotion rising in his throat. "My own daughter! My own daughter is the first to come! Will you join her? Cleanse yourself of your sins and ask for his forgiveness?"

Goody Brewster and her husband, William, stepped forth to kneel in prayer. "We seek forgiveness for our hardened hearts! Our wicked resentment is surely the reason we are unable to bear a living child!" They fell in tears at his feet.

Aye, it was good.

"Shake off the yoke of this sinful bondage that is not of God! Come to him, the altar is open!" Reverend Winslow walked with haste through the crowd. "*We* are the elect! Among the chosen for salvation while the rest of humanity is condemned to eternal damnation. Let not yourself be counted in those numbers, friends. Seek a cleansing! Wash away your sins and begin anew!"

Jonathan Carver and Agnes Dare were next to join those in prayer. "Through the word, sacraments, and prayer, we would find ourselves wrapped in the grace of—" he paused, shocked to see Ananias Dare and Alice Tilley rise to join in prayer as well, "—our Lord."

"Help me to commune with Him,
Depend and follow after Him."

23
THOSE OF BEFORE

"On this bright and airy morning full of life and warmth of the sun, Lord, I am encouraged that today will be the day that our fate will improve in this, the colony of Roanoke. Perhaps it is because I am filled with excitement, Lord, as one of my dearest friends, Ambrose Wythers, and I are headed to the edge of the sea in search of berries and herbs for the making of jam. With the work of our households a never-ending list of tasks, our days are filled with little joy and time for merriment, as are our ways, yet today will be different in that we have many hours to spend together on the shore, foraging together with a chance for laughter and pleasure. I pray for our safety, God, as I have seen what darkness lies within the woods, lurking in the shadows, and yet as I venture out beyond the walls of the palisades, I have no feelings of fear. The ocean calms me. Mother left us near six months ago, and I've come to think she may have joined with Manteo's people, or another such tribe, with the grief of little Henry's death too much for her to bear. I pray she's safe, Lord, wherever she is, and for peace to come into mine own heart at this new presence of Alice Tilley in our home. I don't agree with it, Lord, yet Father's choices are not mine own, and I daily try to right the wickedness that burrows in my heart. Give us this day, and help Ambry and I find the last of nature's sweetness before the bitterness of winter comes. Forgive me of my sins, and shelter me always. In your name I pray, Amen.

Agnes and Ambry held tight to their pine needle baskets, the sea breeze threatening to whip their coifs from their hair. Agnes bent low, the soft sand tickling in between her toes as she reached for another shell, this one with the shape of a star upon it. She placed the shell in her apron pocket, its cousins already clanking against each other as she walked. She loved the shells, and cherished this moment by the ocean with Ambry, as they had both lived far inland back home across the sea.

"It's so vast, isn't it?" Ambry said, shielding her eyes from the sun as she looked out beyond the shore. "I can hardly believe we sailed across it," she laughed, "but then again I'll not easily forget how sick we were as the deep waves rolled around us."

Agnes grinned. "I think you suffered worse than I, Ambry."

Her friend nodded, "Aye. And you were holed away with *Jonathan* below the decks. It's a wonder your mother and father didn't suspect anything even then."

She cast her a withered glance. "Oh please. They were too busy quarreling with each other or chasing after Henry as he tried to climb the sides." They laughed again. Poor little Henry. Such promises for a better life he had back then, and still yet her sadness at his passing burrowed deep within her heart. No. Not today. She wouldn't let her thoughts of what could have been consume her. Today would be good. Pleasant. "Remind me again of the plants Manteo told us we would find here?"

Ambry pulled the scribbled drawings he had made for them a few days prior. "Lettuce of the sea. He said we'd know it as a bright, green blade with a wave to it, looking much the same as lettuce we've eaten before. He said we'll have to wash the sand from it, and can eat it raw, or we can lay it out to dry and crumble into our soups."

Agnes nodded. She noticed a strange looking bird with a white belly and soot-colored head poking its long, orange beak into the sand. A tiny, soft-feathered bird, clearly its young, scampered around on the sand beside it. She smiled. A mother and her babe. Such sweetness.

"And then there's the beach bean vine, which we can find over by those dunes. He says we'll know it by the pink and purple flowers with seed pods that resemble our garden green beans." Ambry walked closer to the water's edge, dipping her toes in it as a wave crawled up the shore towards them. "Let's go for a swim, Aggy." She turned, a mischievous glint sparkling in her deep green eyes, much like the sea foam Aggy had spotted a couple hundred paces back.

"Ambry, no! I'd not like to walk back to the colony soaked through in my dress." She raised her eyebrows at her. "Surely you aren't serious."

Ambry had already set her basket down by the dunes, removing the outer layers of her dress down to her knee-length tunic and shift. "Oh come on! It's so hot. And we've been gathering for a long time. Have a bit of fun, Aggy!"

Her friend ran without abandon into the crashing waves, shrieking with joy and splashing water up around her. Agnes wasn't the strongest swimmer, the real reason she hesitated to join her, but Ambry wasn't going out too far.

Ambry floated her toes to the surface of the water, laughing as she lay back, allowing the waves to rock her, move her– carry her closer to the shore. "Oh Aggy, come *on*! The water is divine!"

Agnes looked around; she wasn't sure for whom, considering those that attempted to fish for the colony usually stayed to the west of this shore. She shook her head, but felt the smallest of smiles spread across her own lips as she set her basket on the dunes. "You'll be the death of me, yet, Ambry!" She laughed, pulling at the strings of her own dress to join her friend in the waves.

The water was cold, sewing needles of ice stabbing into her skin as she slowly walked into the water. Sharp, broken shells drove into the bottoms of her feet until she made it in up to her knees. She bent to run her fingertips through the water. Ambry was further out now, beyond the swell of the larger waves, swimming then turning to float on her back, only to turn and swim again. Her laughter was intoxicating, even if her teeth shivered as she tried to get used to the cold.

"Come for a swim!" Ambry called. Slowly, Agnes moved deeper into the water, first up to her thighs and then further until the water rose clear to her chest. The sand shifted beneath her, pulling her out further each time the waves crashed into the shore.

"I–" something small bumped into her leg and Agnes jerked her feet up underneath her, shrieking. "There's something in the water!" she cried, but Ambry only laughed.

"It's fish, Aggy. We're in their home. Calm yourself and just enjoy it!"

She wasn't sure that she and Ambry shared the same understanding of enjoyment, yet she tried again to find the peace and tranquillity her friend seemed to have. Ambry slapped her hand across the water, showering Agnes with a cold spray. She could taste the salt of it in her mouth. Swimming in the ocean just wasn't her idea of fun. "I think I've had enough of this," she called, ready to head back to the shore and the comfort of the warm, dry layers of her dress.

"Oh boo!" Ambry laughed, laying back again and swishing her hair back and forth in the water.

Another wave, this one larger, lifted Agnes from her feet and pulled her closer to the shore, but as soon as it swelled, the ocean ripped again from under her feet, driving her further out to where her feet no longer touched the bottom. Her heart thumped as she struggled to swim with her arms, desperately clawing at the water, trying to get herself back to the shallows.

"Ambry! Ambry, I can't swim in this! It's too fast. Too harsh! I–" Her words were stolen from her tongue as another wave crashed upon her head, this time throwing her underneath the surface. She gasped, water filling her mouth and burning her lungs. A thunderous roar pounded in her ears, she couldn't breathe.

Dear God above, she was going to drown.

She kicked her legs, moving her arms, trying...trying. Her head crested above the surface for one moment. "Ambry!" she cried, but as soon as she choked out her plea, the water shoved her downward again.

She opened her eyes to try and see, but the water burned. Oh, how it burned. Her chest. Her lungs. She kicked with what remaining strength she had. So cold.

She was going to die.

****

"Aggy! God help her. Help me save her! Aggy, can you hear me?"

The sand. It was hot against her skin. She heard the rush of the waves. The ocean. Ambrose. She coughed. Choked. Salty water spilling from her mouth as she felt hands rolling her on her side. Her head pounded as she opened her eyes, the bright sun nearly blinding her as she tried to sit up. Ambry clapped her on the back, helping her expel the last of the sea water from her lungs. Everything hurt, but worst of all– her pride.

"I'm so sorry, Aggy! I never would have asked you to come out further if I had known." Her friend stared at her, tears falling down her cheeks and her wet tunic clinging to her skin. Agnes shook her head, unable to speak her thanks so instead grabbed onto Ambry's hands.

"Thank you," she whispered, "you pulled me out of there. I thought I would drown."

Ambry nodded. "Well, you nearly did!" They clung to each other on the shore, Agnes noticing they were far removed from where they'd entered the sea in the first place. "I think it best we head back now."

Ambry nodded. "Agreed."

She rose from the sand, strength filling her muscles once again as they walked towards the dunes where they'd left their baskets. Thankfully, all they'd collected remained, untouched by any of those strange-looking birds or any other wildlife. She turned her back to the ocean, looking instead beyond the dunes to the small, dark shapes far removed from the shore.

"What are those, Ambry?" she asked, wondering if her friend had seen them as they had come to shore earlier in the day.

"Hmmm. I'm unsure. We walked along the beach for at least three hundred paces before going in the water, and then the ocean carried us farther, so I've never been over here before." Her friend narrowed her eyes, straining to see. "Let's have a look, then."

While Ambry's adventures had already led her astray this day, curiosity overwhelmed Agnes as she, too, wanted to know what the small dark shapes protruding from the earth were. They walked in silence, and as they drew near, her breath caught in her throat.

They were tombstones. Wooden. Weathered only slightly but clearly engraved with names.

She turned to Ambry. "Perhaps a native burial ground?" Ambry shrugged. But why would the natives, who lived deep within the woodland areas surrounding them, bury their dead this close to the sea? They walked closer, further from the ocean's edge and sand dunes, with the tall, soft grasses tickling in between her toes.

Agnes bent low, perching her basket on her hip as she read the words carved into the wooden tombstones.

William Backhouse: Death by Plague 1586

Anthony and Rise Courtney: Consumed Sick Cattle 1586

Edward Ketcheman: Death by Plague 1586

Jane Pierce: Succumbed to Boils 1586

"Dear God," Ambry whispered, "do you see what that says? Death by plague." Agnes nodded, the full weight of their own colony's trials heavy upon her shoulders.

"1586," she whispered. The date of the previous attempt at Roanoke settlement. This wasn't a native burial ground, but the final resting place of those that came before them. The carved pictures in the wood made sense now.

A frog.

Cattle.

The deaths of those from Lane's original Roanoke Colony.

What was happening to them had happened before, and if the plagues mentioned upon the wood were to be believed– their trials had just begun.

24
COME TO ME, LITTLE LOVE

ALICE TILLEY - OCTOBER 31, 1588

"*Momma...where are you, Momma?*"

Alice opened the creaking wooden door to their room, following the whispered voice of her eldest son, Robert. It was an eerie sound, as if floating through the air yet thundering once it reached her ears.

"*We need you, Momma! Help us!*" Thomas, this time. She scrambled to their sleeping mats, pulling back the linens to see that neither were there.

"*Momma! She's coming!*"

"Robert? Thomas! Where are you little loves? Momma's coming to find you."

She raced around the tiny home that her late husband had rebuilt for them. They hardly stayed here now, yet sometimes they would if the boys wished for it. These walls brought them comfort.

Her heart thumped in her chest. Her boys were in trouble. She must find them. Now.

"*Momma!*"

"I'm coming!" They weren't in the kitchen, but in the darkness of this moonless night, she watched as the front door swung on its crude hinges. The trees groaned in the wind outside. One little shoe rested on the doorstep. The hair of her arms prickled, chilled from the sight of it as the cold night air blew inside.

"Thomas! Momma is here. Come to me, little love!"

A piercing scream ripped through the silence of the night. She ran to the barn, lightning flashing in the sky yet it made no sound. Chickens roused from their roost as she struggled with the door, the damn handle always sticking, goats bleating and horses whinnying as she startled them.

But they didn't have horses?

As she flung open the door, lightning flashed again but this time with a thunderous clap piercing straight into her ears.

Dearest God.

Swinging from the loft above, their backs turned to her, were both of her boys, hanging from nooses, one without his little shoe.

She ran to them, clutched at their small, cold bodies, trying as she might to lift them. Their eyes were open...glassy.

Dead.

In the throes of her anguish, a visceral scream ripped from her throat, chickens crowing and flapping away at the sound.

"My boys! Not my boys"

Suddenly, her arms were empty, they stood before her on the ground, wide eyes staring up at her yet both faces were gaunt and grey. Their lips were blue, their tiny necks broken.

"Hello, Momma." Thomas grinned but narrowed his eyes. This wasn't her boy. God, no, it couldn't be.

"We need you to help us." Robert stepped forward, a carving knife gripped tightly in his hand.

"Yes, Momma, please." Thomas reached out for her, stepping forth as if to hug her.

Alice trembled, gasping for air, unable to make sense of anything at all. She reached for them, but backed away.

Blood dripped out of their eyes now, her two precious boys moving closer, their innocent faces twisted into snarls. Cold sweat dripped from her brow, her blood running cold.

"I–" she tripped on the rope lying on the ground, falling backwards. She scrambled back, but still they came.

"Help us, Momma." Robert raised the carving knife before her, plunging it deep into her shoulder.

"NO!"

Alice clutched at her linens and sat upright, the window of her small room crashing open in the wind, waking her from the terrible nightmare. Heart still pounding, she raised her fingers to her shoulder, checking for the wound she was so sure had been there.

She rose from her bed, heading straight to the room where the boys slept. She had to check them. To make sure.

There, exactly where she'd left them when she bid them goodnight, lay her two, innocent boys. No carving knives, no noose, no blue lips or wicked sneers. Only two brown-headed boys with no knowledge of her nightmares.

Thanks be to God.

She returned to her room, closing the window shutters and pouring a small bit of water into her basin to wash her face and clear her mind.

The nightmares came for her daily now. She'd thought, perhaps, that staying again in her own house would ease the innor torments she suffered and bring about a small bit of peace, but that didn't seem to be the case.

She settled again in her bed, thankful for the fresh hay gathered by Ananias to keep her more comfortable.

He helped her, as she did him.

Alice lay back down, first on her side, then with one knee hitched as she lay on her stomach. She never cared for sleeping alone, but surely the nightmares wouldn't last forever. Pulling the blanket to cover her back, she suddenly felt a cool breeze gently blow on the nape of her neck.

But, she'd shut the window.

Alice froze, lying still as stone to hear if anyone were in her midst. Perhaps one of the boys had risen to play a trick on her, but no...she knew that wasn't the case.

She forced a swallow as the thunderous beat of her heart once again met her ears. It wasn't a dream, this time, but the breeze had stopped. A trick of the mind. She needed more sleep, was all.

She stretched out her extended leg, one foot sliding out from underneath the covers. Not too hot, not too cold. She placed one arm under the pillow.

Something sharp, a nail...a claw...scratched along the bottom of her uncovered foot.

Alice froze as a solid board.

She shut her eyes tight, praying this was yet another nightmare, but it felt too real this time. The claw trailed from her foot up her legs, over the covers. Fingers reached into her hair, gripping at the scalp, colder than ice. It turned her head, forcing her to face whatever demon held her, but she kept her eyes closed.

"Our Father, who art in Heaven, hallow–"

"HA!" Her captor laughed. But wait, that was no demon. It was a voice she knew.

The voice of a girl.

Agnes Rose.

25

INNOCENT GUILT

Ananias Dare - Nvember 1, 1588

"We seek ye, Lord, in this our troubled hour, with hopes that thou can shine a light upon our settlement and guide us out of the darkness which swirls around us. It's all consuming, the stain of sin, and yet while we scrub at our tattered selves in order to wash it away, we know in our own hearts that the blood of your son is the only way. I confess my sins privately to you, yet I know it deep down that I must profess them widely, in a larger circle, in order to truly repent and be made whole again. Try as I might, I am moving forward with my life. Eleanor has not come back to us again, and I fear she never will. I believe she was taken, Lord. Taken by those in the woods my Agnes Rose spoke of those many months ago. I intend today, to gather those in the village who are of a praying mind, to wrap ourselves in your word and prayer to find an understanding to these trials, to right our ways, and to seek the cleansing Reverend Winslow speaks of. In your holiest of names, Amen."

Ananias glanced at those gathered round, perched upon cut logs and what chairs they could scrounge from the surroundings. Today they would pray, seek counsel in the word, and just as the men of the settlement fortified the palliside upon their first arriving at Roanoke, so now they would fortify their hearts against the sins of this world.

He would start anew and begin again as a cleansed man, a whole man, away from the stain of his own past transgressions against his former wife and God. There was William and Mary Brewster, Reverend Winslow, Bennet Chapel and Walter Mill. The man upon which Agnes looked kindly also joined them, Jonathan Carver, and Goody Chapman and Goody Warren, both of whom were the most knowledgeable women of the Bible he'd ever met.

Together, they would search the Word for findings related to witchery, seeking guidance if these trials of late were actually what they had experienced. He had not shared his visions of Henry, for fear of being accused of witchcraft himself, yet with the warnings of Emme and Agnes at the meeting for the frogs, he couldn't deny an otherworldly presence might be at work here. At this point, they weren't sure what to believe, but he'd seen the plagues of a biblical nature with his own eyes, more than once, and feared that if such trials continued they would not survive.

"Bloody water, frogs, and lice...all things we've seen come to pass here on Roanoke Island." Good Warren opened her word, no doubt searching for the passage in Exodus in which they are described.

"And yet," William Brewster pinched his brow, "we've all experienced lice...even back in England."

Ananias cleared his throat, "Aye, we have, but how can it be that even the days after we rounded up the frogs, they were gone within a week? After bagging and bagging, it seemed it would never end and yet they were suddenly gone?"

"So you think it be witchcraft then, Ananias?" Goody Warren looked to him with a questioning eye.

"I–" Ananias prepared to answer her, but Reverend Winslow cut him off.

"The girls mentioned witchcraft, and if I do recall, Ananias, your daughter saw them with her own eyes!" The reverend raised his eyebrows at him, releasing a puff of smoke from that damned pipe he always kept. He wouldn't know the man if he didn't reek of the stench of tobacco, easily noticeable even from where he sat, ten metres away.

"In my questioning of the girls, they spoke of witches, dancing around a fire, sacrificing a goat and drinking its blood. Surely you, Ananias, of all people, believe the words of your own daughter as she speaks of this Devilry?"

Ananias nodded, lowering his head in respect for the Reverend. He would know more of these unholy works than he, as all who felt the call of God to minister were taught about such things long before taking to the pulpit. He'd seen it in England. They all had. The muffled screams of the accused from within the fires of the stake, still echoed in his ears.

The reverend continued. "And yet, I question, as we speak about in Sunday prayers, if sin doth not also play a part in these trials. If witches it yet be, then why would they invoke plagues of a biblical nature to haunt us? Hmm? Could it not be that God is sending us warning signs to address our own sins, to ready ourselves in a fight against the evils of the woods?"

William and his wife Mary, Goody Brewster, nodded in agreement.

Ananias couldn't disagree with him.

"Exodus, Leviticus, and Deuteronomy...that is where we begin our search for methods in defending ourselves against such evils," Reverend Winslow said.

Just then, across the clearing between their houses, Ananias noticed the shape of a woman draw near, her two sons in tow.

Dear Lord. His neck stiffened. It was the last person he wanted to see today.

Alice Tilley.

"Speaking of sin–" Walter Mill spoke before instantly clapping one hand upon his mouth. Jonathan Carver glared at his friend.

He felt a fire burning at the tips of his ears.

Goody Warren rose, "What is she–"

"I–I've no idea." The rage and fear splashed across Alice's face could surely bring any other man to his knees. Something was wrong.

"I *knew* it!" she shouted. "Ever since you've graciously offered to help me and my boys, that daughter of yours has had it out for me. She *lies*! Wickedness yet stirs within her heart, Ananais, and you best be the one to deal with it!"

Ananias rose. "What say ye, Alice? Surely you're not placing blame for our trials on Agnes Rose this day?"

She stopped, clutching at both of her boys. "Aye, that is exactly what I'm meanin' today. She visited me last night. I heard her voice. She's the cause of my nightmares, I'll have you know."

Gasps rang within the circle, Goody Warren placing one hand upon her heart.

He rose. "Alice...enough."

"She didn't see any witches in the wood by chance, Ananias. Your eyes are clouded by the love you have for your daughter, preventing you from seein' what lies before your very eyes! *She* is the witch, I say!"

"Agnes Dare?"

"It's not true."

"This harlot speaks lies."

"A witch!"

"Come now, come now, settle down, kindred, and let the woman be heard." Reverend Winslow moved toward Alice offering his hand to her. "Speak freely and release yourself from this burden. How can thou know Agnes to be a witch?"

Alice glared past him, straight at Ananias.

"Last night, as me and my boys were sleeping in the night, she stole into our home and ran her claws up my legs. She grabbed me, suffocated me.

Put terrible thoughts in my head as I dreamed. She tried to rip me from my bed, but God held a mighty hand upon me last night, and she could not."

Ananias shook his head as all eyes fixed upon him. "Alice, you shan't... you don't really believe–"

Jonathan Carver stood. "You saw her with your own eyes, then? Agnes at your bed?"

"Aye! Well–" she paused, casting her eyes across those gathered, "well, I felt her claws upon my skin and heard her voice, but I know it was she!"

Ananias clenched his fists at his sides, glancing at Jonathan. The man's face had drained of all colour. Surely this couldn't be true.

Jonathan turned. "But you didn't see her, Alice. Perhaps the voice you heard wasn't hers at all."

"I–".

Heat rose to his cheeks as anger flashed within his heart. How dare she say these things. "Take back these accusations against my daughter, Alice. God condemns a liar, that you know is true!"

"The witch! She lives among us!" Goody Warren had fallen to hysterics. They tread in dangerous waters now, with accusations such as these.

"Silence!" Reverend Winslow narrowed his eyes. "We will question the girl, that is for sure. Ananias, bring her to me in the meeting hall. We will speak there."

"But Reverend–"

"Enough! Ask yourself why you wouldn't want to root out the cause of these accusations and rid ourselves of the very evil we gathered here today to discuss." The Reverend trained his eyes on him.

If Ananias could bury himself in the ground with a thought, he would do it now.

"Your son...your wife, their demise cannot be ignored in this, Ananias." Goody Brewster stood next to him now, grabbing his hand in both of hers, trying as she might to bring him comfort. "There could be more to this, dear friend. Agnes may yet not know she is afflicted, or possessed, if that's the case. Questioning will do her no harm, and perhaps that can help clear her name of this?"

He nodded.

"Prepare the jail."

He heard the words, but couldn't believe that they came out of the Reverend's mouth.

"*Jail*!" The fires of anger ignited within him again. Jail was no place for his little girl.

"Absolutely not! I agreed to questioning, in the prayer house. That is *all*."

Jonathan Carver spoke. "Surely there's no need for all that, Reverend?"

Reverend Winslow turned and nodded to Walter and Bennet, both who raced off towards the one-room shack they'd appointed as the jail after some of the men who'd joined them were in need of it. "And you, Jonathan Carver."

The young man paled white as milk as the reverend turned to him.

Ananias moved toward Jonathan. "Reverend Winslow, there isn't any need–"

But the reverend raised his hand to silence him, turning to face Jonathan. "Did we not also hear testimony of your consorting with the witches in the woods along with Agnes?"

The young man trembled, knowing the outcome of such a crime. "No...no! We were not conjuring with any witches in the woods, sir. We–."

"Then what, pray tell, would have you and Miss Agnes out in the woods at night at *all* young Carver?" The reverend's wheels were turning, Ananias could see it, but even he wanted an answer to the latest question.

"We...uhm...we were–"

But the reverend wouldn't hear it. "Sin! Unbridled. Take him to jail along with her, but put him in the other room."

"Reverend!" Ananias shouted.

"Ananias." Reverend Winslow shot him a glare. "You'd do best to reign in the happenings of your household, sir." He held his bible close to his heart. "God speaks to me often, kindred, and I have known it for a while that evil galloped among us. Even still, I believe that when the whispers of sin surround us we must not allow it a chance to do more harm. Agnes Dare and Jonathan Carver, guilty or innocent of witchcraft, will wait in jail until the time of questioning." He paused. "And until then, I will seek the guidance of God in this matter."

Ananias raced after Walter and Bennet. Two more men appeared to take Jonathan away.

Someone called for him, it sounded like Alice, "Ananias!" but he didn't slow.

He must speak to Agnes before they took her away.

26
SHACKLED

AGNES ROSE - NOVEMBER 1588

"*Witness me now, oh dearest Lord, that I am not as they say I am. A witch, they've called me, like the ones I saw in the woods. God as my witness, I never lay a hand upon Mother or Henry as I am so accused, for I loved them with every thread of my heart, and still mourn their absence from us. I do not yet know which of my kindred hath accused me so, but in my heart I fear it be the same woman who has tightened her grip upon Father, even before Mother had yet gone. God, I beg of thee, I pray with all that is in my heart and soul, to help them know that I am true. Yes, I know of my wicked thoughts and how easily I succumb to the temptations of the flesh, but I have never, and* will *never turn my eyes from God and forsake him for the Devil. I'll not do it. I am an innocent in this. Please help them see. In thy holiest of names I pray, Amen.*"

Agnes lifted the metal cup full of water to her mouth, her shackles raking against the sores on her wrists. Stale bread lay on the ground beside her. Sometimes she dunked it in the water to soften the bite, yet nothing could improve upon the taste of it. How she pined for the custards and sweets from England, or even a pumpkin cake, long ago baked by her and Mother back before everything changed.

Two weeks, she'd been here, chained to a barrel full of grain, fed only by the food which Father so dutifully brought her twice a day. The food sent by the reverend was hardly more than slop for a pig, and even as hunger stirred within her, gnawing and clawing at her middle, she couldn't bring herself to eat it. She thought of Virginia, of Henry, of Mother. How far her family had fallen in this new world. And now she, herself. She thought of the vile, putrid thoughts of resentment she'd harboured every day since their arrival, staining her relationship with God. In the night, by the grace of God, she and Jonathan could whisper to each other through the wall, which brought about a small bit of comfort. He fared no better than she, but Father brought food for him, too, God bless his soul. Somehow, Jonathan managed to keep his faith in the villagers, holding strong to the belief that they would soon realise the mistake they'd made.

"It can't be long," he'd whisper to her.

Tears stained her father's cheeks each time he opened the door, allowing a much needed breeze of fresh air to lighten the stench of her cell. They'd provided a bucket to relieve herself in, and with the shackles she couldn't keep it far away. She'd never given a thought to the conditions of their jail until she, herself, sat in it, but when she got out, it was surely something that needed to be addressed. The nights were quite cold, but the days were tolerable as far as temperature went.

Best not to anger them further, though, as she waited for the damned Reverend to "complete his findings" or whatever falseties he'd told them.

She saw it clearly now, more than she ever had before. While, yes, they were not perfect as a people, God himself only extended his hand upon the fallen in order to correct them, using these lessons to help them lift *themselves* out of tribulation. She'd been taught to believe that her entire life. It was almost an awakening in her soul, to come to terms with her own fault, to re-train her focus on being the best she could be once she got out. God was not to blame here. It was Alice...and the reverend.

Her friends had come to visit her, but there was one who stayed away. The one she'd most hoped would come, so that she could help them see the wrongness in this accusation.

Emme.

She knew that Reverend Winslow had spoken at length with Emme, and cursed herself for ever mentioning seeing the witches in the first place, since Emme was the one to sell her out in front of everyone. Alice must have taken that moment to latch on to opportunity, especially seeing as they didn't mince words when avoiding each other in Father's presence.

Ambry and Winnie did come, though, and brought news from the village to keep her spirits alight. They spoke through the slats in the walls, wide enough for Agnes herself to watch the goings on of the village, just outside of reach, yet close enough for the icy stares and hurried whispers as people walked by.

"Wouldn't I have escaped, if I was a witch?" she'd asked them. Ambry and Winnie laughed, agreeing with her at every turn. They knew it wasn't true, this talk of Agnes dabbling in witchcraft, and had stopped sitting by Emme at prayers or talking to her at all.

"You won't be in here long," and "your Father is gathering testimonies of your good works," they'd told her, and that brought about a small bit of comfort, at least. It wouldn't be long before she'd be out there again, and she would do everything in her power to make sure she'd never come back to this wretched place.

An owl hooted in the distance. A witch's familiar. She remembered the poem, far back when she and the girls had had their picnic in the woods.

Damn them all. The true woman of wicked intentions should be in here, not her. And when she got out, Agnes Dare gripped tightly to her thoughts of how to move forward. She would bring forth the reckoning of Roanoke.

27
A QUESTIONING

"*Dearest Lord, I fervently pray to thee today for guidance against these wicked ills of the world. There is a resistance here, whether from man or from thine own hand, and I seek to cleanse this village of the scourge in your holiest of names. Bring me strength, Lord, that I might shine a light unto this people, shepherding them in the ways of righteousness for your glory. As thy kingdom come, we wait for thee on this barren rock called Roanoke Island, as thy will be done for us to forage a new life in the wilds. I pray to thee that the crops which thankfully came in this season will last through the winter for the nourishment of our bodies. Forgive us our trespasses, as we know from the word to forgive those that trespass against us. Temptation runs as a rampant bull among us, but with the strength that I know only you can provide, we will be victorious over all evil. Help me find the truth in the Dare girl's words, and the Carver boy, to snuff out any flames of wickedness which might rest within their souls.*

Lord, I also pray for a healing upon mine own, as I have awoken this morn with hot bumps under my skin, reddish and purple in hue, tender to the slightest of touches. If it is your will, remove these blemishes from me as I am in a great amount of pain because of it. In your holiest of names I pray, Amen."

The lumps didn't downsize, rather, they grew into painful, pus-filled boils near to bursting on his skin. They grew in clumps, all over his body, meaning each movement brought with it excruciating pain. He surveyed his naked body in the mirror, his bloated stomach was covered in the sores just as his legs and skin-flaked tops of his feet were. Was this a disease? His family's linens were washed regularly by the ladies of the church.

Perhaps it was sabotage. Too much lye in the washing or poison oak soaked in the water. And if it were, there would be a reckoning. Or...it be the Dare girl, casting her magic upon them. He could delay no longer.

He carefully slid one arm into his linen shirt and then the other, saving his breeches for last. Wearing a doublet and cloak today was completely out of question. Emme, unaware of his plight, still slept in her room. Dear God, let her not be afflicted as well. Let her not suffer as he did. He had only just noticed the pus oozing from his arms, wetting his shirt, when there was a sudden, short knock on his front door.

"Reverend Winslow! I think you'd better come outside and see this."

It was a man's voice, one with urgency laced within it.

Knock. Knock. Knock.

"Reverend Winslow! This is urgent. I ask that you answer the door at once!"

He heaved the heavy wooden door open, swinging it wide to allow the morning light to pour inside his humble home. Ananias Dare stared back at him.

Also covered in sores.

The man's lips were pulled thin. Stern. "Reverend, God hath smite us again. The whole of the village is taken with it." Ananias looked at him from the top of his bald head, down to his leather shoes, "and I see you have it as well–".

"Aye. I do." He straightened to his full height, still one head below Ananias. "After great consultation with the Word and highly intentional prayers, I will speak with Agnes and Jonathan today."

Ananias scoffed. "A bit too late for that, I think. I went to bring breakfast this morning, and the both of them were taken with the plague as are we."

Reverend Winslow stood still as a stone as a sudden coldness crept inside his core. They were covered as well. Surely everyone in the colony hadn't contracted the same sickness, overnight, without so much as contact with each other. He thought of the little ones among them, the babes still suckling at their mothers' breast. Such pain upon the skin. Exodus came to mind. God, spare them.

"But...how can this be?"

Ananias turned, heading to where Agnes and Jonathan were kept. "Because they *aren't* witches, George," he sighed. "I, myself, doubted for a moment, but I see the sores on the both of them clear as day, and no man nor witch would cause such an affliction upon themselves."

Reverend Winslow opened his mouth to speak and then closed it again. Surely God was not punishing them further. But this, well it was certainly in line with the likes of biblical plagues.

"Fetch Roger Bailey, and meet me over there. We question them *today*."

Ananiass nodded and disappeared without a word, off to find their physician. He was young, and poorly trained, but, other than prayer and sacrament, was one of the only hopes they had right now.

"Reverend! Reverend Winslow! Has God spoken to you of these sores?"

He made his way through the crowd, careful not to touch any of the slimy pustules covering everyone's skin.

"My babies! My babies are covered in them. Please help them!"

"Please...ladies and gentlemen. I have a questioning to do and then we can attend to your needs. I know...I know it's hard. Just let me have this moment–" His heart thundered in his chest, sweat pouring from his brow now, stinging as it covered the sores on his face.

"Ambrose Whythers, sir, covered from head to foot in em'. Dead in her bed!"

He whirled to the voice that spoke. "Dead, you say?"

"Aye sir," Christopher Cooper covered his hand as he coughed, "the boils covered every inch of her." Reverend Winslow noticed a bit of blood on the cloth Christopher held to his mouth.

Good God. Were the boils inside them, as well?

He turned and headed to the small log cabin inhabited by the Whythers family. Marke Whythers, his wife Margery, their eldest Winefred, and three smaller children all made the journey so that Marke could serve as treasurer of Roanoke Island. Not that he had much to treasure, seeing as money had little use here when the villagers did their best to barter what supplies were left to them.

Death was not an unusual thing, at least not here in the wilds where sickness or struggle or any manner of things could lead to one's demise; yet the death of this young woman from what can only be assumed is a plague weighed heavy on his soul. These plagues were progressing beyond mere nuisances into life-threatening and life-*ending* affairs.

And his Emme and Ambrose were friends. She would be crushed.

"She's GONE!" Goody Whythers bolted outside of their home, clutching her aprons with sore covered hands. "Dear God above we are damned! We are damned this day to burn in a blazing fire! Marke! Come quickly!" Her husband rounded the corner from the back of the house.

"What, what?" The treasurer could hardly see them from under the swollen pustules above his eyes.

"Her body is *gone*." Margery shrieked as she flapped around their yard. She looked like a chicken, clucking and flapping as if a fox chased after her. "I left her in her bed, to give Doc Bailey a chance...but she's *gone*!" Goody Whythers, bloody sores and all, sank into the arms of her husband.

"Reverend, you have to believe me!"

His tongue might as well have been a slug in his mouth, for he couldn't move it or coax it into speaking. Try as he might, all he could do was open and close his mouth, uttering sounds that surely made no sense to anyone but him.

"Uh–I–"

His heart beat faster at what this could mean. Had Revelation come? Bodies disappearing, amidst a plague of untold origin. God himself or the Devil one had their arms wrapped around this, and for either, he was afraid.

"Marke, search for your girl. She might not have been dead after all and simply risen from her bed!"

"It's witchcraft, Reverend! Of the Devil! God spare us. Save us!"

Lord Jesus, Almighty God on High, if she weren't alive and yet still risen from the bed, he would fling himself from the cliffs at the shore. This cannot be. Any of it. This wasn't of God. Our heavenly father has no use for the empty, earthly shell we leave behind once we die.

But there was an entity that did.

And the stolen body of Ambrose confirms it.

Roanoke Island was indeed plagued by witches.

He stared at the Dare girl, covered in sores just the same as his. "Reverend Winslow, can't you see? If I were a witch, I would surely heal this affliction upon mine own skin, and Jonathan's too. I've nothing to do with this...nothing at all. I merely viewed those that bring about these evils as they were dancin' in the woods. That's all." The Dare girl had a point. There was no rationale in thinking she would bring about the sores on her own person, or bring about the demise of one of her friends.

Which brought to mind.

"Agnes...are you aware of the condition of your friend Ambrose Whythers?"

The accused narrowed her eyebrows, cocking her head to the side in clear confusion at his words. "I–uh–well, I saw her a few days ago when she visited but not since then?"

The reverend sighed. "Have you heard of her afflictions today, child?"

Agnes Rose's eyes grew wide, her lips parting as she said, "No? She has the sores, too? Is she ill?"

Reverend Winslow closed his eyes, breathing deep through his nose. "Name your commandments, child."

Agnes nodded, worry glistening in her eyes. Her father, Ananias, had wordlessly made it over to their shack now. He stood beside them and watched as she began.

"We should have started with this, Reverend!" Ananias muttered.

He opened his eyes. "Enough." A calm washed over him. "Let the child speak."

"Thou shalt have no other Gods before me. Thou shalt make thee no graven image. Thou shalt not take the name of the Lord thy God in vain." She raised her eyes to the clouded sky behind them. "Remember the sabbath and keep it holy–"

"*To* keep, Agnes." Ananias whispered.

He watched as Agnes nodded at her father. "Honour thy father and thy mother. Thou shalt not steal. Thou shalt not commit murder. Thou shalt not commit adultery…"

Agnes paused.

Her father stepped closer. The air held thick as her silence grew. Agnes flitted her eyes around them, looking upward as she tried to remember. "The last one Aggy. What's the last one?"

She faltered in word. A single bead of sweat rolled down Reverend Winslow's face, waiting with bated breath. If Agnes were a witch, she could not utter the commandments in their entirety.

"I–uh–thou shalt have. No, Thou shalt–"

Ananais pulled at his hair. "Agnes Rose!"

"Covet! The last commandment, that's it! Thou shalt not covet thy neighbour!"

Relief washed over him as a bucket of warm water in the weekly bath. She had spoken them true.

He pulled the key to her shackles from his pocket, handing it to her father. "You may release the girl."

"And Jonathan, too?" She cried.

"He must speak for himself the commandments this day, and if he can name them, then he too is found innocent of the crimes of a witch."

Agnes Rose from the ground, her shackles unbound. "Praise be to God, today!"

He nodded, forcing a smile towards her. "Yes, yes. Remember your prayers." Reverend Winslow watched as she hugged Ananias, a father embracing his eldest daughter. Both grimaced, pulling apart and staring at the pustules that pained them.

"Emme will be so glad to hear of it."

Agnes paused, with a hesitation in her smile. "Yes, sir, I'm sure she will. I'm sure they all will. Ambry and Winnie, too." She stopped. "Why was it that you asked me about Ambry? Her condition?"

He sighed. He might as well tell her, as they were no closer to finding out the cause and still had a day of trials ahead of them, what with the sores and all.

"I'm afraid...well, I'm sorry to tell you this Miss Dare, but your friend seems to have suffered the worst from her wounds–"

Agnes released her father. "And?" Such worry in her eyes. Why did he have to be the one to tell her now?"

"Agnes...she's dead."

28

TO FLY

Lenorea twirled around in the old, musty hut given to her by her sisters. So generous. So giving. She was careful not to bump into the large wooden table by the fire, nor knock over the shelves littered with clay pots filled with all manner of curious things.

Oh, what life *was* now. Chirp, chirp, chirp goes the little birdie outside.

"Hello, little bird. Come to help me?" She busied herself collecting each knife she would need. The long one. The short one. The knife made of stone.

Cut the bones and carve the skin.

Lenorea sang to herself as she worked.

Remove the insides from within.

Ambrose Wythers lay upon her table, removed of all clothing and covered from head to foot in the sores. It had worked. Her first attempt at sending a plague upon the colonists had been a success. She had watched them this morning. Wailing. Crying. Miserable at their condition. A pang of sadness almost broke through, knowing this was Agnes' friend– but it didn't. She needed the fat. Today. One step closer to having her revenge.

Following in her sisters' plan, she had unleashed this plague of a biblical nature upon the settlement. Mocking their God. The God of pain, of suffering– the God of silence. Yes. Yes. Such a pretty one, this girl was.

She licked her chapped lips, staring with greed at the girl. If they'd follow in the ways she knew all too well, they'd blame this plague upon God, himself. Her sisters had intended to root them out by the stem, driving them from these lands, as Latsvna had done before. That she, herself, could help in this, and have her revenge against them, was bliss.

Few had consoled her when Henry had died. None had told her of Alice and her charms. Believing they were right in claiming the lands of another for themselves. No. The colonists be damned.

She sliced from chin to mound, sinking her hands deep into the flesh to remove the girl's entrails. These would be of no use to her, no. It was the fat she was after, and bones.

Splat.

Oh dear. The heart of Ambrose had fallen to the floor. Oh well. Food for the rats.

How easily the skin parted from meat and fat, much like the deer and pigs she'd helped butcher a thousand, thousand times. The girl's blood ran down her arms. Lenorea ate mostly berries and dried fruits these days, but maybe she'd feast on this flesh tonight.

She hadn't considered it before, but it would be a waste if she didn't.

The large, clay pot waited upon the smouldering coals leftover from the morning fire. She'd separate the fat from the meat, cooking it slow until brown cracklings separated and floated among the clear fat. She'd have to watch it, so it wouldn't burn.

If only that bastard had watched little Henry.

But soon. Yes, soon! With this fat she could fly to meet him! Yes, little Henry. Momma would see you soon. They had promised, and unlike God, her sisters kept their word.

Now where were her bottles? Ahh, yes. There they were. She'd have to sift the mixture through a cloth to collect the fat once clear.

Nightshade, Devil's Helmet, cinquefoils, smallage, and sweet flag, all to be added once cooled. Blood of a bat with the dead girl's fat, and soon she'd see her son.

"You could fly!" they'd told her. Shown it to her in a vision. Both in spirit and through the air, aided by a broom.

She'd fashion her own handle now, as part of the ritual, while she waited for this fat to boil.

The sun sank low behind the horizon as night fell and their familiar creatures woke. The gentle croak from each frog that lived in her small pond was silent as the air turned brisk. Cold, even. Their sound was another reminder of the gifts her sisters wielded, and yet when that plague had befallen the settlement she was still on the other side. One who suffered. One who pined for a new start in life. She'd known it in her heart that coming to Roanoke would grant such a prayer, but never expected it to be in this way.

Yet this way was better.

The plagues were to weaken them, uproot their lives, but never intended to kill them all.

No. That would come later. With the passing of time, her former kindred were lulled into a false sense of security, believing their devout prayer and worship had saved them again and again. Little did they know, she and her sisters waited on purpose.

She'd finished her mixture and sat by the renewed fire, watching and waiting for the moon to fully rise, the warmth of the flames licking at her skin and singeing the hair on her arms. Only fire could harm her now. Yes, yes, grandmother moon. It spoke to her, much the same as the whispers in the trees and the groans from the earth did as it stretched and breathed and teemed with life she'd never known of. She hadn't cared to listen before, but now that she could hear it, commune with it, she realized just how powerful the earth beneath her feet was.

Lenorea felt the change within her, her old self slipping away in the breeze with each passing day as she invited the darkness of Roshef to take hold. It grew within her, she knew, waiting for the moment in which she would need to birth it into the world and assist in wreaking havoc upon the one she sought revenge.

The love she lost.

The one who betrayed her.

The man she watched every day– Ananias Dare.

The snapping of twigs and crunch of dried leaves met her ears. Her sisters were coming to join her this night. Together they would twist their bodies, exalt in His presence, and dance around the fire, using this ointment to fly.

To *fly*! Oh, to fly!

Tonight she would see Henry, her little boy, and wrap him in her arms once again. Aye, he might not recognize her, with wild golden hair, clawed nails, and bumps across her skin, but in his realm, her sisters had assured her she would present again with beauty untold. Yes, he would know his Momma.

And after, the ointment could help with her blemishes. If she used it regularly, applied as a salve upon the skin, all who looked upon her would see beauty beyond their wildest dreams.

She relished it. Waited for it. Soon enough.

Into the light her sisters came, naked on this wintry December eve. She knew that none of them could feel the cold against their skin, as with the darkness inside came a comforting warmth, tingling just below the surface. It numbed some sensations but encouraged others. Always. Their beings buzzed with gifts she had yet the opportunity to explore.

Croatoan.

Sister Rikka began to beat on her drum—human skin stretched thin, painted in the blood of those who'd wronged her. Her tight curls were matted with moss and foliage, flames of the fire dancing in her eyes as she began to sing.

Ayooooo mak bana too loftilen shok
Dayees reshnanon vlesh
We dance tonight, to bring the souls forth
Meeting in spirit and flesh

Lenorea rose with her ointment in hand, passing it on to her sisters. Her feet, moved by the drum beat and stamping upon the ground, carried her between each one. They growled. They moaned, rubbing the ointment upon themselves and their brooms. Latsvna smiled as she smoothed it upon her broom, steading herself upon it to ride. Roshef watched them from the shadows, fog billowing from his snout as he stroked his member.

Yes, there was pain, as the barbs ripped through her skin each time as he plunged deeper and deeper within her, within all of them in turn, but through the blood and sharp sting there was a sensation of ecstasy unlike any she'd ever known before. She wanted it. Craved it. She was desperate for each coupling as he spilled more of the Croatoan gift into her.

"We fly tonight, sisters! We meet them here!" She felt the words, rather than hearing them.

Back and forth, Latsvna rubbed her broomstick between her legs. Others lay upon the ground and inserted theirs. Lenorea reached for the bottle, dipping her fingers into the cool, waxy fat, slathering it upon her own. She placed it in between her legs, the ointment sticking to the hairs of her mound.

Latsvana's voice rose above their chanting and moans. "Ride, my sisters! Ride your broomsticks to the moon and *fly* among the stars!"

She moved faster, sliding back and forth, a tingling sensation hot between her thighs now. Yes, yes. Come to me. Visions of shapes and the shifting of colour altered the sights around her. She closed her eyes, and images formed in the inner world behind her eyelids.

Yes, come now, take me there, let me fly!

Her bare feet lifted off the ground, a whoosh of wind kissing her legs and blowing her tousled hair. She threw her head back, sensations of the flesh rolling as waves through her body, tightening her muscles and releasing in euphoria.

If this is what witches burned for, it was worth it.

Above the trees they rose, flying faster through the blackened sky, the earth, the sea, the stars beneath them. Visions of her former home, her former life, flew past.

Bring me to Henry! Bring me home.

29

TENDRILS TO THE SHORE

Agnes Rose - December 1588

The ocean stretched out in front of her, calm and gentle at the farthest reaches of her eyes, yet crashing and angry as the waves met the sand. Slowly reaching, clawing at the sand as it came in, then carried away as the water went back out to sea. Father had thought it would calm her spirit to rest upon the shore for a while, taking a break from the relentless daily chores she had to complete in order for them to survive. And even though it was a clear day, sitting among the rocks and sand on the shore, the bitter cold of the ocean breeze stung her face. She wouldn't sit here for long.

Fetch the eggs, refresh the hay, milk the cow. The cyclic nature of her life was so different from what it used to be. How she pined for England. For her warm bed, the hustle and bustle of town. Even though they weren't the richest among men they had managed, and she sorely missed those days.

Agnes dug her fingers into the sand. So cold, yet the feeling was nice. Her sores had all but cleared up by now, as had everyone's that survived the scourge. They'd lost near a dozen from their numbers. Their scars served as a constant reminder of the power of prayer, for God had healed them in their plight.

Slight marks remained on her wrists from the shackles, and looking back, the anger that had once stirred in her heart at those conditions had all but floated away. They thought her a witch, and were only doing what they thought best. She wasn't even sure how she, herself, would react if she was trying to protect the village from one. Not like that, but those things were beyond her power. Every day since she had combed the Word for guidance and prayed for a solution to their trials. Aye, there was evil in the trees, but surely God would root them out eventually.

Looking out to the water she thought of Moses and the Red Sea. *Let my people go.* If only he were here, and could part this sea all the way to England so that they could cross back and leave this dismal island of Roanoke.

"A bit cold to sit on the shore, isn't it?"

She turned to see who called, hair whipping around her face. She wasn't of a mind to converse with anyone today.

Oh, thank heavens. It was Jonathan, and he was holding something in his arms.

"My love." She smiled. Jonathan sat beside her on the beach and wrapped her in his warmest blanket. God bless the man. She leaned into his strong arms, resting her head on his shoulder.

"Did Father tell you where to find me?"

He nodded. "Aye. Said you were in your feelings today and could use a bit of comfort. I think he's come 'round to the idea of us, Aggy."

She raised her eyebrows. "Is that so?"

He grinned. "Soon enough, when our lands are plentiful and the settlement thrives, I'll have enough to take care of you on my own. We can start our life together, here, in the new world."

Agnes scoffed. "The moment I see the great sails of John White's ship will be the happiest I've been in a long time."

Jonathan frowned. "But...won't I make you happy?"

She lifted her head to meet his eyes. "Of course, sweet man. I only mean that when he brings provisions for the settlement, we will be much happier—feel more settled." She looked out at the ocean again. "My dresses are loose, my hair is thin, and I'll never be able to remove the crusted mud from my shoes."

He laughed. "Crusted shoes are hardly a concern of mine, Aggy. We've our whole lives together! And even with the trials of man, we came here to pioneer a new way of life beyond the ills of England. Surely you haven't forgotten?"

She shook her head. "Nay. I haven't. I remember well the rolling tide of the Church of England and what blasphemies it brings. But what of the witches, Jon? Are they no closer to finding the true ones among us?" He didn't answer, just squeezed her tight, rubbing her shoulder. "Jon. I like that."

Agnes held his other hand in hers, running a finger over the scars on his wrists. "You struggled too hard against the shackles, love." A pang of sadness wracked her heart.

He looked down. "I had to strain against them to get close enough to the wall to speak to you."

She gasped. "Jon, you didn't! You only made it worse on yourself." She brought his wrist to her lips and kissed it.

"Aye, love, but those whispered nights meant a great deal to me. They kept me going, a light in that dark, cold cellar. I knew we would come out of it together, just as we will each time life throws a boulder on the pass."

She gave him her tight-lipped smile, swinging one leg over his to sit facing him in his lap. "Kiss me, you fool."

But as he leaned in, Jon glanced behind her, grabbing her by the arms and moving her to the side.

She frowned. "Wha–"

"Look there. Out to sea. What *is* that?" Agnes squinted at where he pointed. Dark, swirling tendrils rose from the sea. A faint buzzing was growing louder, coming closer with the blackened fingers reaching into the sky. She'd heard of water columns just off shore before, but this wasn't the same.

"We need to go. Now." Jon hurriedly rose from the sand and grabbed the blanket, shaking sand from it as the wind blew stronger.

The tendrils were almost to the shore now, but they weren't fingers, nor the likes of anything she had ever seen here in the wilds or in England.

A single fly landed on her hand.

"Ouch!" She saw a tiny speck of blood where the fly had landed. "It bit me!"

"Aggy, listen to me. We need to warn the others. Something evil is afoot again."

"Damn these witches! I'm of half a mind to go out there and bring them to justice myself!" They swarmed her now, flying in her face, her neck, her eyes.

Jonathan grabbed her hand as they ran into the trees, a small bit of comfort, and the flies were just behind them. "I think we should. Maybe if we can find them, we can find out what they're after. We've seen them once. We can do it again!"

30
A BLESSING

Dear Lord. I pray to thee and give thanks for the removal of the blood-drawing flies. As those in Exodus, we, too, suffered greatly from their presence. One of our elders succumbed to them by choking after too many entered through his mouth. Lord, the sights I witnessed in those days have surely burned a terrible image into mine own eyes. Mothers shielded their children with their skirts. Strong men were brought to their knees as the columns of flies engulfed their bodies, bleeding them. My own Virginia and her unrelenting cries as they landed on her rosy cheeks and sparkling eyes. Eyes like her mother's.

I bring thanks for our deliverance from this curse, for all agree that it is surely a curse upon us, from those that practise their devilish witchcraft within the trees. Those that took her from me and ended her life. I pray for her soul, and rest easier knowing she is with our son, with you in heaven.

I do not dwell on it, nor idle in my time by questioning why she was taken, and yet, still I harbour guilt in my own heart. Forgive me, Lord, for I know the strength of sin and how firmly its grasp has held to me, but I am trying. I pray and fast, intentions fully turned upon minding the commandments of the word. Lead me not into temptation, and deliver me from evil. For thine is the kingdom, and the power, and the glory for ever. Amen.

Ananias rose from his prayer journal and turned to watch as Alice and young Virginia were snuggled together in their bed. He twisted the small knob on one of their many oil lamps, dimming the flame in preparation to go to sleep himself. Such long days, these were, and not without their trials—two goats had passed in giving birth just in the last few weeks. They couldn't stand to lose any more.

He viewed the crooked clapboards and walls packed with thick layers of straw and mud, bathed in cool blue as the moon shone through their grimy windows. He stoked the coals of the fire, the smell of it always bringing a small comfort to his hardened heart. Best to add another log lest it putter out in the night—then they'd suffer much more in the winter cold. Alice's boys were asleep on the floor, having moved their bedrolls closer to the warmth of the fire for these frozen nights.

Yet, he looked around, stepping with care down the hallway to her room. His heart thumped in his chest, blood rushing louder in his ears. Agnes Rose wasn't in the house.

This wasn't like her. She never left without telling them where she was headed off to. Something was wrong. Perhaps someone had taken her.

Dear God. The witches.

Ananias scrambled to the door, pulling on his boots with shaking hands. He grabbed the lamp, turning the wick to strengthen the flame. He would go out into the night and find her.

Thoughts raced in his mind. Should he wake Alice and alert her? No. He'd let them sleep. Heaven knows they needed the rest to save their strength. Food was scarce and hardly filling these days. No. He would shoulder this worry by himself.

Once out into the biting night air, he searched. Frantically. Combing their small plot of land in the hopes that she had merely gone for a walk.

But that wasn't like Agnes. Not at night. Not with her fears.

"Agnes!" He rounded the corner to the back of the house. "Agnes Rose!"

Soft flickers of light shone between the cracks in the boards of the barn. What on earth could she be doing out there? At this hour.

Ananias trudged toward the barn, icy wind stabbing at his skin. He'd forgotten to put on a coat, but no matter, there was no time for that now. He needed to find Agnes. Now.

He listened as he drew closer, voices whispering inside the barn, rustling in the hay. "Agnes Rose! Are you in there?" He opened the door, and all thoughts of worry melted into anger at the sight of his little girl, naked, wrapped in the arms of Jonathan Carver.

"Father!"

"Mr. Dare–I–I'm–please." Jonathan Carver scrambled to cover himself with his clothes, clothes that had been cast off to the side.

"Father, I'm sorry! But we love each other! We will be together always."

"God condemns a whore, Agnes!" He couldn't comprehend why rage filled his mind in such a way. For in this barn he had forsaken the vows he'd made to his own wife, her mother, to lay with another woman. Perhaps it was that he had hoped for better for Agnes. A good life. A pure life. He couldn't judge their actions himself, but knew of the penance from God.

"First Corinthians, chapter six, verse eighteen," he muttered. "Flee fornication: every sin that a man doeth, is without the body: but he that committeth fornication, sinneth against his own body."

"We are married in our hearts, Father! There be no time nor resources for a wedding here in the wilds!"

Ananias groaned. Of course she would think that. "Ye are not your own, Agnes! Your body is a temple of the holy ghost! A Godly temple! And yet ye besmirch it with fleshly sin *in a barn*."

Like he did. But he prayed she would be better than him.

"Oh, as if you and Alice are keeping your bodily temples holy," she shouted, enraged, "is this not true, Father?"

"Agnes." He closed his eyes. "That's enough. I am but a lowly sinner, but I wish more for you. No blemish shall stain your name or your crown that awaits you in heaven, child." He looked at them again. "If you and Carver see it fit–"

"You don't understand!" Agnes had fully dressed now.

"To come together as one, then it is my right as your Father–"

"Father, *please!*"

"...to bestow my blessing on your marriage."

Agnes froze, mouth dropped open.

Also now dressed, Jonathan Carver grinned, stepping forward to shake his hand. "Oh thank you, Mr. Dare. I'll make an honest husband for her, I promise. I've nearly fixed my place up by now, and she can come and–."

"Nay." They both paused, staring at him in confusion once again.

"With dwindling supplies and hard enough work to go around, how would it be if *after* the marriage ceremony you stayed in Alice's old place? We can supper together and share the load of the farm, without the need for you to plant your own crops or try to start fresh?"

It was the least he could do.

Agnes nodded. Alice's house was much larger than the small shack Jonathan had been given upon arrival. She smiled. "We can consider that, I think."

"Then it's settled. A marriage there shall be!" As unorthodox as this was, there was no place for him to harbour anger at her sins. They were young, in love, and memories of he and Eleanor back in their beginnings had risen to the surface. He understood.

3I
BLOODED

Our Father, who art in heaven, hallowed be thy name. Bless this day which we are given, and bless this sow so that she might provide much needed milk for our family. Five nights have passed since Father discovered Jon and I in our sinful transgression, and I ask again for your forgiveness. I am weak. I am a sinner. But I swear it, Lord, that each day I am renewed in hope to walk the straight and narrow. Hell's gates are hot, Mother used to say, and I have no intentions upon finding that out for myself. Send your blessings upon our family, upon the settlement, and upon the natives living outside these walls. I ask ye, Lord, to handle the witches in whichever manner is best, or provide the knowledge and tools for me to seek out and destroy their evils myself. I ask for guidance...for love...for you to wrap me in your arms of protection and shelter me from this storm. In your name I pray, Amen.

The wet and sparkling morning dew still rested on the grass as she made her way to the barn. They were in dire need of milk, and their faithful heifer had slowly produced less and less through these winter days. Perhaps they weren't feeding her enough, or she was taking ill, but Agnes prayed that today she would have enough to get them by.

She swung the pail in her right hand, skirts clutched in the other so she wouldn't have to suffer through damp bottoms during the rest of her morning chores. Five nights ago, in this very barn where she lay with Jon, Father had given his permission for them to be married in earnest. While yet there was a great deal to be troubled about on the island, this blessing helped her heart soar to new heights, the very thought of joining with Jon bringing with it a small bit of peace. They would be happy together and make the most of their conditions, maybe even having children of their own in the coming years. She prayed for John White's safe and swift return, for without it, hopes for that future were slim to none.

Father was already hard at work, shovelling muck and mire just outside the barn doors.

"Good Morning, Agnes." He looked up, giving her a soft smile to show his love. Father was a hard worker.

"Morning, Father."

She swung the barn door open, the familiar scent of musk and hay filling her nose. "Good Morning, Flossy." She stroked the heifer's coarse hair, thick for the winter and warm. "Let's see how much milk you have for me today, eh?" Placing the stool beside her, she settled upon it, preparing to begin.

The barn door opened again, and Father stepped inside.

"Agnes, I've been meaning to talk with you in earnest. To ask forgiveness for my reaction the other night." He leaned on his shovel, boots and trousers covered to the knee in mud.

He rested his scruffy chin on top of his hands. "I think it was a bit harsh of me to speak to you so."

She paused. He had every right as her father, the spiritual leader of their home, to call out sinful actions and lead her back towards the light. She shook her head. "You did as a father should. It was improper of me. A stain upon my flesh. I knew better than to seek gratification, even if it were with a man I dearly loved."

Father sighed. "Aye, child. I know it be true, more than anyone, perhaps. And yet I still wish to tell you that I am sorry."

She nodded. "Your blessing upon our union is apology enough, Father." She looked at him and smiled. "But now we'll have a weddin' to plan out here in the wilds." And even though the spark of happiness lit a flame of hope inside her, it was quickly doused with thoughts of Mother.

Mother wouldn't see her married to Jon. She wouldn't know. She sighed. "I only wish Mother could see it herself." Flossy moo'ed, reminding her of her task at hand.

Father straightened. "Aye. It will be a long, long time, if ever, that our sorrow over your mother will subside."

Flossy's udders were swollen and red, as hot as coals as she reached to grasp them. She stretched and pulled at them, the heifer taking a step back.

Father stepped towards them, reaching a calming hand to stroke Flossy's head. "Easy girl, easy."

The tension in her shoulders released as Agnes watched the pure, white milk slowly filling the bottom of the pail.

"There you go," Father whispered.

Agnes raised her eyes to look at Father again. "Why would the witches take her from us, Father? What did we do to anger them so?"

He pressed his lips together as he inhaled a deep breath. "I know it not, child. Your mother was a good woman. A Godly woman. And she didn't deserve the pain that I put her through."

Agnes stopped, teet in hand. "What pain?"

Father opened his mouth then shut it again. "I—well, what I meant was—" he stepped away, turning his back to her.

"*What* pain did you cause her?"

Father looked at her with pleading eyes, nervously wiping his worn linen shirt across his mouth. "Agnes, I...wasn't always the best of husbands to your mother."

She froze. Of course. She'd always questioned how quickly Alice Tilley came to be in their lives, but if they had come together before. Yes, that would explain it.

"Alice! Here? With a new settlement and little Virginia to care for?"

"Agnes, I–"

"How *could you*?" She closed her eyes, milking faster now, thankful that Flossy had more than enough milk for today yet seething with rage at her father.

"It was a moment of weakness, child! I thought you might be able to understand..."

"Understand!" She couldn't believe her ears. "Fornication with the one man that I love hardly compares to the breaking of one's vows, father. And with our neighbour! You were friends with her husband before his death!"

Father thrust his fists at his sides, heated now. "I know this be true! I was sick with myself and thought it best to tell her the truth. She forgave me before, and I–"

"*Before?*"

Agnes looked upon the man whom she thought she knew, thought she could believe in. Her own father had broken his vow even before Alice.

He leaned against the wall, resting his head in his hands.

"God forgive me, it's true. I strayed before the crossing from England. That was one of the reasons we came here. To get away. To start fresh." He kicked the hay beside him. "And look at us! Scraping to get by and Eleanor *dead*! Why, God? Why!"

Heat flushed in her cheeks as she pondered his words. The reason they came here. To run away from sin.

But sin had followed.

Father was moving now, staring at the floor, manically pacing. "Perhaps it was the witches that did it. Just as they sent us the plagues." He slowed.

"Yes, yes, that's it. They came into my heart and festered lust for Alice Tilley. They turned me from a Godly path."

She huffed. "The witches had nothing to do with your previous offence, Ananias Dare."

Father stopped, his breaths slowing as he dropped his arms from above his head. Her strong, hard-working father, reduced to this.

"Aye. You're right. It was my own sin that did this."

Agnes rubbed her hand on Flossy. "Thank you, girl, for your milk today."

She rose and grabbed the bucket, but immediately dropped it on the barn floor.

"Ahhh!"

"Agnes! What on earth?"

"The milk, Father! Look at the milk!"

Sloshing out of the pail, spreading among the hay and sinking into the ground, was a pail filled with a liquid that wasn't milk at all.

It was blood.

32

THE BAKER

JONATHAN CARVER - FEBRUARY 1589

It was late afternoon, and he was of a mind to settle Agnes's fears by bringing home a few loaves of fresh bread. The good Hugh Pattenson had told him any time he was in need, he would trade him any of the supplies that he wanted for a bit of honest work on his own plot of land. He had been a plentiful baker back in England, and used that skill to keep half the village fed with his loaves.

He made his way through the main houses of town, heading to the opposite side of the village where Mr. Pattenson lived alone. He'd no wife, and never even sought one out, perfectly content to stick to his prayers and knead his dough into old age. Jonathan always enjoyed his visits with the man, as he was somewhat of a storyteller, reminiscing of travels across the greater parts of Europe.

"Sitcha down a spell and I'll tell ya a tale, m'boy!" he'd say, probably glad to have a bit of company every now and then that wasn't just looking to be fed. Jonathan helped him often, patching holes in his thatched roof, and fixing the back door that always stuck on him. He'd even helped wash his laundry in exchange for bread before.

But there wouldn't be time for stories today. He'd promise the man some honest work in return for the bread, and he really needed to take it back to Aggy and ease her troubled soul.

Blood in the milk.

Sick cattle.

It could be that this was yet another plague cast upon them by the witches in the wood, but there would be time enough to ponder on that troubling thought. For now, his suspicions and future plans would have to continue their rattle in the back of his mind. No time for that, now.

Jonathan crossed the path, turning east to draw nearer to the baker's home. His curtains were drawn shut and chickens loitered about, kicking up dust and pecking at the cold, hard ground as they went. They were searching for food, as he was.

Knock. Knock. Knock.

He waited, listening for the ever comforting, "Jonathan, m'boy!"

But it never came.

Knock. Knock. Knock.

"Mr. Pattenson? Good Morning! It's Jonathan Carver. I've come to trade for a loaf of bread, if you've any to spare!"

Yet only silence greeted him. 'Twas odd. Perhaps he was visiting elsewhere, or attending to chores out back in his makeshift greenery. He might not hear him calling. Yes, that was it. He would just have to check around back and see if he could find him. "Mr. Pattenson? I'm stepping 'round the back. Are you here?"

Again, only silence. He pulled his coat closer around himself, blowing into both hands in a feeble attempt to keep warm. In just a few month's time, he'd welcome spring and warmer temperatures when they came. They'd start again in the planting season, this time more prepared to care for their crops than the last, as they knew how harsh and hot the summers were in this New World. Mr. Patterson's butcher table sat untouched, his milking pails still stacked along the back wall. Where on earth could the man be?

Icy, winter wind whipped at his face as he looked at the patch of trees not far beyond. If he walked through them, he would yet again find himself at the ocean's shore. He thought of the flies and the swirling columns of misery they brought with them the last time he stood there.

Damn witches.

An owl hooted in the distance. Was it a familiar? Or just a simple owl? After Aggy's encounter with one, every creature he encountered was suspect.

Oh no.

There, just across the clearing, lying at the edge of the forest before the shore, was a large shape lying in the grass, chickens pecking at it. It was too long to be a boulder, too small to be cattle. A rounded belly faced the sky.

Dear God. It was Hugh Pattenson.

Jonathan quickened in step, pushing his legs forward into a run to the man. Perhaps he had fallen, was injured, but as he came upon the body his blood ran cold.

This man was long gone. Never again would his heart thump within his chest.

Dead.

The baker's body was covered in spider webs, trickles of blood running down the sides of his head and onto the ground as the chickens pecked at his flesh, his eyes. His mouth agape, Mr. Pattenson seemed stuck in a scream, his fingers tensed and frozen as claws, his legs twisted and broken.

"Away! Be gone, ye beasts!" He waved his arms at the pecking poultry, trying as he might to preserve some dignity for his friend. "Help! Someone help! There's been a murder, this day!"

Small shapes moved in the distance, running towards him from the other buildings in the town.

He knelt beside Mr. Pattenson, examining the body. There were scratches and holes in his flesh, no doubt from the chickens, but as he looked closer he saw more.

Dearest Lord.

There were symbols. Markings in the flesh.

He stepped back, wiping his hands on his pants, a chill running the length of his back and reaching the nape of his neck. He unwillingly trembled.

Whooohooo. The owl again.

Jonathan looked between the trees, a cracking and rustling of dried sticks and brush noticeable above the wind.

"Come quickly, now!"

Those that ran from the village drew closer, as the dark shape in the forest ran further away.

Perhaps it was lunacy, or the sheer need to understand, but before he could give it another conscious thought, he raced after the shape in the woods. He lifted his knife from its holder on his trousers, readying the blade from when he caught them.

He'd finish this witch once and for all.

"Jonathan! What happened?" Familiar voices called to him but still he ran.

Oh my God!

Hugh Pattenson!

Carver!

He turned at his name being called, and as he looked back, the shape in the woods was gone.

"Damn you to hell!" he called. "God will bring a reckoning! I swear it!"

Defeated, he trudged back towards those gathered around the body. Another soul, taken for unknown reasons. They could not let this go on. Something must be done.

He would call for a hunt. And this time, it wasn't animals they would search for.

33
EMERGE

Salted pork and stewed potatoes filled his belly with a much needed warmth on this chilly, still wintry and not yet spring day. Ananias leaned back in his chair, resting in Alice's arms as she wrapped around him, stroking his chest.

"Was your supper to your liking, Mr. Dare?" She whispered in his ear, nibbling on the bottom of his ear.

He closed his eyes. "Aye, woman. You treat a man rightly so."

Agnes and Jonathan had taken little Virginia for a walk. The boys were playing at the Brewsters' until sundown.

For the first time in too many weeks–they were alone.

He rested his fork on the cleared plate and wiped his mouth clean. Their fire licked and crackled in the hearth across the way. It had been a long time since he truly felt euphoria, but today, he was sure this was as close as he could get.

She leaned down, trailing kisses down his hair and on the side of his temple. He turned to face her, meeting her lips with his.

This was the time, on the cusp of lust, in which he typically noticed the sting of emotions welling from within. But this wasn't infidelity. Not now. Eleanor had long been gone, and he must carry on with his life in her absence.

Or, at least, that's what he told himself to right it in his mind.

Alice trailed her kisses down his neck, onto his chest, pinching the few exposed hairs between her lips as she went.

Enough thought on Eleanor. She was gone. Dead. No more. He had Alice now.

She untied his breeches, pulling them down, spreading his legs to take him in her mouth.

God, this woman. Full of excitement. Vitality.

Alice stood before him, slipping her dress off her shoulders, wiggling to slide it past her hips. She kicked the dress from around her ankles, stepping forward, full breasts and brown tufts of hair just before him. He gasped at the sight of her swollen belly.

Alice nodded, confirming his thoughts.

He reached for her as she leaned in to kiss him. As he grasped for the back of her neck, running his fingers up into her softened hair, his fingers grazed over something raised–an old, healed wound, perhaps. He'd never noticed it before.

Her lips met his as she led his free hand to her most delicate bits. She slid on top of him, rising and falling with each breath, tracing her tongue in and around his ear.

She set his world on fire.

"Do you like that, Mr. Dare?" Alice moaned in his ear. "Pleasure me. Deeper."

He placed both hands on her hips, rocking her back and forth upon him.

He grunted, nearing his release but still holding on. "Alice. God. Yes." He could hardly speak as she rode him, circling her hips and thrusting forward faster than he could handle. Her skin felt rougher than before.

"My seed comes..."

She paused, slowing her hips, taking him in fully. "Did your wife pleasure you like this, Mr. Dare?"

He froze. How was he to answer that?

"What?"

She rocked her hips again, slowly, cautiously. "I've asked a question of ye, Mr. Dare."

She kept calling him that.

"I–Just–Why are ye asking that of me?"

"Answer me." She quicked again. Back and forth. Bringing him to the edge.

"She—."

She grasped his shoulders. "Answer me!"

His breath caught in his throat as she slammed on top of him. "No! She didn't. Only you, Alice. Only you!" He shuddered as he spilled his seed inside of her. She slowed, shifting back and forth, wrapping her arms around his neck and stroking his hair.

Alice rubbed his arms, sliding her hands down the length of them until she reached his hands. He worked to settle his breath. She placed his thumbs just below her eyes, his fingers wrapped around her face to the back of her head.

"Alice...wh–?"

She pushed his thumbs into her skin, hard, as she sneered.

Bile rose in his throat as he sat, still pulsing inside her, while she used his hands to slide the skin off of her face.

"Aaaaah!" He shoved her off of him with shaking hands.

It could not be.

She stood and stepped out of the skin. What was left of the true Alice landed on the floor with a sickening *splat*.

Hell had come.

Emerging from the skin as his worst nightmare- was his lost wife, Eleanor.

34
RISEN

He wanted to run, to flee from the very presence of evil that stood before him. He choked on his words, struggling to breathe. It wasn't her. It couldn't be. Not really. The woman who stood before him radiated with a beauty beyond that which his former wife had held. Golden curls spilled down to her waist, much longer than he remembered. Her teeth, stretched in a malicious grin, sparkled as white as a bleached bone.

"Have you missed me, Ananias?" She smirked.

Eleanor's words rolled off the tongue as smooth as butter, matched only by the supple, rosy skin she now had. She was a vision on earth—with the devil in her eyes.

Heart clenched in his chest, Ananaias froze, unable to move, unable to breathe. Visceral stirrings in his stomach rose to erupt from his mouth. Heaving, he retched onto the floor, careful to turn away from all that was left of what used to be Alice.

Dear God. Alice. His Alice. Crumpled on the floor.

"I-wh-how are you here?" He clutched his middle, wiping his face as looked up at her. His cheeks were wet with tears. She stared with a wicked grin stretching farther than should be possible, rubbing her belly that was, to his horror, still swollen with child.

Yet none of this should be possible.

He yanked up his trousers, scrambling to get across the room. Away from *her*.

"Tsk. Tsk." She followed him, advancing to back him into the corner. "Come now, Ananias. I've returned to you." She held out her hand, nails as long as talons. "Forgive my little ruse, husband, it was only a bit of fun." Eleanor cackled. "Let me show you what I can do for you *now*!" He trembled as she reached for him, unsure of what to do or say.

This was of the devil. Darkness had changed her.

He stared into her speckled eyes.

Dearest God. That was how she did it. How she murdered Alice and wore her skin.

Eleanor was a witch.

Perhaps the very witch that plagues them so.

"Be gone from here, devil woman!" Broiling rage stirred within him. Her betrayal upon God, their family, her life, to him, was a dagger to the heart.

"Mr. Dare. But there's so much I want to *show* you." Her grimy nails were nearly upon him.

"Be *gone*, I say!" He grasped her hands, shoving hard to throw this wicked being away. She stumbled backwards before falling to the floor on her back, quickly spreading her legs and wiggling her hips and the tuft of hair between her thighs towards him.

This wasn't his wife. Not anymore.

Her grin twisted into a snarl. "Don't you want it, Ananias? You were so eager when I was your little Alice!" She cackled again, rising and cracking her back, unnaturally twisting her neck. Her hair greyed, growing in length until it nearly reached the floor. Her face was weathered and worn, leathery, with large bumps replacing the smooth complexion of her skin. Her teeth, yellow and broken in shards, putrid breath spilling from her rotten mouth. Her hands weren't really hands anymore, but rather claws, dirty and covered in grime.

Now he could see her as she truly was.

If she hadn't been standing just before him, now, he wouldn't believe this creature to be her.

Witchcraft.

He trembled. "Eleanor, why! What have they done to you?"

She hobbled over to the crumpled form of Alice, crouched low with her back to him, grabbing the chestnut brown hair he had only just ran his fingers through this morning.

"If you'll not have me, how about we bring your old whore back, hmmm?" she croaked. Her raspy voice sounded as two boulders scraping together, as if someone had taken a blade and run it along the inside of her throat. "Would you like that, Ananias?"

His heart yet thundered in his chest. Fear danced with rage in the deepest corners of his soul. Whatever evil she was about to perform, he didn't want to see it.

"Eleanor. No!"

"Alice Tilley...rise." She cackled.

The crumpled form of his former lover, commanded by his former wife, pushed itself up from the ground, skin inflating as a water skin, stretched taut, eyes but mere pockets of darkness. Alice was only a tanned hide, risen again by the purest evil on earth. She rested on all fours, head whipping towards his witch wife waiting for direction. He'd think it was a person kneeling on the floor, without eyes, if he hadn't seen the skin swell to its current form himself.

"Bark, little bitch."

The sound that came from the swollen skin was unlike any dog he'd ever heard before.

Hau. Hau.

Maybe a demon.

"Wag your tail, little bitch."

"Eleanor, enough! Stop this, now!" He backed against the wall, knocking a pitcher from the table so that it shattered on the ground. What used to be Alice wagged her naked bottom, tongue hanging limp out of her vile, evil mouth. She advanced towards him.

"Go to him."

He searched the room for something, anything, that could help him keep this beast at bay. A knife. A weapon. Anything. Come on, Ananias. Think! The skin beast, the husk of a human, crawled towards him, the cavity of her lungs rising and falling with each pant.

Dirty fingers reached his boots, crawled up his legs. *Hau. Hau.*

"Awww. She misses you, husband." His witch wife watched from across the room, long, leathery arms crossed in front of her and face splayed with the foulest grin he'd ever seen.

His hands shook as he raised them, kicking at the beast as she slowly sniffed at his trousers, but still she came. "Call her off! Eleanor, please!"

The skin beast growled, snarling and snapping its jaws. He could see clear to the back of her head, on the inside. She was a hollow shell, born again by witchcraft.

Chestnut brown hair nuzzled into his stomach. This had to end. He summoned his strength and swept the beast away with the back of his hand. It whimpered, falling to the floor.

"Now, Ananias! That's no way to treat a woman." His witch wife glared.

"This is no woman! I'll kill you both myself!" He kicked the beast, lunging for Eleanor, content with the fact that the only weapon he had upon him was his hands. He'd have to use them.

She crouched low, swaying from side to side as if in a learned dance with him.

"Ananias wants to *play*, does he?"

Quick as a flash, she escaped his reach and stopped beside what used to be Alice. He strode for her again, but this time Eleanor wouldn't get away. She backed against the table. He wrapped his fingers around her thick, wrinkled throat, squeezing as hard as she could.

But she smiled.

"Ye cannot harm me, Ananais." She leaned forward, the stench of her breath gagging him. "And you will pay." She brought a knee to his nethers and pushed him back, running with her skin beast to the door.

"Aughhhhh!" He doubled over, darkness clawing at the edges of his vision.

"Come, little bitch." She stroked the top of Alice's head, caressing her new pet. "Until we meet again, husband."

And then she was gone.

35
FOR THE GREATER GOOD

"*Heavenly Father, I come to thee today seeking strength in my bones and a productive outcome to my impending hunt within the woods today. While the wildlife are few, we, as a family, are in desperate need of nourishment for our bodies in order to continue on. My clothes hang from my frame even as I pen this prayer, knowing that we, as a people, have taken far much more than the forest can provide. I do not enjoy it, Lord, taking the life of an animal in order to feed myself and my kindred, but as in Genesis with your promise that every living thing that moves is to serve as food for us, I still struggle with it in mine own heart. Give me this day, Lord, and make my aim strike true, as painless as possible, so that I might not mourn the death of the animal I seek to take today. As now I suffer with a hunger settled low in my belly, I am thankful for all that I have had until now, and recognize your gifts upon my life that have led me to adulthood. Greed is a wicked sin, one I experienced in my old life and in the coming to Roanoke. While we had been promised a plentiful land, it was not, and through prayer and counsel, I seek to dampen any envy I might now have. Forgive me of this sin, Lord, for I envy my old life, the plentiful life, where meats and cheese and sweets were of easy access back across the sea. Help me to lead this colony into a better growing season, with thriving crops and fish from the sea. Forgive me of my lustful thoughts, for each day I strive to become the man deserving of Agnes, able to provide for her and make our way with grace, yet I am stained with the sinful thoughts of an earthly man. Lead me not into temptation, and deliver me from the evils of this world. In your name I pray, Amen."*

Jonathan crouched low with his back against the rough bark, settled, quiet, waiting for the kill. Smaller animals such as squirrels and rabbits had crossed his path, yet he waited for something bigger. He hoped for a deer, feared a black bear, but he needed something large enough to feed the whole of his new family. They would butcher it together, salt curing some of the meat and smoking the rest. Venison would do. Now if only a deer would cross his path.

Manteo had often come with him and some of the other men into the woods to teach them how to hunt. It wasn't something he had learned in earnest back in England, as he'd lived in the city centre and simply purchased meat from the butcher's shop. Such comforts he had grown used to, and hadn't given much thought to when he decided to join this venture. He knew it would be hard, of course, but hadn't grasped the full gravity of what would be expected once they arrived. Spoiled, his mother would have said if she could see him now, yet she had died long ago from a raging scarlet fever. Life had never been easy, but it certainly didn't compare to this.

A twig snapped and flung him from his thoughts. Dearest Lord, an answered prayer. There, just within reach if he could shoot his arrow true, stood a beautiful golden-tan doe. She was bent low, facing away from him, with the tiniest of white beards under her chin. His heartbeat quickened as he readied his arrow, careful to pull the drawstring back with as little sound as possible. As the birds chirped to each other in the trees, he thanked the lord for this moment of grace, of provision, for tonight they would have meat to nourish their bodies. He waited, slowly exhaling in the hopes that she would turn and give him a clearer shot. Manteo said he needed to shoot for the spine, in line with the shoulders or above to the head or neck, for immediate death.

Just then, his heart sank and fire crawled up his throat as a fawn stepped out from behind a tree. A child. Her child. The child of his dinner who would soon be motherless. The hand of pain clenched tightly around his heart in his chest. He needed to do this. He must. They would slowly starve if he didn't. But to think of taking this fawn's mother from it for his own selfish desires twisted his thoughts into doubt.

No. He must. For Agnes.

Suddenly, the mother doe rose from her stirrings on the forest floor and looked straight at him. Whether she saw him or smelled him he knew, this was the only warning he would get. Now was his chance. One warning and the animals froze, but with the second warning, they were gone. It was now or never. Take the shot and provide for his family, or let them leave and hope to see another. Even worse, as the day got away from him, he might have to return home empty-handed and hungry still.

He loosed the arrow, closing his eyes and collapsing upon himself, the sound of the deer as it was hit a dagger to his heart. He had to– there was no other choice.

But as the fawn ran away, he knew that there was.

The mother doe kicked her hind legs outward, running hard for at least 20 metres before slowing to a staggered walk. Blood dripped from her wound, the arrow having cleared through her. Manteo would be proud of his aim, of his kill, but still the whole of it horrified him. This was the first animal beyond a squirrel that he had killed in earnest. The mother doe's tail twitched erratically as she stumbled and fell, trying to gain her footing once more. A single tear rolled down his cheek.

"Forgive me," he whispered.

He was glad it had gone through the heart, a shot for killing quickly, without the risk of having to track the deer for long. Death spreading through the meat would make it tough. If he had missed the heart and shot solely through the lungs, the deer would have run hard and fast, belly low to the ground. But that was not the case with this mother doe, meaning his aim was true.

He stepped towards her, gently, softly, and kneeled beside her as her thrashing ceased. Jonathan reached out with one hand, the hand that had loosed the arrow, and caressed the coarse hair on top of her head. She wouldn't die alone, at least. At last, she blew one final, heated breath from her wet nose, one glassy eye staring at nothing.

He remembered his teachings, and reached for his knife. The key to quick work was a sharp and sturdy blade. He propped the mother doe on her back, placing two large rocks under her shoulders to create an uphill slant, with smaller rocks beneath her hips. He started behind the hind legs, making a short cut down into the pelvic bone. Cutting on one side of the udder, he sliced a shallow slit up to her jawbone, into the white fur. He cut through the muscle layer along the same line, careful not to puncture the organs and spoil the meat. Jonathan worked to cut a hole around the anus, tying it off so as not to have spillage.

Next came the windpipe, cut in two as far up the neck as he could, putting aside the knife so that he could now pull out her entrails. Hard. He stifled the bile as it rose in his throat. For Agnes. For their family. They needed this meat.

He finished with dressing the mother doe, wiping his hands as clean as he could on his trousers. When he looked down, the smeared crimson handprints gagged him. It was time to head home.

****

Jonathan paused at the edge of the trees to catch his breath, the sun slowly making its way back into slumber as it had taken him much longer to dress the deer than he expected. Even longer to carry her back to the home of the Dares. Agnes would be so proud of him. He hoped Ananias would, too.

As if summoned by thought, his future Father-in-law raced across the yard towards him. "You got one! Gods be praised, Jon. Well done! And you've dressed it yourself!" Ananias lifted his hands as he came near, whispering praises as he drew near. "I'm proud of you, son."

Jonathan paused, fully aware of the word Ananias had just used. He met his eyes, smiling back as the hoisted the deer together, moving it towards the butchering table beside the smokehouse.

"Thank you, Sir," he muttered in return. They set the deer upon the table, and Ananias clapped him on the back.

"You've done well today. You'll make a fine husband for my Agnes."

Again, Jonathan was speechless. Compliments were few when they came from Ananias Dare.

"I thank ye, Sir. I want to make a good husband for her."

Ananias nodded. "But promise me this, boy." His eyes darkened with his words as a serious calm fell between them. "The moment you're able, say when the Governor returns, you'll take Agnes back across the sea to a better life back in England." Jonathan froze. Ananias spoke again, leaning close so his words wouldn't carry. "This is no place for a new couple, Jon. These wilds. The darkness in the woods. I've seen myself as I know you have, too. It's evil, m'boy. Evil. We can't sustain our settlement against such."

Jonathan tightened his lips, pulling the cool, evening air in through his nose. Ananias stared at him, waiting for an answer. Slowly, he tilted his head forward, a sort of half-nod, hardly committing to Ananias's words but appeasing him, yet. "I'll be good to her, Sir."

Ananias nodded and they set to work on the deer once again.

36
TAKEN

Dearest Lord, I come to thee today in fervent prayer and forgiveness upon my sins. I am a spiteful woman, a jealous woman, a woman who's heart you know through and through and who is in desperate need of comfort. One month it's been since Alice Tilley left us, or was murdered, it's hard to know the truth of it anymore.

But the way Father described...skin crawling around on the floor as a witch bid her to do, I find that part hard to believe. Maybe it was a nightmare, Lord, cast upon him by the witches in the woods. Or maybe they really did *turn her into a dog, crawling around on the ground. I cannot know. But what I do know, is that now in addition to caring for little Virginia, Jonathan and I have had to take it upon ourselves to raise the two Tilley boys, Robert and Thomas.*

I'm jealous, Lord, of my friends. Winnie and Emme, whom I hardly ever get to see anymore, who don't have the weight of a thousand boulders crushing upon their shoulders as they try to raise three children that aren't their own, like I am. I'm spiteful, Lord. Towards Father. Towards the witches. Towards this New World that is, in fact, an unforgiving wilds.

I want to go home. To sleep in my old bed, in my old home, with my old family.

But that family doesn't exist anymore, Lord.

I, too, fear for Father's sanity, as he's let his daily tasks and prayers fall by the wayside in the pursuit of "the witch that killed Alice," as he says. I asked him if he knew her, this witch. If she were one of the women in town and perhaps we could stop her from releasing all hell and its fury upon us, but no. Father won't say who it is. Says he doesn't know her. But I know he does, Lord. The look in his eyes tells me more than his words do, and I know it in my heart that he recognized the witch that day.

I pray for peace, Lord. For your comforting arms to wrap around this colony of Roanoke and bring about the promises we held dear when we arrived. Help us, Father God, to understand our wrongs and help us to make them right. Help me with these children, Lord, and guard my heart from the wicked thoughts that stir within, resentment and chaos and fear. In your holiest of names I pray, Amen.

The wind whipped at her face, stinging the reddish skin from where she'd been out in the sun too long yesterday. The sheer amount of soiled linens her growing family produced astounded her, but whether or not they had room on the lines for drying didn't matter, she'd have to make more. Always more. More mouths to feed, hair to comb, trousers to mend, meals to make, and on, and on, and on. The work never ceased, and she found herself committed to daily prayers asking for help to make it through.

Father was having a rough time. The reverend stopped by ever so often to inquire as to why he'd stopped attending the weekly sermon. She and Jonathan prepared the children as best they could, traipsing along through the dust or mud, depending on the day, to take the children to the meeting house. If their family would fail in these wilds, it wouldn't be because of her.

Reverend Winslow wasn't happy that she and Jonathan had not yet married. She knew it. He didn't speak on it, but the way he wiggled a mention of it in conversations, far more often than was necessary, told her it was so. There just wasn't time. No time for anything.

"Boys!" She called, watching as Robert and Thomas played in a sword fight with two sticks, edging closer to the trees. They stopped, branches falling to rest beside their legs, Robert cocking his head to one side, wordlessly asking her what was wrong with their game.

"Just be careful with those sticks!" Agnes yelled into the wind. "I can't have either of you poking your eye out!"

She wanted to believe that she kept such a close eye on them for their own safety, which, of course, was true. But it was also true that if one of them got injured, that would mean more work for her in the long run.

No, they couldn't have that.

Come to think of it, they were playing a bit too close to the trees for her liking.

"Move back from the trees, boys! Stay where I can clearly see you, please." Robert and Thomas nodded, letting her know that they had heard.

She turned back to the washing. Little Virginia toddled around her legs, running through the linens she had hung on the line, tiny, muddy handprints marking her presence.

"Virginia! Darling, please don't touch the linens with the mud. Please. I beg of you." She wiped the sweat from her forehead with her arm. "Go wash them in the bucket beside the door. That's a good girl."

The clack of sticks and the ringing of the boys' laughter brought a small comfort to her heart. As much as she tried for them, they did seem to enjoy life among the struggles. It had been a tough couple of weeks after their mother had turned up missing. *Dead! By the witches!* as Father reminded her at every turn. Thankfully, he hadn't shared that bit with the boys, but with as much as he talked about it in town, she wondered if the whispers had reached their innocent ears. They weren't at fault in any of this. They didn't ask for their mother to steal into the Dare home, to replace Mother, to disappear. They didn't wish for the lice and bugs and hungry tummies they were so often met with. None of them asked for it, least of all she.

Virginia giggled as she splashed around in the water bucket. Agnes smiled. She turned to check on the boys, their sticks having fallen silent, probably because they found a frog or snake or something else entirely to capture their shortened attention.

But they weren't there.

Her breath caught in her throat as all she could see was the swaying of trees in the breeze at the edge of the forest.

No sticks. No sounds. No boys.

"Robert!" She rushed to grab Virginia, slinging her on her hip as she headed towards the trees. "Thomas! Where are you?"

She raced through the field, eyes scanning the surroundings for any sign of Alice Tilley's children.

"Jonathan!" she screeched. "The boys! I can't find them!"

He was around the front of the house, chopping wood, and surely he would hear her. Sure enough, she soon heard the thud of boots running around to the back of the house. "Aggy? What is it, love?"

"The boys! They're gone!" She frantically looked in the woods, drawing closer to the edge of the trees.

"Where were they?" Jonathan called.

"They were right here! Playing swords! I only just spoke with them! Rooooobert! Thomas! Quit this game, now!"

But they didn't come to her. A chill ran from the base of her spine, creeping and crawling all the way to the back of her neck. She shivered, clutching closer to Virginia who had started to call out as well.

"Wober! Domas!" But her little cries were in vain.

This wouldn't be good. Father would think she had done away with them. But she hadn't! She hadn't. She cared for them. For all of them. God, *why* was this happening to them?

37

A DISCOVERY

Jonathan Carver - April 1589

"**R**ooobert!" he called.

"Thomas!" Mr. Dare searched to his left. They were back, in these unsettling woods, but this time, instead of searching for Eleanor Dare, they were trying to find the Tilley boys. How many of their number had succumbed to these witches in the woods? Ten? Twelve? The number escaped him, but the threat of what it meant remained.

If they didn't extinguish the flame of these witches in these woods, surely they would all be lambs to the slaughter. It was only a matter of time.

And time was something they didn't have, right now, as night would soon fall upon them. He gripped his torch, keeping it at the ready, for whether he would ignite it in a need to see or bash one of the wicked on the head, he was ready for it. The last dregs of sunlight passed through the trees, the orange and yellow hues bathing the path ahead, yet casting no light on any signs of the boys.

They couldn't have simply vanished. No. While the townsfolk ignored the ravings of Mr. Dare about Alice, surely the disappearance of her boys was a sign that he spoke the truth. They'd seen the plagues for themselves! Felt the wrath from within the woods. His own eyes had seen their dancing on that night so long ago, and yet, still, there were those who doubted.

Cling to the word, they said. God will provide.

Well, so far God had allowed them to be picked off one by one under the supervision of these wicked women. If they lived among them, he'd seen no sign of it, and Aggy assured him that Ananias knew at least one of the witches, but he wouldn't say.

Damn these woods! The wild! The moment John White returned he would gather Aggy, Virginia, and the boys, if they could find them, and load them up on the ship to return home. He was done with this forsaken land, biding his time until White returned.

"Thomas!" His calls were pointless. Deep inside he knew they were lost, but caged that thought in the hopes that maybe there would be a sign of what had happened to them.

"Any sign?" Ananias asked him.

"Nay, sir. None to be had. I fear our presence here in the woods might stir trouble if we stay when night arrives."

"Aye. But we mustn't stop searching. They're out here. They've got to be. Those wicked women won't have hurt them, yet."

He wasn't convinced of that.

The calls of the others faded in the distance, as he and Ananias had trudged ahead of the group, foraging deeper into the woods than either of them had gone before. They'd passed the clearing he knew of, the one with the stone table, and could practically taste the wickedness in the air.

Yes, there was evil about in these woods.

Suddenly, a glimmer in the trees caught his eye, accompanied by the caustic taste of smoke in his mouth. There was a light.

He stopped. "Ananias."

His soon to be father-in-law, whenever they could manage it, halted in his search and turned to him. "What is it, Jon?"

"A light." He pointed. "Just there, not 100 paces ahead of us. Can you see it?"

Ananias coughed as he, too, realised the smoke. "None of our number live this far within the woods, Jon. Could be Natives. Be at the ready." He untied his knife from his belt, grasping with the blade held out in front of him as he stepped between the brush.

They were moving from the path now, far from it, in fact, following whatever light they saw ahead of them.

The silence of the night sliced through him. No frogs. No crickets. Only the sound of their own boots stamping along the dried underbrush below. He carefully stepped over a root that rose up and out of the ground. The trees were older here. Twisted, gnarled branches reaching out, tangling their clothes, scratched at their faces despite weaving around the dense underbrush. Perhaps the forest would swallow them whole as they plunged deeper into it.

Ananias slowed, placing a finger to his mouth. The thatched roof of a small structure stood before them, clay walls mixed with straw crumbling away. There was a fire pit out front, yet the flames came from inside. A small chimney puffed with the smoke that filled their lungs. Jonathan worked hard not to cough. To breathe.

His eyes grew wide as he took in the full sight of it. Bones of various sizes arched around the door, a single skull protruding out from the middle of it.

It was human.

The blood rushing through his veins froze at the sight of it. Around the hovel, animal caracasses littered the ground, which explained the scent that now filled his nose.

The stench of rot. A smell of decay.

Death.

Someone lived here. Someone he didn't care to meet.

"Ananias. I think we should go."

"Quick," Ananias whispered to him. "Light your torch, but stay behind this bush. We can't let her know that we've found it." His eyes blazed. "Let's burn the bitch out."

Jonathan rounded on him, keeping his voice low. "We don't know who lives here! It could be a native. We can't burn down someone's house without knowing whose it is." Ananias paused at his words. "Besides, we might set the whole forest ablaze!" he hissed.

"Fine. I'll do it."

Perhaps the townsfolk were right about Ananias.

"But what if the boys are inside!" he muttered in return.

Ananias thinned his lips, narrowing his eyes. "True. Hand me the torch. Go see for yourself. I'll wait until you give me the signal." His father in law licked his lips in anticipation.

Good God, what were they doing?

"Do *not* set anything on fire unless I say so."

Ananias narrowed his eyes, but nodded.

Jonathan passed him the torch and moved slowly toward the hovel, careful not to step on any of the slain animals that surrounded them. Surely it was a Native's home. Not a witch. But maybe it was. He could almost convince himself it wasn't, until he saw them.

There, standing upright underneath the window was a pile of brooms stained dark and slathered in a shiny substance. A crimson colour.

Dear God.

Blood.

His mouth ran dry at the thought of where exactly he stood, now, just outside the window, a mere six paces from the doorstep of one who actively consorts with the devil.

But he couldn't shout to Ananias and confirm. Not yet. That man would surely stir the wicked from inside as he set the home ablaze. No. He needed to check for the boys first.

Jonathan reached for the window, straining to see beyond the grimey film that covered it at least as thick as the tip of his finger. He pulled out the small cloth he used for wiping sweat and blood off his arms from the briars and rubbed in a small circle, trying, hoping, to see.

From what he could tell, there was no one inside. He would have to be quick, and careful, but if he could make *sure* that the boys weren't tied up and lying in the floorboards or already stewing in her giant clay pot on the fire, then he could give the go-ahead to his manic, fire-wielding father-in-law and burn this wickedness to the ground.

He crept to the door. The skull of God-only-knew-who was staring right at him.

"Good God," he whispered. The handle was a rat, dried, shrivelled, but somehow not swollen or bursting in the flesh like the dead rats he'd seen on ship during their crossing. He curled his fingers around the coarse fur, holding back the bile filling in his throat. Just a quick look, a confirmation, that was all he needed.

"Jon!" He turned around. Ananias had poked his head out from behind the bush, and even from here the shock was clear on his face.

He held up one finger. A moment, if he could have it.

He swung the door in, creaking as it went. A dank, musky scent filled his nose, yet it wasn't as unpleasant as the carcasses outside. All manner of dried herbs, flowers, and bones hung from the ceiling. A simple wooden chair sat beside the hearth, the clay pot bubbling with something unthinkable inside. He scanned the room. A bed heaped with rags, a large, wooden table in the centre. Furs lined the floor in a soft carpet, for which he was thankful as it dampened his footsteps.

"Robert? Thomas?" he whispered. "Are you in here?"

If whatever witch lived here *was* near, she would surely hear the thunderous beat of his heart as it threatened to thump right out of his chest.

Bones. Knives. Tools.

More brooms. A bucket of blood. All were exactly as he would expect from a witch's lair, just like the ones he'd heard about back in England during the burnings. But he couldn't believe he was here, standing among it, in the home of Hell's minions themselves.

He stilled his breathing, listening, waiting for either of the Tilley boys to answer, but it never came. They weren't here, or at least from what he could see.

He turned to leave when suddenly an owl hooted from rafters. It watched him.

A familiar.

He'd been seen.

"Ananias!" he yelled, scrambling to make it back out the front door. "Ananias, now!"

Bursting from the brush as a frightened soldier wielding his flaming sword, Ananias Dare ran to the hovel and set to lighting the thatched roof. The owl screeched, exploding from the door in a flash of feathers and claws. His soon to be father-in-law cackled as he ran around the house, touching his torch to the thatched roof every few steps.

A shriek shattered the air around him, threatening to explode the inners of his ears, as a naked woman with long grey hair ran with the force of a gale wind out of the trees.

The witch had come.

38

THE HAND OF GOD

ANANIAS DARE – APRIL 1589

Dear Lord, I know it's been a while since I have attended any weekly prayers. I am a sinner as thick as sin can get, this is true, but I beg thee to take mine own hands and use them as you will to bring about the will of God. To rid this world of the evils which hath been sent by the Devil himself to this land. The bible tells us not to suffer a witch to live, and I shan't, Lord. I won't allow this scourge to sweep across our colony any longer. They might think I'm exaggerating my experiences, even having seen the works of the devil with their own eyes, but I am right in this! I am right! The bible speaks of witches and I beg of thee to smite them down! Reign Hellfire and damnation upon them that are the most wicked of this world. She's not my wife anymore, Lord. She's not. Those in the woods have turned her and she hath sickened poor Alice Tilley into a skin beast not of the world. Smite them, Lord! Bring about their end! Use me to do so. I will do what is needed to bring about an end to this madness! In your holy name. Amen.

Ananias flexed and curled his fingers, having gripped the torch too tightly as he ran. Burn the witch! Bring her fire! Today she meets her end! Even though Jon hadn't said he'd seen her, the look on his face as he shouted for fire meant he had. It had to. He'd wanted to save the boys today, but this was even better! He tipped his head back, barking laughter to the sky at this small victory. Yes, there were many witches, but today, at least, he'd ruined the shelter of one. Perhaps they all lived here, in this wretched, putrid hole of death and despair. Ha! Haha! Victory upon sin!

His breaths came fast, lungs filling with air and smoke and the sweet, sweet breeze of a triumph. He watched as the flames enveloped her house. Evil burning before his very eyes.

But before he could celebrate for long, a ripping scream erupted to his right, with a flash of naked flesh and long grey hair sprinting towards the home. He locked eyes with Jon.

"The witch returns!" he shouted.

"Ananias, no!" Jon threw his hands up, signalling for him to stop, but Ananias never slowed. He was already after her.

"I'm the hand of God now, Jon! I'll do his bidding in this!" He licked his lips, spit dripping down his chin. He would end this. Now.

"Aaaarrrrgh!" his witch wife screeched, her face full to the hairline with hatred and rage. She flung her arms out, and he might as well have been yanked back by a rope tied around the waist, for Ananias flew in the air, landing hard on the ground on his backside.

He looked over and saw that Jon had suffered the same. Her witch-craft had sent them back, but he wasn't about to stop trying.

"It ends now, witch!" He coughed, smoke from the fire filling his throat and nose.

She raised her arms to the sky, ignoring his cry as she ran towards the front door which was already engulfed in flames. From beside the door, she grabbed a broomstick, the tail of it already singed and smoking from the licking flames. He raced towards the house, holding in his scream as he grabbed a flaming handful of straw from the roof and threw it on her.

Shrieking and wailing rang through the woods as she looked down to see the blisters already forming on her hands. So fire *could* hurt her.

The fire spread from the middle of her head, all the way to her scalp. She yelped, patting the flames with her own leathered claws, trying as she might to put it out with the broomstick in her hands, beating her hair with it. Smoke rose from her singed hair. She turned and growled, swinging one wrinkled and leathery leg over the pole, her pregnant belly much larger now. Between her thighs she slid on the broom, up and down as her hovel burned behind her. A desperate, filthy noise escaped her rotted mouth, high-pitched shrieks of pleasure followed by sudden gasps.

It was ungodly in the worst of ways.

"Enough, witch!" he shouted.

She grinned, throwing her head back and cackling towards the sky, wisps of smoke still floating up from her burned hair. Ashen clouds rolled in that weren't there earlier, and before her laugh had even finished, raindrops fell.

First they were a patter, tapping on the burning thatched roof with small hisses. Then, the rain fell in sheets. So fast. Unnatural.

She was doing this.

His witch-wife slid on her broomstick again, moaning in pleasure. She rocked her hips forward and for one, sick moment he remembered when she'd rock her hips on him like that. But she's evil now. Manipulating the weather, even! She must be stopped. Faster and faster she rocked, gasping for breath as she rose on the broomstick into the rain-filled sky.

Dear God.

She flew above them, circling as a vulture waiting for its next meal, and then she spoke.

"Ohhhhh Alice!" she called, in a sing-song voice unlike the gravelled tone he'd heard before.

Bounding out from within the trees, the skin beast that used to be Alice Tilley galloped on all fours towards him. Jonathan shouted, searching the ground for whatever weapon he could find and try to help.

Grrrrraah. Grrrraah. The skin beast growled, twigs and leaves stuck in the chestnut brown hair that he used to love.

This was madness.

A sharp pain met the top of his head. Then his shoulder, and his arm. The rain let up as small balls of ice fell from the sky.

"Another plague for you, darling. Hail!"

The flames of her hovel were nearly gone, smoldering and smoking as a result of the rain. "Come on, Jon! Let's go!" He kicked the skin beast, Alice, away as he ran with all of his might back into the woods. It howled in return. He wasn't confident in which way he was going, but he surely needed to get away from here. They needed to prepare. To come back. To end this wickedness brought to them by this bitch.

39
HEALING

"*Scatha Morain Vesti Bordue*

Cover my skin, bring it anew

Kleshta Crimsa Diack Lafin

Restore the scalp, life within"

Damn the fire. Damn that man. How had he come to know where her new home was within the woods? And the younger one, Carver, is working with him now. Aiding him in his feeble attempts to bring her to ruin. She shuffled around the blackened innards of her home, the roof completely gone, but that was ok, she enjoyed the night sky.

She'd have to fix the roof, but she'd have help, yes, help. Her sisters would help her build it again. But first she must tend to her scalp. It burned, yes it burned. She reached her fingers to again touch her scalp, skin falling away with her fingers. It hurt, but distantly, as if she experienced the pain elsewhere, in a dream.

But, it hadn't been a dream. Ananias had come to her doorstep, and Jon had come inside. Even among the musk and smoke of the charred remains, she could sense the stench of religion still upon them. It reeked of goodness. Of salvation.

Things she'd long been rid of.

Yes, she'd mourned it. But when her heart finally escaped from the dungeon of despair that it was held in, she was finally able to claim her true self, her new ways, serving Roshef and heeding his call.

She thought back to that night in the woods. The night she gave herself to him entirely.

Yes, worse things have been done to her than a simple burn upon the skin, yet now his gift grew inside of her, soon to be born and assist her in damaging the colony. And Ananias.

But for a just cause, it was. She'd never even tried to bring about the rains until she needed it, but as her sisters had told her, she'd only need to believe she could have it, and whatever she wanted was hers. She'd wanted the rain. And it was hers.

And now, as was her new purpose. She wanted revenge.

She stared into the eyes of the two children her sister had stolen from the edge of the woods for her. They stood unmoving, their eyes black orbs absent of any light, any life. Yes, they lived in a physical sense, but no longer did they carry about life as they had.

No. Alice Tilley's children served *him* now.

They would be useful. The first of many, an army of first borns and siblings, if they could get them. Those in the colony would be much less likely to resist if it was their own children they were up against.

It was all according to their ways. Use others to do their bidding, and do it yourself if you must.

Roanoke Colony would have their day. Their day of reckoning. She smiled, smoothing the salve that had just received her gifted words onto her scalp. She would be healed. Reborn.

Ready.

40
TO WED

Dearest Lord, I thank you from the bottom of my heart for the gift which thou hast given me today. A day to celebrate love. Life. The coming together of two souls who will work hard at our match and keep you at the centre of our hearts and our marriage. As I serve you, I will now serve him, as he will serve me in return. While I know the preparations are not as grand as one would have expected back home in England, the prospect of finally uniting with my Jon, under the clear, blue sky on this mild, summer day fills my heart to the point of bursting. He is kind, gentle, caring, and unquestioning in his faith and devotion; all of which are laid out in the Word as a worthy husband. He is a leader, Lord, and I thank you again for bringing him into my life. Help us grow together, Lord, and protect us from the evils of this world which are many. Bless our union, our life together that officially begins today. While our hearts have been joined for many months, now we join in earnest. Forgive us of our sins, and lead us down the path of righteousness. For thine is the kingdom, the power, and the glory forever. Amen.

"Love is a duty, a requirement by God to enter into a marriage covenant." The words of Reverend Winslow echoed in her ears as she stared into the warm, bearded face of her forever love, Jonathan Carver. The makeshift arch, which they stood in front of, piled with fresh-cut greenery and interwoven with her favourite purple and red columbine flowers, swayed ever so slightly in the midday breeze. She was thankful for it, as even with all of her hair perched on top of her head, the heat of the day brought about a sweat unbecoming of a new bride.

Jon smiled at her, hands clasped tightly around hers. Mr. Brewster had allowed him to borrow some finer clothes than he usually wore, matched by the new handmade dress she and the other ladies had worked on for a fortnight. The whole of the village had come, as reasons for celebration were few and far between out here in the wilds. Manteo and some of the other men, including Jon and her Father, had cut logs into benches, providing ample seating for all of their guests.

They shared this day with them. A day of happiness. Mrs. Brewster sat near the front holding a squirming Virginia who'd rather run and play in this field than sit while the Reverend spoke. She smiled. It was just like in weekly prayers, only this time she wasn't the one tasked with wrangling the small spitfire. Next sermon, she'd have the opportunity to choose their topic of discussion, as was custom, and still she hadn't chosen what that was. She had a bit of time, but not much.

"Let there be a joining of the heart and knitting of affections with one another, coming together as the sky meets the sea." Reverend Winslow smiled, looking between them both. She remembered the sneer from that same face as he looked down upon her in her prison. No. Not right now. Things were set right. In the midst of their trials with wickedness, she told herself to put those thoughts from her mind today. Today was a day for celebration, and by God's will she would have it. As they'd proven, their enemy watched and waited, never rushing in their attacks against the colony. They would be there on the morrow, and with the might of God her people would overcome it. Today, she would rejoice.

"Let the practices, duties, and ethics of marriage flow out of the literature and into thine own hearts."

Father sat stiffly, but the small, tight-lipped smile he wore on his face showed her he was happy. He liked Jon, trusted him, leaned on him in the tougher of times.

"Love each other with a pure, Christian, tender, abundant, matrimonial love."

She would.

Now for the rings. Father had given Jon the ring Mother had worn. While it did bring her joy to have a small piece of her here today, it also served as a reminder that perhaps Mother had gone seeking something in the woods when she met her demise. The ring had been left on the table, after all.

Jon squeezed her hand, a comfort to her. He must have seen the glaze come over her eyes. Stay present. Stay focused. This is the happiest day of her life.

The reverend continued. "The three pillars of marriage are this, I say to thee, they are of a spiritual nature, of a superlative nature, and–" he paused, "of a sexual nature."

Her cheeks flushed and she took great care not to meet Jon in the eye. Right here, in front of all of these people. She'd rather not think on it.

"Only within the confines of this marriage are these three pillars appropriate and warranted, as if either were to stray, it would be an abomination against God!" The reverend grew louder, teetering on the edge of blasting into a full blown sermon.

"Companionship and mutual assistance. These are the first of reasons for marriage. From this day, to their last day, Mr. Jonathan Carver and Ms. Agnes Rose Dare shall be joined in holy matrimony, under the eyes of our Lord. Let us pray."

One long, floral garland of Rhododendrons stretched along the mismatched wooden tables the colonists had cobbled together for their wedding celebration. Feastin meats, salads from the garden, and even a few cakes were available all the way down the line. The spicy yet sweet smell of the flowers, reminiscent of cottage pinks, cloves, and carnations intoxicated her. Of course, that could be the rum. The warmth of her cheeks summoned a blush. Jon stretched out his hand, offering the opportunity to dance within reason with him. One must not allow their work or their life to be consumed with a lust for leisure, but on this, their wedding day, a small bit of dancing was allowed.

Manteo sang, the beautiful sound of his native language ebbing and flowing with the water drum he played. The children stood around him, shaking dried gourds filled with beans, stamping and laughing as they played.

Their colony had not seen happiness like this in quite a long time. Too long, she mused. Her cheeks would surely be sore from all the smiling she was doing today. Jon reached up to fix the flower crown along her hairline, twirling a finger through one of her fallen curls. His eyes shone with the bright fire of a new beginning, matched only by the silly grin plastered on his face.

Goody Carver.

That's what they would call her now.

"Aggy!" Winnie and Emme swirled into her presence, stamping their feet to the drumbeat as Manteo continued to sing. They wrapped her in a hug. The warmth of friendship. Soon they, too, would marry one of the men from the village. She just couldn't believe she'd been first.

Winnie leaned close and whispered in her ear, "All ready for your wedding night?" Her friend giggled.

"Winnie!" She laughed, heat rising in her cheeks at her friend's words. "Enough of that. You *know* we've been waiting a while now."

Winnie smirked. "Aye. Since the *last* time!"

She rolled her eyes. "Away with ye, you dog!" They laughed as she squeezed her friend tightly and sent her away. What had happened to Jon?

Ahh. There he was. Deep in conversation with Father. Surely they weren't plotting, on this their wedding day.

"Father! Jon!" She waved her hand for them to rejoin the festivities, when suddenly a hush fell over the crowd.

Manteo and the children had formed a circle in the centre of the crowd. For a performance, or prayer, possible. He produced a small reed with holes in it, placing it just against his lips, blowing into it to make it sing like a bird. He motioned for her and Jon to step forward.

"A prayer," he said, "for the newly united."

"God in heaven above please protect the ones we love.

We honor all you created as we pledge

our hearts and lives together.

We honor mother-earth - and ask for this marriage to

be abundant and grow stronger through the seasons;

We honor fire - and ask that this union

be warm and glowing with love in their hearts;

We honor wind - and ask we sail through life

safe and calm as in our father's arms;

We honor water - to clean and soothe this relationship -

that it may never thirst for love;

With all the forces of the universe you created,

we pray for harmony and true happiness as

we forever grow young together. Amen."

All gathered broke their silence with a rapturous roar of applause. Jon cupped her cheeks in both of his hands, drawing her in for a long kiss in front of the crowd.

"AMEN."

Screams ripped through their peace, coming from the colonists.

No. Not today.

She opened her eyes and saw at least ten women, maybe more, all with long, stringy hair. Their naked bodies were painted in mud, clawed hands as black as the night, as they stood around them in a circle.

They were surrounded.

Their small celebration fire roared to the sky, logs cracking and burning, the rush of heat from it stinging her face. The witches laughed, all at once, their voices rasping as stone scraping against stone.

"Fire, Jon! Use the Fire!" Father ran in a headlong rush towards the flames, removing his shirt as he went. The crowd scattered, mother's clutching at their children as they tried to run away, the men drawing knives, eyes wide in fear. Her heart pounded in her chest as Jon kissed her once more then rushed to the fire along with the rest. They were going after them.

It was only then that she saw their brooms, the witches sliding back and forth to ride them as they stood upon the ground. Their maniacal laughter rang in her ears as heat rose in her cheeks.

The witches rose, circling above them on their sinful sticks. They looked down upon the colonists. Their prey.

God, save us all.

Someone, she couldn't see who, produced a bow and arrow and shot arrows towards the sky.

Manteo.

"Heavenly Father!" Reverend Winslow cried, "Save us from this wretched scum that crawls upon your earth. Deliver us from evil!" He rushed towards the men at the fire, some throwing flaming sticks and others throwing knives. But it was of no use. The witches flew too high above their heads.

"Enjoy," one of them shrieked, the sound of it clotting the blood as it rushed through her veins.

Agnes slapped her arm as a giant fly landed on her. Then another. Then another.

The colonists' screams rose as a swarm of the winged beasts swirled into the presence. She smacked one that landed on her chest with a sickening crunch beneath her palm. She held the fly, but it wasn't a fly at all. Its body was black with fiery red eyes and orange veins running through its wings. Were these the locusts from the bible?

No, those were like grasshoppers.

Women and men ran in every direction, crying out as they crashed into each other, trying to block their faces from the swarm.

One among them produced a matchlock, aiming at the witches as they flew above them. They fired, the sound of it pounding in her ears. She peered at the witches through the tears in her eyes, whispering prayers for this chaos to end. A sharp pain shot through her chest, her heart, and she clutched it as she watched one of the devil's daughters raise the man who had fired, dropping him amidst the flames. He landed with a hard thunk upon the table, the flames licking at his body. She could hear his screams, smell his burning flesh. Others ran to the trough, clamouring to douse out the flames.

When she again looked to the skies, expecting to look upon their sneering faces, there were none. As quick as they had arrived, the witches were gone. They'd flown back to their safety within the trees. The swarm followed with them, their presence, unquestionably, irrefutably, known by all.

Father tried running after them, but Mr. Brewster stopped him.

"I'll kill them all!" he shouted.

Mr. Brewster slapped her father. "Dare! Dare! Keep your wits about ye! We follow them prepared. This is a trap. A wish. They beseech us to follow them this day, but we shan't grant them that wish! Weapons! Arms! When we go to them, we'll be ready."

Father threw his stick to the ground, stamping in rage. He clearly wanted to chase them now, to end it.

She pulled her arms close, doubling over at the sight of their ruined affair. There was more than one fire now.

Dear God.

One of the flaming sticks, desperately thrown by one of their own, had landed on their feast, the rhododendrons burning, spreading the flames to everything on the table.

"The fire!" she called, "The tables are on fire!" She turned to Goody Chapman and the ladies beside her, screaming, "We need water! Now!" She gathered her dress in both hands as she ran, passing Mrs. Brewster who held the now-wailing Virginia in her arms.

Buckets of water quenched the fire on the table with a gut wrenching hiss, their cakes and meats and salads charred beyond saving. Her wedding. The day which she had anxiously awaited for so many years, crushed beneath the souls of the damned.

They needed God more than ever now, to help them, to save them, or this colony wouldn't last much longer at all.

41
PREPARE

Provisions tending to force. An all-consuming, ever exhilarating command agreed upon by those of the colony. We will ruin the filth of the forest today.

He surveyed the spread that lay before him, muscles quivering and shaking, readying for his attack upon them. This venture would need more than knives, than torches. Yes. Today they would make those that plagued them rue the day they soiled themselves with Satan's sinful whisperings.

He'd heard their call from the woods, of late. But he wasn't going to answer them. Not even *her*. He'd seen Henry again, too, standing at his bedside whilst he was trying to sleep. The sight of his dead son curdled the blood in his veins. Especially since none were there to tell him if what he really saw was true. Alone, in his bed, no longer warmed by Eleanor nor Alice nor any other women.

He was done with those days. His sole purpose, in the preservation of their settlement, was to rid the world of their scourge. Some of the other men feared them, but not him. He had known one of them far better than they knew.

But they didn't believe him.

It didn't matter. Provisions of force, guided by the hand of God, would fill him with the strength needed to do what must be done.

He would start with her.

How could she do this? Forsake God. Life. The hope of salvation and an everlasting home. The steel sword, taken from out of their locked armoury, still held a keen edge, useful for cutting and thrusting. The pike, the chiefest weapon to defend, held a small pointed spear atop a shaft of ash, ready to pierce through the heart, if he got the chance. He even had an arquebus, a smooth-bore muzzle loader with a barrel at least three foot long. Those witches stood not a chance against it.

But they, (he peered out the window as an owl screeched outside) wielded weapons of an otherworldly design. A weapon more deadly than any he held here.

Magic.

Reverend Winslow did well to prepare them, reminding them of the mentions of magic in the word found in Exodus, Leviticus, and Deuteronomy. Works of sorcery as described in Acts, as a baneful opposition to the will of God.

He would face Satan himself if it meant they could be rid of them.

His new son by law gathered his own provisions across the room. Together, they would search in the forest once more.

Thump. Thump. Thump.

Three sharp knocks sounded on the door as their signal to join. They'd waited only a day, some gathering weapons and supplies while others fortified the palisades. He opened the door to what looked to be a solemn, silent mob, packs thrown round their shoulders and torches tucked at their sides.

It was time.

"Do ye remember where exactly you saw that hovel in the woods, Ananias?" one asked him.

"Aye. Well, not exactly, but I'm confident that God will guide our footsteps in the same direction as that day. We will find them."

Jonathan clapped the backs of his friends, not a smile among them as they nodded.

"Let's go."

They trudged along into the trees, the gathered crowd of those they left behind tearfully bidding them farewell. Agnes stood with Goody Brewster, Virginia clutching at her skirts. With one last look, he turned and crossed the threshold of the forest, into *their* territory.

But it wasn't really theirs. It was God's. They had stolen this forest and all of its wayward pines and oaks, perverting the land with their very presence.

"God give us this day," he whispered, "guide us to their hovels and bestow upon us the strength to root them out."

His murmured prayer went unheard by the others as the cracking and breaking of dried sticks and leaves filled their ears. They'd started on the path, the path he'd walked before but was unsure of who created it in the first place. Manteo's people, perhaps.

He'd asked him if they would join in the fight, but Manteo was unyielding in his response. He wouldn't endanger any of the native folk further, and Ananias respected that. There was no sense in bringing the wrath of these wicked beasts upon anyone other than themselves.

Truthfully, he should be at this alone, as he was the one who'd angered Eleanor so with his actions. But the plagues came before. The death of their son. This fight had started long before his former wife had fallen.

Squirrels scampered in the branches above them, causing some of the more skittish men to jump at the sound. The birds continued in their song, a sign that they weren't as close as they needed to be to the hovel he knew of.

He'd know they were getting close when the stench of it again filled his nostrils.

Jonathan must have remembered, too, as he had struck out among the brush, twitching his nose ever so often.

"Ananias..." Richard Berry called to him from far to the left, waving his arms for them to join him. His face was ashen, drained of blood and comfort.

As he drew near, his eyes were met with a sight that surely signalled they were getting close. It was a deer, ropes tied to all four legs and fixed between the two trees as a splayed man. Its belly had been split clean from the neck down to the white underside of its tail. Blood still dripped onto the ground, landing in a circle of stones beneath it.

"A sacrifice," he whispered.

Men uttered prayers and branished their weapons as they turned, searching around them for a sign of the ones they searched for.

"Let's keep moving."

They'd know it when they got to the stench.

"Ananias, I think we should spread out. Cover more ground." It was Jonthan.

He narrowed his eyes, pondering the suggestion. If they split up, their number of thirty would be easily overtaken if only fifteen, but then again, they *could* see more of the forest that way.

"Stay within earshot, son." Jonathan nodded, leading his crew further off the path, deeper into the left side of the woods.

Soon, they made it to the clearing with the stone table at the centre.

Yes, sweet Lord, guide my footsteps. Help us find them.

They crossed the clearing, acutely aware of the sun slowly setting between the trees, brilliant, blinding yellow light fading into orange and pink.

Cu-caw! Cu-caw!

A murder of crows burst forth from a nearby bush, their wings flapping and beaks snapping as they rushed he and his men. He shielded his face with his arms, praying that one of their beaks wouldn't soon sink into his eyes. They ran, deeper into the woods, some losing their footings or ducking behind trees, others fell to the ground pulling their arms above their head for relief from the pecks of the crows.

Ananias fought them off, swinging wildly with his unlit torch, knowing this be one of their tricks against him. They must commune with the crows, as they did with the devil.

"Away, beasts!" He swatted at their feathers, whacking one or two with his spear, stabbing straight into the meaty chest of one.

In an instant, they ceased in flocking him. He stood, surveying how far off the path he had travelled, and found himself alone.

Should he call for them?

No. This was his battle to fight. Eleanor was *his*.

As if summoned by his thought, a grey-haired woman, her long strands packed with twigs and leaves, stood before him. She reached for him with soiled claws, sharp teeth bared behind her rotten mouth.

"You've come," she growled.

His words nearly caught in his throat, heart galloping as a wild horse, pleading with him to run away. "Aye. I have. They'll be no more of this Eleanor. No more of it."

"But how about a dance, first, sweet husband?"

As she sauntered towards him, the vision of hell in the woman melted away. Her hair shrank back into her head, shortening in length and colouring once more. Her claws returned to fingers, smooth and tinged with peach as they were before. Her eyes bored into him, yet even though he knew he should feel angry, afraid—at this moment, he didn't.

Warmth spread along his skin, burrowing down into his bones. His heart felt lighter. Unafraid. No feelings of rage or anger stirring within.

This was Eleanor.

His Eleanor.

"You've come back," he whispered.

She caressed his face, her soft fingers a reminder of before. How she'd loved him. Doted upon him. And yet, he had betrayed her.

Tears welled in his eyes as he faced the beautiful soul that she was. She was no witch. Not his Eleanor. Not this perfect picture of grace and purity that stood before him now.

"I'm *so* sorry, Eleanor. For it all. I was a wretched husband to you then as I am now."

She gathered his hand in one of hers, the other placing a single finger on his lips. "Shhh, now, sweet husband. Dance with me again."

She placed his hand on her hip and turned, guiding them between the trees, twirling around under his arms. Faster and faster they moved as he drank in the scent of her. She smelled of warm honey and a mulled spice ale, a sweetness welling on his tongue.

"Oh, Eleanor. Forgive me."

They danced around a tree, the moss-covered ground soft under his footsteps until he felt himself floating, rising higher and higher in the sky, his sweet wife wrapped in his arms. They were flying.

Flying. This cannot be. It's the devil's work!

"Aaarrrggghhh!" he screamed, pushing her backwards and falling with a hard thud upon the ground. Pain shot up his back as he landed with a raised root jamming into him. "You have bewitched me, devil woman!"

All of the fire and fury and vengeance that had sheltered away behind her magicks came welling back with a thunderous rage. "I will see you dead, woman!"

She threw back her head, returned to grey and weathered, laughing towards the sky.

Ananias scrambled to his feet, drawing his short sword and brandishing it. His helmet was lost to the leaves, but no matter, he wouldn't be needing it much longer.

"Eleanor!"

"It's Lenorea now, ye git. And I'm not her," she laughed.

This was a different witch entirely.

Between the trees, he saw them come. Dark shapes, unclear to him as the last of daylight had faded, quickly replaced by shadows. All at once, they sprang. He readied himself for more witches, but saw that it was Jonathan and a few others, and they now had the witch in their grasp.

"Do it, Dare! Now!"

He held the knife to her neck, preparing to slice, when one of their wicked number spoke.

"But wait–"

Ananias trembled, sweat slicking between his hand the hilt of the sword as he held it to her throat.

Suffer not a witch to live. He ran the blade across her neck, blackened blood spilling down along her naked form. He'd done it.

With the help of the others, he'd lessened the stain of evil upon this world.

42

HER

ANANIAS DARE - MAY 1590

The fire burned his face as he stared into the flames. He'd taken a life today, but it was the right thing to do. The only thing to do. There had been no choice. Whoever she was, she was a witch, a servant to the devil himself. Not of God.

He did the right thing.

He hoped.

"God hath smiled upon us today, boys!" Charles Costmur settled on the bench beside him, clapping his back and raising a tankard to his lips. Ale spilled down along the sides of his mouth as he slurped and drank the honey-ed water that tasted closer to piss than a beverage. The sight of it sickened him.

He'd no desire to drink, eat, or celebrate in this moment, which in and of itself was an odd sensation. He should be rejoicing. Victory! But the pit in his stomach prevented it. They used to be humans, if Eleanor was any proof of that. And today he had taken away any hope for that one's renewal. He'd seen it done, back in England, when one witch repented of her sins, clinging fast to the words and reciting her commandments just before she took to the gallows. The crowd was astounded, as they ought to have been, since a witch is known to be unable to name the commandments in full, and this woman had. She'd renounced her ways, begged forgiveness, and that moment remained burned in his mind, as did the face of the woman he had slain today.

"Why the long face, Ananais?" His old buddy Brewster called from across the way. "You've taken one down, which shows that we can! Soon enough we will be rid of them entirely!"

Which also meant Eleanor. She, too, would be slain.

He forced a small smile, knowing it didn't reach through to his heart. "Aye. We did. And the lot of them are next."

"Here, here!" they cheered.

"God will surely place another jewel in your crown in heaven, Sir." Ambrose Whithers offered him some bread. "I made it myself just yesterday." He took it, half expecting the bread to turn to ash in his mouth, but it didn't. It was warm. Refreshing.

They were right.

He must put aside these willful thoughts, as they were on a mission for God, now. These witches had already damned themselves to a fire everlasting, anyway. He would simply see them there at a brisker pace.

"What of the other men?" he asked.

A quarter of their number hadn't returned when they'd made it back through the forest, surely guided by God to find the way home.

"No sign of em', Sir." Jonathan sat on a bench to his right. "They'll come, Ananais. The night has not yet thickened and the moon shines bright. They'll find their way."

"But what if they have fallen?"

Just then, even as he spoke the words, six men burst through the trees with a woman in tow.

Dearest Lord.

They'd captured one.

Shackled at the wrists and feet, chains clanking with each step she took, the witch stared straight at the ground as they moved forward. She was naked, as they usually were, and had the same, long, grey hair that he'd seen before.

Hushed whispers permeated through the crowd, a slight panic rising among them.

They've brought her here!

Kill her!

We've not a need for a witch among us.

Burn her at the stake!

Ananias rose, knocking Cotsmur's tankard of ale to the ground. But Charles didn't even notice, as he, too, watched as they brought her into the light. Bennet Chappell and Walter Mill stood on either side of her, grinning from ear to ear.

"We got her," Bennet said, standing a bit taller as he gazed around the crowd.

Walter added, "She climbed on Bennet's back, bringing him to the ground, but we managed to slip the chains on her!" They were both breathless. Naturally effervescent.

The witch woman growled and Ananias stepped closer.

"Be careful, Mr. Dare. This one bites." Bennet chuckled, brandishing his arm in the firelight to show what were clearly teeth marks in the skin.

"Foolish boys!" Reverend Winslow made his way through the gathered observers. "You should have killed her where she stood! What possessed you to bring this evil here!" The witch struggled, fighting to wrench from their grasp but couldn't manage it.

Both of their faces fell, if only slightly.

"For questioning, I'd imagine." Ananias moved ever closer, wanting to catch a good glimpse of the witch's face. He needed to know if it was her.

The reverend paused. "Aye. Questioning. Perhaps we can find out where the others reside."

Bennet and Walter nodded with such veracity he was sure their heads would break off of their shoulders and tumble to the ground. "Aye, sir. Yes! That's exactly it. We thought she could be questioned, sir."

"Lock her up in the cellar, and keep the chains on her," said Reverend Winslow.

As they dragged her away, kicking and spitting and clawing at their arms, he caught a full view of her face, curtained in familiar wisps of greyed hair.

His breath caught in his throat as he saw her swollen belly.

It was her.

43
BURNED BY FIRE

REVEREND WINSLOW – MAY 1590

It is May, this the year of our Lord 1590 and even as the birds sing their songs to each other and the shining sun and plentiful rain hath brought forth the flowerings, we in Roanoke are up against a darkness of a most terrible nature. We are face to face with one who hath penned their name in the devil's book, a ghastly creature, one that growls and spits and bites when we come near. Lord, I ask for strength, that I might smite the devil from this servant of earth, bringing them back into the fold with an opportunity to instead write their name in the lamb's book of life. Help me to save her, Lord, if there is any humanity that remains within her, yet I fear there is not. I will try, Lord, as I am charged, but I will not hesitate to cleanse this stain upon our village as is my duty. Protect my faith, Lord. Protect my earthly body as I look into the eyes of the unholy, keeping mine own hand out of her filthy reach. We shall suffer not a witch to live, if this witch cannot be saved. Give us strength, Lord. For thine is the Kingdom, the power, and the glory. Amen.

He gripped the flaming torch in one hand, ascending the hill upon which she was chained. Fire, if he needed it. Witches could be burned by fire. Two boulders rested on either side of her, the frail, naked woman kneeling between them facing away, her wrists in shackles and head bowed low. Deep wounds covered her back. The forty souls brave enough to join him, to witness to this resolution, whatever it may be, followed behind.

The early morning fog crept just above the ground, blanketing their surroundings in a white mist. They should have waited for midday, but the sun was hot and he knew if they left her chained outside for much longer this woman wouldn't survive it. He had questions.

She had the answers.

Ananias Dare had tirelessly joined him in study and prayer, working hard to convince him to try and save this woman from her contract with the Devil. He'd sworn to have seen it done before, that the possibility of saving a wretched soul was possible, yet Reverend Winslow had his doubts.

Once one had turned from God, forsaking the righteous light of his unending love, they broke his covenant. In his eyes, and in the eyes of the church, this woman was already damned. But, for the sake of hope, of peace, of righting their wrongdoings– he would give this woman a chance. Ananias felt guilty for taking the other witch's life; he knew this to be true. He had prayed with him, and fasted, yet try as he might, he feared that something else was lost in Ananias that day.

Reverend Winslow looked to his right, where Ananias, Agnes, and her husband Carver stood. Grim.

Together, they were shepherds in God's work today.

The chains binding the witch to stone clanked, breaking through the deafening silence. Head still bowed, long, greasy hair falling forward and covering her naked flesh, the witch rose to stand.

Reverend Winslow cleared his throat. "We've come to question you, witch. To bring an opportunity to step from the shadows of evil back into the light!" He steadied his words; if the others heard the tremble in his voice then fear could strike in their hearts. They must be united in this.

"What say you, witch? Why hast thou come upon us on this island?"

She lunged, straining at her shackles, hissing and spitting as she clawed away from them. He was but twenty paces from her now.

The Holy Ghost surged through his veins, the righteous flame of God enveloping him entirely, strengthening his resolve. Hounds growled beside him, their owners holding fast to their ropes as they tried to reach her. She twitched her head towards them, and the dogs yelped and whined, shrinking back behind their owners.

"Leave me." she hissed.

Where fear once played at the edges of his mind, now only buzzed determination.

"Why hast thou come?" he shouted.

The witch woman shrieked, the sound of it piercing his inner ear as if with a hot stoker from the fire.

"*We* were here first," she cackled. "The daughters of the forest."

"The daughters of the Devil!" shouted Agnes Dare.

She swung her arms, the chains swinging with them, clanging in the way the prisoners' lines used to back in England. Still he had not seen her face.

He wished they'd never left.

"Speak your purpose, daughter of the Devil! Why hast thou plagued our colony so?" He handed his torch to a follower behind him, reaching instead for his bible and small, iron cross.

"You've a chance to cast aside your wicked ways! To rejoin the world of men, if any part of you that remains is yet human!"

"Aye, I am human," she said, in a voice unlike the gravelly one before. Familiar. A voice he'd heard before. "And a bit of something more." Her neck cracked and surely broke as she turned to face him, turned completely away from the front of her body, pregnant belly still facing behind.

Dearest God. He trembled at the sight.

Her eyes rolled back into her head until he could see only the whites of them. Her body shook with a violence that surely tore her muscles inside, twisting unnaturally like a snake over coals.

"Forsake him! Forsake the Devil and claim your human form yet again, woman!"

She twisted her neck even further. "Satan is only one of whom I serve, now."

"I beseech thee to try!" Even he could hear the desperation in his voice. There was no hope for this woman. She must be extinguished. Now.

"Ready the logs, men! And the flame!" He signalled for them to move forward.

The witch woman laughed, head snapping back to face away from them again. She exhaled a long breath of black smoke, and as she did, her blackened feet lifted from the ground.

"The fire! The fire! Light the logs! Now!" The chains still held her, but as she rose, her feet lifted far above her head, arms stretched out to either side, grey hair falling towards the ground.

Dear God. She was an inverted cross.

Many of those that had joined him ran, heading for the safety of the colony. But not him; he would see this through.

"By God's command, I sentence thee to die!"

Spoken through lips that did not move, her gravelly voice filled the air around them. "I welcomed him inside me. His seed filled me, black as coal, as cool as the stream, burning once inside." Raising her voice and speaking in tongues not of this world, the witch thrashed between the chains. The words that spewed forth from her mouth surely came straight from Hell.

"Our Father! Who art in Heaven!" One of those present began the Lord's prayer.

"Sew your lips, you filthy pig!" The voices welling in the woman's throat were not her own, gravelled or otherwise. "Damn your Christ! Damn you all! She will have her revenge!"

The one who'd spoken grabbed his face in a muffled scream as his lips melted together, sewing shut as she'd commanded. If this continued, he'd lose his flock to fear.

The flames beneath her climbed higher, singing the bottom of her hair. The sudden realisation of what they had captured fell over him as a load of bricks.

She consorted with a demon.

"This witch houses a demon! Stoke the fire! Rise the flames. We must burn them out!" He undid the clasp on his belt, grabbing the last bit of holy water he'd brought across the shore.

"I cast thee out, demon!" Where the water touched her skin, boils raised and popped. Her shrieks changed from laughter to agony.

"I am within her," the deep voices of a thousand called, "You cannot rid her of me. Her mind. Her body. Her soul is mine!"

"In the name of God, I cast thee out!" In this moment, he knew there was scripture to read, words to say, but God grant him mercy he couldn't remember them.

"I help her," the deep voice called.

"God is her help! You infest her. Speak your name. Tell us who resides within her now." He sprinkled the holy water again.

"No!"

"Speak your name, demon!"

The poor woman laughed, black smoke again spilling forth from her mouth. "I'm perching in her. Inside her. She is damned to you all, now."

"In the name of God, in the name of the Father, I command you to die!" Reverend Winslow threw the last of the holy water on this unholy possession. God help us. Save us. Give us the strength to rid the world of this evil.

"I am a gift to this world," the thousand voices boomed, "I am...Roshef."

The chains binding the woman to the boulders broke free, her body righting with her head above her feet once again. Her scream ripped through the air as antlers burst forth from her skull in a spray of black blood, spattering the faithful that remained.

"Help me! Reverend, help me!"

Dear God! The woman yet lives!

"God sees your strife, woman! Fight this abomination. Reach for God's hand and tear yourself free from its grasp!" Her body moved away from the flames now, resting in front of it on the grass.

Ananias Dare lunged forward. "Come back to us, Eleanor! Please! I need you! We need you to fight!"

Dear God. Eleanor. That was the voice he knew. Gasps rose from the remaining crowd.

Eyes still white, what used to be Eleanor twitched her head towards Ananais. "Eleanor is gone, Ananias. You killed her soul when you coupled with your whore while your son died cold and alone. He cried for you, Ananias."

He watched as Ananias trembled, hands shaking as they covered his mouth. "No. No. I'll not hear it."

She moved toward him, slowly. "He begged for his Papa to help as he shivered and died."

Ananias shrank back beside him, tears streaming down his face. An otherworldly laugh escaped her. "I speak no lie. I can hear him, even now." Her eyes rolled back to again only white, inches in front of them.

The words came, though her lips didn't move, in the voice of a child. "Papa, I'm scared! Pwease Papa, I'm cowd. Where are you?"

Reverend Winslow's breath caught in his throat. It was the voice of the Dare child, there was no doubt.

"Enough!" he cried, reaching forward to place the iron cross on Eleanor's forehead. "I command this to end. Let her go, Roshef. Leave her be!"

Eleanor screamed as the cross burned her flesh, poisonous words spewing from her mouth, scrawled letters appearing on her chest, carved into her skin, dripping with blood.

Croatoan.

The voices of a thousand rose from her once more as she squirmed. "I lived long before your God was invented, Reverend Winslow. Know me, and suffer!"

Eleanor's head snapped back as black birds flew out her mouth, their numbers astounding.

She couldn't possibly live through this.

When the last of the birds had flown from her mouth, Eleanor doubled over, vomiting ichor with a sickening hiss upon the ground. It splattered him, and Ananais, and burned. God, it burned, worse than any flame. A white-hot brand would feel as ice by comparison. The stench of his own burning hair made him wretch and the vision in one eye went dark.

He would show no weakness. The armour of the lord was firmly upon him and his impassioned righteousness drove back this madness that threatened to overcome them all. He grasped Eleanor at the back of the neck, turning her face up towards him as she sneered.

The Reverend shouted. "You hath burnt my flesh and broken her bones, but my soul belongs to the one true God! You will not take this woman!"

She cackled.

Once more. "Roshef, I name you and command thee to flee this host! By God, by Christ, exit Eleanor's body and return from whence you came!"

Eleanor's form convulsed, quaking and twisting. Her mouth foamed as a rabid dog.

But then, by a miracle only befitting of God Almighty, her elongated claws sank back into her flesh, revealing the fingers of a human again. Her antlers fell away, thudding upon the ground where they landed. Her skin and hair were the same, but she again seemed closer to the woman he knew from before.

Black smoke poured from her eyes, dissipating into the mist. The fire from before crackled beyond them as all fell to silence.

Eleanor stilled. Unmoving, but breathing. Ananias cradled her and cried.

"She is healed!" Reverend Winslow proclaimed.

They would have to watch over her, that is sure, but today had been more proof than he'd ever seen before.

God was real, and he'd saved Eleanor.

44
WHAT NEEDED TO BE DONE

Jonathan looked down at the woman who should be his mother-in-law. She should have been there to celebrate when he and Aggy joined in marriage. She should have been there to care for little Virginia, safe and healthy within the Dare home.

But she wasn't, and yet, here she was.

She lay on the table, clothed for the first time in who knows how long, arms stretched out on either side. He studied her, her chest rising and falling with each breath. She could have been asleep if it weren't for her eyes being open. Wide open, hardly blinking, never shutting.

Truth be told, the sight frightened him a bit. Her arms were loosely tied to the corners of the bed in this shed. Those in the village took turns watching her, feeding her, bathing her. The lesions on her skin started healing around three weeks ago, and yet she never made a sound. Even at night, which thankfully he'd only had to sit through with her once or twice, her eyes remained open.

Staring.

Watching.

At first, he had tried to talk with her, tried to tell her of all the wonderful things that had transpired since she'd been taken. But as far as wonderful things go, the list was few. He wasn't sure of her involvement with the plagues or dancing in the woods, those that had disappeared, or if she was the one who had stolen Ambrose from her bed– and he wasn't planning on asking.

Not that she'd answer.

He'd tried that, too, as they spent the long hours of his watch together. Tried asking her questions about the night she'd disappeared, about Ananias, and Aggy. But still as a stone she sat. Mute. Unmoving.

It made for long watches, that was for sure.

At least, as far as he could tell, she wasn't able to wield any witchcraft and she had no special powers about her anymore. The demon hadn't made any appearances, but Reverend Winslow still wouldn't chance it. He also kept Ananias at bay, who desperately tried to visit with her every day, since he wasn't given any watches himself.

Eleanor's pregnant stomach had grown a bit in the weeks since her exorcism, a sign that she was at least swallowing most of the food fed to her, which was a good sign. The colour had returned to her cheeks–also good. Jonathan prayed that whatever lingering hold the devil or that demon or whoever still had upon her would dissipate soon.

This was no way to live. No way to *be*.

He and Aggy had made up their minds last night. If Eleanor didn't "wake up" from whatever trance she was in before the harvest season, they would help her cross over into Heaven.

They wouldn't share these plans with anyone, of course, but it was the right thing to do. The Eleanor they knew wouldn't have wanted to waste away her life like this.

Nay. If it came to it, they would do what needed to be done.

45
HEAR MY PRAYER

ANANIAS DARE - JUNE 1590

Dearest Lord, hear my prayer. You know that I am a wretched sinner better than I. A wicked man. A lustful man. But a man with a heart and mind set upon making things right in this world and in the eyes of God. My wife, oh my precious wife, undeserving of her fate and possession at the hands of those that still lurk in the woods, sweet Lord. I pray that you wrap your healing hands around her and bring her mind out of the shadows where they are shackled. Her heart is surely held in a great dungeon of despair, as mine is, and I fear we may not ever see her the same as before but I'm asking for a chance. Give her a chance, Lord, a chance to find her way among us in the righteous world again. I believe that day when you scourged the demon from her soul you were setting us upon a new path. A new life. A life free from the stain of our prior sins and transgressions against thee. Yea tho I walk through the valley of the shadow of death, I fear no evil. For thou art with me. Thy rod and they staff, they comfort me and guide me. Guide Eleanor. Guide our family, our colony. Help Roanoke to be the plentiful settlement and outpost of the Lord's work as we so intended when travelling to these shores those many months ago. In your precious name I pray, Amen.

Today was the day. After four weeks under the watch of others, he would finally have the opportunity to sit with Eleanor and beg her forgiveness. He would cast aside the happenings of before, in the woods, and with Alice.

He wouldn't think of any of that now, because she was under the dark magics of a demon then. Possessed. Unable to make those choices herself.

It wasn't her. It couldn't have been.

Now the town knew it was she that had plagued him so. They knew him not to be of an addled mind, but strong, sure, resolute in his standing. Today, when Reverend Winslow had knocked upon his door with the offer to see her, he had fallen to his knees and wept. Weeks, he'd waited. No spoken words had come from her, and yet, he was sure that he could help her return.

He moved closer to the door of the shed in which they kept her. Charles Cotsmur stood outside, no doubt gleeful that such pain had befallen the Dare family, but he never spoke a word of it. He was an envious man. A man threatened by any who rose to perceived power within their colony. Charles nodded at Ananias and took his leave.

He opened the door, surprised that no stench or sense of evil filled his senses. After their last encounter, he wasn't exactly sure what he would find within these walls. Aye, he'd received many an update, but all were the same, and the same as the sight that met his eyes just now.

As he entered the room, he swung the door inward, its hinges creaking and moaning as he closed it.

"Eleanor. Darling? I–" He was suddenly at a loss for words. What did one say to the woman whom he loved with a fire brighter than any flame, yet betrayed, and had then suffered greatly at the hands of her possession?

He thought of Alice, or rather, her skin, crawling along as a dog.

No. Put these thoughts away. She didn't mean it.

"I've come to take you home." The words flew out of his mouth faster than he'd even realised. What was he saying? Reverend Winslow would smite them all! But it felt right. Like it needed to be done.

Yes. That would help her come out of this shell that consumed her very being.

Her head snapped towards him, not violently, more out of surprise.

"Home?" she said.

Ananias couldn't believe his ears. She spoke! For the first time in over a month, and as a consequence of him, she responded. He steadied the nerves that rattled him.

"Yes, darling. Home. If that be something you would like?" He moved closer, slowly settling beside her on the bed. He'd felt no evil among them, yet. This was his wife. The wife that he'd betrayed.

"Home," she said again, this time trying to sit up on the bed, but unable to because of the restraints. She looked at him, nodded at the cloth tied to her wrists, then looked up again. Wordlessly, he dipped his head and set to untying them.

Yes. Take her home. That's exactly what she needs.

But she was a witch.

No! He wouldn't blame her any longer. He shoved the thought away, training his efforts on the here and now. The frail woman that sat beside him on this bed in her prison shack.

"How are Agnes and Virginia?" she asked, rubbing her hands on her wrists, smoothing the fresh nightgown that someone else had dressed her in. She pulled at her grey hair, pondering it, twirling it around one finger.

"They are well," he responded. "The young Carver man has taken Agnes as his wife, and they seem to be elated together."

She nodded. "So he mentioned."

Ananias paused. Should he question her further? There'd be time for that. He must tread carefully for fear that she would resume the catatonic state she'd been in. Perhaps one question more.

"Are you all right, Eleanor?"

She stared, unblinking.

He cursed himself inside. A daft question after all that had transpired, he knew, but he could scarcely find the right words to say to her at this very moment.

"Let's get you home, then." He rose from the bed and grasped both of her hands in his. They were cold, unusually so for such a hot, summer day, but he paid it no mind.

"I've no shoes, Ananias, and my feet are tender," she whispered as she placed both upon the dirt floor.

"I'll carry you."

Eleanor nodded and wrapped both hands around his neck, a feeling they hadn't shared in far too long, long before they'd traversed to these shores. It reminded him of before, back in England, back when happiness and love crossed between them rather than this stoney, awkward silence.

He carried her to the door, desperately trying to ignore her swollen, pregnant belly. He opened the door slowly, peering outside to make sure none would see their quiet escape from the shed. Reverend Winslow would know of their doings soon enough, when the next watcher came to relieve Ananias, but he'd hoped that by then he could prove that Eleanor was safe and happy at home.

He was trusting in it. Trusting in God.

The walk home wasn't far, and they could keep to the edges of the trees to shield them from greater view. They could slip by, unnoticed, as long as he was careful.

"Hold tight," he whispered in her ear.

Soon enough they would be home. Safe. He wasn't sure if they could ever reclaim that happiness from before, but he knew he would do whatever he could to try.

His footsteps squelched in the mud with each step. They'd suffered many a day of rain, and today was the first break in it, thankfully. He loved the way the earth smelled after a rain, especially on a hot day like this as it all dried up. The weight of his frail wife in his arms was a welcome one, and he hoped that together they, too, could dry up all of the fear and mistrust and settle back in together.

"Aggy and Jonathan should be here. And Virginia. They'll be waitin' to see ye." He couldn't believe he was doing this, what life they were living now, with demons and witches and hellish plagues on earth, but so it was. The front door was slightly ajar, so he nudged it open with his muddied boot. "Aggy! Jon! There's someone here to see us!"

But no one answered him.

He looked at Eleanor, who had fallen back into a silent trance, and gently set her in the largest chair they had. "Virginia?" His heart thumped a bit faster than it had before, but there was nothing to fear. Surely they had gone for a walk or to the well or along the back pasture to the stream.

Where Henry died.

No. Surely they were all right.

He glanced at Eleanor sitting unmoving at the table before he crossed to the hallway that led to the room where little Virginia slept most nights. There, nestled in her bed, slept his toddling babe. She was safe. But where were the others?

Ananias went back out and saw that Eleanor had risen in that time, busying herself in the cupboards that so many months ago she used to prepare meals at. She moved slower, more carefully than before, as she was surely soon to give birth. He tried to think of the last time they'd coupled, before she went missing among those demons in the woods, but it seemed longer than the proof of it before him.

Surely, Lord God, this was his child. Surely.

She settled back in the chair with a pitcher of water, a small cup, and a piece of bread torn from the loaf Aggy had made just yesterday. Slowly, she dipped the bread in the water and raised it to her lips, just like she used to do before.

He never understood why, and didn't dare question it considering she was showing a small piece of the woman she used to be. If it weren't for her singed, grey hair and weathered skin, he'd think no time at all had passed since she'd last sat at their table.

But it had.

A loud shriek from outside startled him from his thoughts. "Father! Jon! Come quickly!"

It was Aggy.

"You'll be all right here, Eleanor?" He rushed to the door, turning back in the hopes that she'd answer him. She dunked the bread in the water again, wordlessly nodding.

He raced outside, around to the back of the house where he'd heard her shouts coming from.

Ananias froze. There, spread across the ground in a pool of blood seeping into the dirt, was their one and one milking cow. Aggy stood beyond it, pale as a linen sheet, with Jonathan at her side.

"What the hell happened out here!" He passed by their hanging laundry to get to them.

"We heard the cow moaning outside, and came to see what the matter was, but by the time we made it out here she was already down." Tears streamed from Aggie's eyes, no doubt the same thoughts running through her mind as were his. Milk. Virginia. Their only source. Gone.

"Could have been a coyote? A wolf?" He reached down to rub his hand along the terrified cow's head. She was still breathing, if shallow, as her insides spilled forth upon the ground.

Jonathan kneeled beside them, surveying the wound. "It looks like a clean slice, Ananais. No teeth marks. I'm not so sure an animal did this."

Ananias couldn't wrap his mind around the thought. "Let's go inside. There's...well there's something I need to show you."

"We can't leave her, Father." Aggy kneeled beside their cow as well, whose breathing had sharply stopped. Glassy, black eyes stared beyond them now.

"I–well–this is important. Jon, we'll cut up the meat and set it for drying in just a bit. I promise this won't take long."

They followed him back to the house as he thought of what he could possibly say. How would he explain bringing Eleanor home? They'd see it too. That she'd changed. She spoke now. She had spoken to him, hadn't she?

But as he crossed the threshold to go back inside, there was no Eleanor at the table.

His heart raced. "Eleanor?" He searched around the room, but seeing as it wasn't large there wasn't any place that she could hide.

"Mother? You brought her *here*? Does the Reverend know? She wasn't speaking!"

"But she was, Aggy! She spoke to me today! And moved! I carried her here, myself!"

Aggy's eyes were wide. "You carried her here, and now she's gone?"

"Virginia!" Jon raced back into the room after checking on the little one. "Virginia's gone!"

Oh No.

No. No. No. No.

"Father, we left her! She was asleep. And you left her in here with a demon-possessed witch!"

"I–I..." He couldn't move. Couldn't breathe. He'd consumed the lie that she'd been made whole again. A fresh start. Virginia. How could he have been so foolish?

46
SWALLOWED

"I ait the bred n drank her water. She's gone now. Eleanoor. She's a witch still. Demon. I find her. God bless. Amen."

He was unworthy. A piece of meat. No better than the chicken feed they were about to run out of. He pioneered this strife upon his family. His colony. Ruined their chances at success by bringing evil into this land. The witches. The bitches. They hated him. He hated them.

Why hath thou forsaken me, God?

Henry!

Virginia!

Eleanor. His sins have led to their demise, but why did God let it be so? If this is punishment, he wished it had been upon his own flesh, his own mind. Not the innocence of theirs.

Ananias stumbled back to the cask of ale he'd hidden away way back when. He'd stolen it. A thief. Taken from the supplies when they'd first made it ashore. He knew better, but at the time didn't care. None would miss it, he'd said to himself. None would know! He'd sneak a drink every now and again, to settle the nerves or end a long day of hard work.

Nay, they'd never know.

But now they would! He. He. He. He'd swallowed himself in it, wallowing in the creamy, buttery taste of ale until he'd thrown up half he'd drunk of it– and then drank some more.

Maybe he'd die. End this life and move on to the next. Then he could swim in ale for eternity. But they didn't have ale in Heaven, did they? He was probably going to Hell. The lake of fire. Torture eternal.

And he deserved it.

Though perhaps it was better than this hellscape on Roanoke island.

"I'm married to a *WITCH*! A *DEMON*!" He cackled at the absurdity of it all. More ale. More ale. He'd hate for Virginia, no Agnes, that were the eldest one, to find him swallowed up whole from the barrel, but he just couldn't take it anymore. Too much. It was all too much.

God hath forsaken him. Marked him as a beast, no doubt. The plagues. Temptation. Alice. God allowed the devil to prance upon his lands and settle into a kingdom of sin.

No.

God did not earn the entirety of the blame. It was *him*. He was the sinner. The scoundrel. The cause.

None of this would have happened if he'd stayed true to his wife back in England. They'd never have needed a fresh start, never boarded the ship for the crossing, and never fallen victim to the curses upon this land.

They should have known it. The first colony was a well-known failure. Who were they, the prideful, pious, poppycock phoneys hiding their greed behind the shadow of righteousness? That's all he was. An ill-fit man, stained by sin.

And how to reclaim it? Was there a way to go on, after this?

He hiccupped, slumping over in his chair– the chair Eleanor sat in earlier today.

"Weeeeeeeee'll rise up from the ashes, and work the long, long day
For God is good, it's unnnnnderstood. His Word we'll not betray." He raised his tankard to this invisible crowd, as they cheered him on and

swayed in his mind. "Here, here!" He slammed his drink on the table, ale splashing out and onto the wood.

"But how to catch a beast?" he mused. "There's got to be a way to find them." Jon had gone to rally those willing to search for them *again*. The last time, some had been killed! Nearly he, himself! Didn't they see that devil woman rise from the ground? And there's more of them.

He stumbled to the back door, ready for a piss in the night. The air was cool against his cock.

Heh. He'd made love to a witch. To a skin beast. He was definitely going to Hell. Ananias doubled over, retching into the grass. The ground swayed, back and forth, much the same as that dreadful voyage across the sea. He'd hardly been sick then, but others had.

But how could he find them? Maybe he'd burn the whole forest down. That might work. Then they'd have no place to hide.

No. No. The colony wouldn't survive then, but they barely survived as is with those women in the woods.

"Aarrrrgh!" he growled. "Damn you, Eleanor!" He'd wanted to believe in her, to believe in himself again. He must find the others. Join them.

Out of the corner of his eye, he saw their cow, still lying out on the ground, meat forgotten.

He had an idea.

47

A HUNTING

Lord as we gather arms to again go after the witches, this time in search of little Virginia, I beseech thee to wrap us in safety and care and bring us home safely. Help us to extinguish this great evil from the world, and rid ourselves from this great spiritual plague. If they are following in the order of your word, then already we've seen bloody water, frogs, lice, flies, sick cattle, sores, hail, and the locust plagues. I fear the darkness and dead first male, Lord, I fear it. Keep the witches at bay and protect our children from this plight. Help us to find Virginia, and bring her home safely, even as we are fearful since we couldn't find Alice's boys. Give us strength, Lord, and forgive us of our sins. In Jesus' name I humbly pray, Amen.

He stood before them, torches ablaze in the darkest night he'd seen in a long while. The grim faces of his fellow colonists, eyes that had seen far too much in their short time upon these lands. Eyes filled with fear, but determination for their cause. Theirs was a virtuous fight, backed by the word of our Lord.

"We shall not suffer a witch to live!" he cried. "If any of you see one within the forest, kill them where they stand. We take no prisoners for questioning. We find Virginia! We set things right, tonight!"

"Aye!" they cried, raising all manner of weapons with vigour. Strength filled his muscles, his heart. They would walk away unharmed and victorious this night, he was sure of it.

"Stay together, men! We've seen what they are capable of. Fall not prey to their wickedness. Their tricks. Their might be strong, but ours is stronger. We have the armor of God on our side!"

He turned, taking the lead with his torch held high, ready to face Satan himself in these woods when suddenly, Ananias Dare staggered up to the fold, arms drenched in blood with entrails draped across his shoulders as a scarf.

"Ananias! What on God's green earth hath possessed you, this night?"

His father-in-law giggled, swinging the intestines around like a rope. "Bait, m'boy! I'm going to bait the witches out with their bloodlust!"

If ever in a thousand years one would have told him that his father in law would stand before him in his current condition, Jon would have suspected them of madness.

Yet here he was. Swinging away.

Ananias fell to the ground, taken with fits of laughter.

"Someone help the poor man," he said. Two men rushed over to help him to his feet, careful not to place their hands on his bloodied arms.

"I'm coming with you!" Ananias shouted.

Jon shook his head. "So be it. Just don't get in our way."

They stuck to the path leading to the clearing in the woods with the stone table. Jon remembered the path well, as it was etched in his mind from before. He'd found them once, and he would find them again. Little Virginia's life, and truthfully *all* of their lives were at stake at this point.

Their colony could not survive much longer with these witches among them.

Eleanor. How he'd hoped she'd pull through. But clearly, after yet another disappearance, she was too far gone to be helped. They'd done what they could.

He almost wished that he and Aggy had acted after they'd decided to put her out of her misery before. Almost.

The thought of blood on his hands wasn't a welcome one, but a necessary action that he wouldn't hesitate to make. The cracking of leaves and sticks as they stepped upon them rattled in his ears, a sound more comforting than each hoot of an owl or sudden rustling of the underbrush as they disturbed the piteous animals that had to share their home with evil.

He remembered well that the closer they came to the witch's hovel that time before, all sounds indicative of life ceased. No birds cawed, no squirrels chattered. Thus, he would listen for the silence as a sign that they drew near to evil again.

There was also the feeling. A sense of dread, a shiver running up the spine, spiders crawling up his arms. That feeling was hard to duplicate, and one he wished he'd never have to experience again– but tonight he welcomed it. He wanted the chance, needed it, to know that they were one step closer in bringing Virginia home. And if they didn't find her, then at least he'd hoped they could rid the scourge of at least one witch or two.

Their number had been many that night he'd watched them dancing in the forest with Agnes. Spied on them, really. Nevertheless, he knew how many they were up against in this spiritual war.

Jon paused, raising one fist as a signal to his men to quiet. He could hear Ananias whispering far too loud in the back. "Does he see one? Lemme at her!"

He held his torch closer to his face as he turned around, ensuring the man could see him. "Enough, Ananias! We'll lose the element of surprise." Ananias nodded at him. "And drop the cattle, for heaven's sake."

His father in law did as he was told.

He turned back, searching between the trees for any sign, and trail in the hopes they'd find their way to Virginia. The crickets and frogs had stopped their chirping, which meant that they were close.

Slowly, gingerly, he stepped forward, eyes scanning as far as the firelight would allow.

"Aaarrrrgh!"

He whirled around, straining to see which one of their number had yelled. Blood rushed in his ears as he noticed one of their number was no longer with them. Walter. His friend.

"They're among us, boys," he whispered.

Another shout, this time from his left, as an elderly man lifted off the ground, ripped from their presence with speed greater than any stallion. They were picking them off from above.

"Take cover!" he shouted, praying they wouldn't claim them all. "Give us Virginia! And then we will leave you. I swear it!"

Cackles drifted around them in the trees, more than one voice, all with an otherworldly feel.

"Hello boys," a gravelly voice startled him from behind. He spun around, lunging forward with his torch held high. "Burn, witch!"

His flame snuffed out.

48
REUNITED, LITTLE LOVE

"Chirp, chirp, chirp goes the little bird." She held the chick in both hands, stroking its soft hair, beckoning Virginia to come see.

"Cup your hands, my little love," she said, watching as her daughter's eyes sparkled at the sight of it. She was a lover of animals, that was for sure, and still had a hard time comprehending why Momma had to kill them for food. She tried explaining the circle of life to her, how they required nourishment for their bodies, but Virginia only saw the death of it.

"Wittle birdie!" she cried, cradling the small chick in her tiny, rosy hands. So precious. So innocent. The perfect age to stay forever.

"Hold tight to him, little love, but not too hard, we shan't hurt the birdie!" She turned to the basket, filled with everything she needed for this particular work. Her sisters had helped her rebuild, using what they could from the old hut and making it a place that she and Virginia were comfortable now. Sure, the child had asked about Aggy and "Papa", but Lenorea had been able to keep her entertained enough with minimal tears.

She was happy here, and safe. A child belonged with their Momma.

It had been Henry's idea, after all. Each time she communed with him, he'd asked about his baby sister, and when she'd be able to come and play. Sister Cecily had raised his body so that his spirit could stay with them. Virginia hadn't noticed the missing pieces or rotten flesh. She didn't seem to care. She watched as they ran together in the grass, a brother and sister reunited as they basked in the warmth of this beautiful day.

It warmed her scorched heart. Yes. Yes. They would be useful in the next step. Her large clay pot, naturally unharmed by Ananias' vengeful fire, bubbled and boiled with the mixture that would help her in the final days. She would test it on Virginia, to make sure it worked, before giving it to the others.

Alice's little bastard boys had gone down another path, forced into the servitude of Roshef, but she'd seen them just the other day, crawling and snarling in the forest on all fours. They seemed fine to her.

Now, back to her work.

Blood of crow. Yes.

Venomous spiders. Yes. Yes.

Poppy seed. Yes.

Blackberry root. She had them all. It was time to begin.

49

THE CHILDREN

Agnes opened the door seeking one last breath of fresh summer air before settling in for the night. The outlines of the other homes would soon be lost to darkness. Against the peach sky, black branches scratched and clawed at the lands beyond theirs, inviting the night to swallow them whole. Tonight should be bright with a full moon, and the extra light would ease her fears of what was crawling around in the dark.

She'd been baking most of the day, thankful that their field had given them the means to make a little extra bread for bartering with the others. She glanced back inside at Father, leaning with his legs straight out and back against the wall, fast asleep and snoring. He'd taken to staring at the woods for many hours each day, slacking on his daily work and all but forgetting any mention of prayers. She feared for his sanity, his hope in these desolate times. Food was scarce, with soups thinner than ever before, hardly enough to soothe the sting of hungry bellies across the town. Their numbers had dwindled, day by day, and now she'd be surprised if even half of their original number remained.

Roanoke. Another failed colony.

She'd given up hope that the governor would return for them with supplies. It's been near two years at this point, and his return seemed less likely with each passing day. They had no way to communicate, to share with him of their trials and spiritual warfare with the witches in the woods.

With her mother.

The men would hardly hunt anymore after their latest endeavour into the woods. She still wasn't sure how'd they made it out alive after what they'd told of it. Wickedness. All of it.

She thanked God for the few vegetables they were able to grow this year, but the summer had been hot, and so very dry, that many of their crops had burned beyond saving.

Lights flickered in windows across the way. More than likely it was Goody. Brewster, settling in the orphaned children she'd taken under her care after their parents died from one thing or another.

Agnes paused, listening to the sounds of the settlement as everyone wound down for a bit of rest. Crickets chirped over near the pond, bull-frogs croaked– though that sound didn't bring her much peace anymore, and the slight swish of leaves in the trees to accompany the cool breeze on her face.

But among the soothing serenade, there was something else.

Something different that she couldn't place. It was a shuffle, maybe footsteps, but there were many and they were moving quite rapidly. She stepped outside and glanced around, but didn't see anyone moving nearby. Strands of hair whipped across her face, as the wind was picking up.

Strange. The skies were clear, but the air suddenly felt as if there was a coming storm.

Never one to leave a question unanswered, Agnes searched for the source of the footsteps, rounding the corner of their home and heading further to the centre of the colony.

She heard the slam of wooden doors from the surrounding houses, but didn't see anyone exiting them. The chickens were roosting. The goats were all bedded.

Where could those sounds have come from?

Agnes turned, facing the treeline that she usually tried so very hard to ignore, and then– she saw them.

Standing in a line, swaying and singing to a song she couldn't hear, was a line of at least a dozen naked women, maybe more. Agnes froze at the sight of it, her blood thickening in her veins as she watched them beckon to the children that walk towards them. The land rose the closer one got to the forest, so she was able to see that some of the children had gone beyond the palisades, walking slowly, hand in hand, heading straight for the witches.

She had to do something. Anything. Now!

A small boy, not even ten years old walked past her, heading for the others. She reached for him, gently wrapping her fingers around his small wrist to pull him away.

"Not that way. Don't go with them!" she pleaded. The little boy turned, rage in his eyes and a thin snarl twisting his lips as he said, "let me *go*!".

"Ahh!" The child bit her, then ran away beyond her reach.

"Help!" she cried. "Someone help! The children! They're going! Please, can anyone hear me?"

She ran between the homes at the centre of town, banging on doors and screaming in between each one. "Awake! Awake! The children have gone!"

So many of their number settled when the sun did, choosing to rise with it and gain an early start to their day.

Mothers, Fathers, singletons, and the elderly rushed from their homes, running in the direction where Agnes pointed.

"Save the children!" she shouted, tears streaming down her face, knowing that the chances of stealing the children back from them was slim, but they had to try.

Mrs. Brewster appeared, a long rifle in her hand. "I've had enough of this!" she yelled, motioning for Agnes to hurry along behind her. "I'll put an end to it myself."

"Aggy!" Father and Jon were right behind them, armed as well.

Agnes hurried beside them. "We mustn't shoot if the children are near! I fear they've been trapped under some sort of spell. A possession. " She turned to Jon. "I tried stopping a little boy and he bit me and ran away."

"We'll kill them," Father said.

Facing off in a war like she'd only heard of through history tellings, she watched as the witches stood before them, arms protecting the children that cowered behind.

Father moved forward, without consulting anyone else and clearly with no care for his own safety.

"You've taken enough, Devil woman! Leave us be!" He marched onwards, aiming his rifle straight for the woman who used to be his wife.

Mother.

An older witch, with even longer matted, grey hair stepped forward. She waved her arms, beckoning something forth from within the trees. Giant shadows, no, horses...no– deer.

Ravenous deer, foaming at the mouth with their eyes glowing red under the influence of witchcraft or demons, Agnes didn't know, leapt out of the trees and stood in front of their masters, ready to defend.

They lowered their horns as a challenge, their antlers larger than any she'd ever seen. Either these beasts were bewitched, or they trampled straight out of the gates of hell. Goody Brewster ran forward, following Father into the fray.

"Father, look out!" Agnes tearfully clutched onto one of the ladies from the crossing that stood beside her. A mother to one of the children. She didn't even know her name.

The deers snorted, black smoke wafting from their flared nostrils. Beasts of the Devil. Bending low and brandishing their antlers, the deer charged for Father and Good Brewster. A loud *bang* thundered out of her weapon as she shot the deer, chunks of flesh flying off of its face– but it didn't slow. Still, the deer came, its skull exposed and one eye dangling from its socket. Goody Brewster screamed. The deer pierced her through the middle, lifting her high into the air and flinging her away.

We were no match for them. Mothers and fathers screamed, desperately running and crawling towards their children, but as the witches disappeared into the woods, the deer kept the colonists at bay.

Who could fight against the Devil himself? Against Demons?

Only God could save them now.

50
BIRTH

Leaves rustled around her in the trees as the branches clacked together, a sign of the winds of change as she would now birth the gift Roshef had given her. Her sisters had told her what it was like, to prepare her, but the last of the shadows born was months ago. It was her turn, and she was ready for it.

Light around them smothered as the sun sank into the earth, and with it her peace. The time had come to bring about a new beginning. Childbirth wasn't an unfamiliar sensation, as she had brought Agnes, Henry, and little Virginia into this world with no herbal support, choosing instead to experience it as her mother had. But this would be different. Darker. More pain. Each of her sisters that had accepted this power had given birth to their Croatoan, yet it manifested in different ways. For Rikka, it had been an animal, a beast that clawed its way out of her stomach with fangs ripping through her midriff, immediately taking flight into the night to hunt. She hoped it would not be the same for her, but trusted in them. In Him.

Sweat beaded on her brow, the rolling pressure in her middle pressing further down about her nethers. She lay upon the stone in the clearing where they met, her sisters stroking her hair, wiping her face with a cool cloth, Latsvna between her legs, massaging her opening to prepare for the birth. They cooed and sang to her, whispering words of comfort and peace as she settled her shaking limbs. Waves of pain rolled through her, bolts of lightning shooting down her legs and deep into her back. Her swollen belly surged, skin stretching out so far she thought surely the gift would break through at any moment.

Roshef waited to the side, hot steam rising from his snout as he waited for the gift, rooted next to the line of children from the colony, all muted, standing still. This gift was needed, to entrance them, to instill the darkness they themselves had claimed into the small bodies of the children.

"Aaaaaaagh!" She screamed as agony shot through her thighs once again. It was all happening so fast, her waters breaking just as the sun sank low, and there was no stopping it now. She tried to remember the pain, the throes of childbirth from before, but this was different. Fire rose in her chest as she heaved with each breath, Hell's gift inside of her clawing to break free.

"Make it stop! Get it out!" Her vision swam as the pain consumed her. They needed her. Needed this gift. There was no other way.

"Bear down, Lenorea." Rikka whispered in her ear. "Give birth to your gift. Push down, sister. You can do this. We will heal you when it's finished." She nodded, sweat dripping down her back. "Bear down. Bring your child into this world."

Roshef grunted. Watching. Waiting.

She pushed down with what little strength she could muster. She'd done this before. She could do it again. Her back arched and then slammed upon the stone, her sisters holding her legs wide as she felt claws emerging from within her. It was happening. Now.

Latsvna's eyes grew wide as she stared at the gift emerging from inside of her, damaging her, destroying her body. She screamed, one of her sisters placing the cool cloth between her teeth. "Bite down, Lenorea. There you go. Feel the pain. The gift. Bring it to us!"

She cried again, biting down on the cloth as she pushed and pushed, ready for this nightmare to end.

She writhed in pain against their hold, her insides surely torn apart as the beast stretched her further open. Black smoke rose from between her legs as the shadow crawled out from inside of her. Long arms with black claws emerged, her gift finally making its way into the world. It clung to the earth as it pulled from inside her, slowly reaching, writhing and gasping as it drew its first breath. She screamed as the rest of it left her, falling upon the ground as black, ichorous liquid spilled from within. Tears streamed down her cheeks as she saw it, unlike anything she'd ever given birth to before, rising from the earth, stretching, growing, standing before her as a full grown man.

Its eyes were scarlet red, shining out in the night as she took in the sight of her gift. Half shadow, half man, covered in a tar like she'd seen back in England. Her gift sucked in a breath, drinking in the cool, night air as it turned to Roshef and nodded. Blood pooled beneath as she felt her own life fading from her. Surely she wouldn't die. She couldn't. Her gift was here to help her achieve that which she most desired. Latsvna was beneath her legs, placing her hands upon her with the warmth she'd felt before, back when she had attempted to take her own life. The warmth of healing. Her breaths settled as it consumed her, burned her, as her fear was replaced with the knowledge that they would take away her wounds.

The shadow man moved from child to child, stabbing out their eyes as they stood unmoving. He filled their empty sockets with black orbs, the same as those Roshef had given to Alice's boys. He hadn't done that for all of them as her service was required for this. Nothing in life was given without a price, and tonight, here in the woods upon this stone, she had paid it. She felt the power of Croatoan grow stronger within her, her own energy healing her torn insides along with Latsvna. She pulled the cloth from between her teeth, using it to wipe away the blood from her skin. Tonight, she would rise.

Tonight, they would visit the colony.

51

A DARK DAY

Dearest Lord, I come to thee in the hopes that thou has an answer, a whisper, a sign of something better to come because I am lost on this day. Some say Revelation has come, that judgment day is upon us, and I cannot find within myself the argument to make against it. We are lost, Lord, both in hope and in our path. Too many times have I feared for my life in these last two years upon Roanoke Island. Too many times have I watched those I love suffer and die from one cause or another. Please, dear Lord, please help us now. Hear our cries as we beg for forgiveness and put our faith in thee. Perhaps it is that our faith hasn't been where it should be. We pray, Lord. We fast. I humbly seek your counsel and resolution in these dark times. Save my soul from the trials of this world, so that I might look upon your sweet face in Glory Land when I am destined to meet it. My body is weak, and my hope is even weaker. Cleanse my soul of all the sins that stain it, wash me in the blood of the lamb, and hear my thanks for your blessings upon me. You've given me life, strong hands, able back to work, and a Godly wife. I am undeserving of any such gifts, and yet I have not spent enough time in thanks, solely focused on my sorrows. Forgive me, Lord, for these are earthly troubles, but my mind wrought with worry o'er our situation. They've taken the children, Lord. I fear they are sacrificed or God help them, possessed as Eleanor Dare. I do not understand it, nor the way in which you work, but God I ask for your healing hands upon this place, these people. Shepherd us through the valley, or at least make it so that our passing comes soon. We cannot bear the whole of it much longer. In Jesus name I pray, Amen.

The sun never rose this morning.

Whether it be an echo of the broken families' hearts or a sign of Revelation, one thing was clear in Jonathan's mind– today would hold the vilest of evils. There was no sunlight, no solutions at hand, and truth be told he wasn't sure there was any hope to be had, either. The air was thick, heavy, and a dark blanket of clouds blotted out any hope for light even if the sun had risen. He didn't understand it, but at this point, he didn't understand the reasoning behind too many things.

Without plentiful meat for eating, their muscles grew weaker with each passing day. Their foe had all but squashed the pillars of their pitiful colony, a valid attempt at settling in this New World, dashed on the rocks of the shore. He knew it in his heart, as he and Agnes had discussed it many a time– they were being punished for stealing the land away from the Natives. They came here in greed, and their vision was destined to fail before they even stepped foot on the shore.

He accepted it; he really did, but that didn't help to ease his suffering in the least. He sat at the edge of the colony, just outside the palisades to serve as a watchman. Why they hadn't had a watcher all this time was beyond him, as that could have saved them from many a surprise from the evils in the woods. He'd volunteered as the first watch, unable to stay inside as the weeping mothers and fathers mourned among their friends.

He pulled a ragged cloth out of his trousers, dunking it in the water pail that rested on the ground next to him. The cold water felt good on the back of his neck, his forehead, wiping away the perspiration of fear.

With the darkness of the day, Ananias had had the brilliant inspiration to place a line of torches in front of the palisades, enabling the watcher to see. If any wickedness showed itself or slithered out from between the trees, he would surely see and raise the alarm. His back to the safety of the colony, it would be a hard-pressed feat for one to sneak up behind him and catch him unawares.

His eyes flitted in every direction. He strained to hear every bark, every rooster's crow. They would not catch him unaware this time.

As if bid by his very thoughts, Jonathan saw movement at the edge of the trees. It was a small shape, larger than a fox but smaller than those demonic deer, crawling closer into the light. It walked on all fours, bouncing as it came.

He inhaled sharply, choking on his own spittle at the sight of what emerged from the trees– the dirtier, empty skin of Alice Tilley.

It walked on all fours, pouncing nearer to him as if it were a dog. He sucked in breath, parting his lips to scream, to sound the alarm– but no sound came. He choked on his own words, grasping at his neck, his temple throbbing as he tried to get the words out.

Jonathan stamped on the ground, turned to beat on the palisades with his fists, only to have those frozen, too.

Gliding out of the trees behind the skin of Alice, what used to be Eleanor appeared, flanked on either side by the children. They galloped as he'd seen a primate do, on the pads of their feet and the tips of their fingers. The closer they came, he witnessed their bared teeth and snarled lips.

But that wasn't the most fearful thing about them... no.

It was their eyes.

Glassy black orbs rested in their sockets where once innocent eyes were. These children were no longer as they were. It was as he feared; they were possessed.

Jonathan tried to rally his muscles, to coax them to move, but against his best efforts they remained still. He was a pillar, unmoving, at the mercy of the coming horde.

"Go, my children," Eleanor whispered.

The black-eyed children crept towards him, pace by pace, licking their lips and imitating the softest of growls. Tears fell down his cheeks as he realised this was it. This was his end– at the hands of innocent, possessed children.

Their fingers crawled up his legs, up his arms. He pulled with every fibre of his being, willing his limbs to move, praying that they would– but no mercy came. Tiny teeth bit into his flesh with hardly a sound. His screams were silenced in his throat. No one would know; none could come to his aid.

For the entirety of his life he had fought. Fought against his poverty-stricken beginnings to rise among society. He'd struggled against his nature, the temptations of his earthly body to try and live as a righteous man. He'd toiled in these wilds, against hunger and plagues and the damned witches themselves, fighting for a better life for himself and Agnes Rose. And yet, here in the end, in a fate worse than the death that now consumed him, he was stripped of his ability to fight and survive. Pain consumed his every thought as the children tore into his flesh. Known as the one who would never give up, there was nothing now that he could do. This was the thread of the coarse rope of death that drew ever tighter around him.

If even he couldn't speak it out loud, he would bid his farewell in his mind. Even as small hands clawed at his skin, ripping him open, spilling his innards upon the ground, Jonathan sought peace. The children forced him to the ground, the wetness of his tears now mixing with blood as they gnawed at his face.

Agnes. I love you. Thank you for the time we've had together and know that I await the day we shall meet again. It is my time.

He closed his eyes, praying for release. *Our Father, who art in Heaven, hallowed be thy name...*

52

FEAST OF THE FLESH

Reverend Winslow – August 1590

"There shall be such a day wherein we suffer no longer, my sons and daughters of Christ." Reverend Winslow stared down at his flock, gathered at the altar in fervent prayer for the children, in a vigil, of sorts, to beg of God Almighty to bring them home.

"I may tell therefore, that this dreadful confusion of the plagues and signs of a darker presence among us does yet tell us of the coming of the Lord. He is establishing his Kingdom. Right here! Right now. We are at the cusp of the very presence of our Lord thy God on earth to rule for a thousand years. We will welcome him. Cherish him."

Murmured prayers that filled their meeting house were peppered with sobs, from mothers and fathers alike, begging for forgiveness and asking for their children. "I beseech thee...pray! Pray for your sons! Pray for your daughters! Lift their names high into the heavens so that God can hear them."

"George! Little Georgie!"

"Marta!"

"Thomas! Bring me my Thomas!"

Reverend Winslow bowed his head low, closing his eyes and whispering prayers over the anguished flock. Their children were as good as dead, but he wouldn't speak it aloud.

No.

This evil might yet be stronger than God Almighty, from what he'd seen– but he wouldn't show it, wouldn't let them know. Peace tames the flock and hope keeps them going.

He heard the doors of the church open and shut. More believers were coming to join them in prayer. He bent low, whispering into Goody Archard's hair.

"Lord, God Almighty bring peace to your children. Ease their tender hearts. Make a lamp unto their feet and a light unto their path, Lord, as they are sorely afraid of the wickedness in this world that clutches their babes, now. Protect the children, set them free from Satan's grip and bring them back home again to join us. We rejoice in you, Lord, and thank you for the blessings of children that these fine followers have been given. Bring their children back to us, Lord. In your holiest of names I fervently pray, Amen."

"Amen."

He opened his eyes only to jump back from the altar. Standing just inside the door, eyes blacker than ten times black, stood the children for whom they prayed.

"Dear Lord." Trembles wracked his body, the bible held within his hands nearly falling to the floor.

Goody Archard looked up at him with tear-stained cheeks and red, puffy eyes. She followed his gaze and screamed, joy intermingled with relief.

"My boy! My precious boy has come home to me!" She ran to him, arms outstretched– but the child didn't move.

None of them did.

They stood by the door, blank stares fixated upon their faces, with a greyish colour to their skin. As Goody Archard drew nearer to them, one little boy, George Archard, stepped forward with his arms outstretched, reaching for a hug.

"Momma's comin' Georgie, Momma's comin'."

"Goody Archard No! Step awa–" but before he could finish his warning, the black-eyed child lept upon his mother, tearing her flesh away with his teeth. Still perched upon her as a predator on its prey, Georgie sneered at them, his mother's blood dripping down his chin. The other parents screamed, diving for safety under the benches of the meeting house with others clamoring to escape through the side door into the night.

Quick. Think. What to do. What to do?

He glanced down at the bible he hadn't realized that he'd dropped on the floor. Its pages were opened to Genesis– the beginning.

Of course.

Genesis 22. The offering of Isaac. The Lord Provides.

"Capture them!" he yelled. The Lord required proof of their devotion; it was all so clear. These children were of wickedness now, and before God would help them vanquish the witches, he required a test of faith– through sacrifice. As Abraham with Isaac, as God himself with their Lord and Savior, Jesus Christ– they must sacrifice their children.

Black-eyed children ran amok in the meetinghouse, pouncing on their mothers and fathers with the single intent to kill. Their parents fought back, a horrific dance of life and death as they endeavoured to keep the children at bay without dealing them greater harm. But this act of mercy was their last. The slightest bit of hesitation allowed the children a chance to strike at the throat.

"They're of the Devil now, kinfolk! Strike them down, but don't kill them! We have a use for them, yet!" As some of the children were held down by their fathers, tied with ripped cloths from their mother's dresses, others escaped out the door. He'd have to deal with them later. He prayed for the other souls unaware in their beds.

Why had Jonathan not warned them? He had been at post this night.

Dearest Lord. The young Carver has a soft heart for the children. He exhaled, slowly. Perhaps they'd already gotten to him. Keep him safe, Lord. Protect thy kin. His heart thundered in his chest as the end of time unfolded before him still.

"Has anyone a knife?" he called.

"A knife? These are our *children*, Reverend," one of them cried. "What do you mean by this? You'll not hurt them!" The parents of the black-eyed children now faced him, their struggling children growling and snapping, restrained, on the floor behind.

Heat rose in his cheeks, the fires of salvation roaring through his veins, strengthening, invigorating him. He knew what was best for them. He knew the word. He was charged by God himself in this.

"As your spiritual leader, I *command* that one of you produce a knife. Either we sacrifice these minions of Hell together, or I'll lock you inside these very halls and burn it down from the outside!"

None spoke. They knew their place.

Good. This must be done.

Just outside the window, a flash of orange met his eye as one of the neighboring homes was on fire. He could taste the smoke of it on his tongue. Someone in the night was already setting their village to flame. Time was of the essence.

"A knife, I say!" he roared.

One older father, his wife long dead from the trials of her final childbirth, produced a knife concealed under his sleeve. He nodded, backing away and never meeting Reverend Winslow's eye.

"And what if it was *your* daughter, Reverend? What if Emme were taken with witchery instead? Would you do this? Offer Emme?" Goody Bishop scowled and blocked his view of her writhing daughter.

"As Abraham trusted in the Lord to bring about the will of God, so shall I."

Crash. The heavy doors of the meetinghouse swung open wide, all hellfire and damnation happening beyond.

Standing in the middle, covered in blood, was Ananias Dare.

53

HELLFIRE AND DAMNATION

ANANIAS DARE - AUGUST 1590

The vision behind the carved, wooden doors of the meeting house was not at all what he expected. Reverend Winslow stood at the pulpit, knife clutched firmly in one fist with his bible in the other. Black-eyed children lay on their stomachs, under the weight of their parents, growling and spitting and desperately attempt to escape. They were small, but mighty. But he knew there were more— he'd fought them off himself outside.

They were overrun. The colony was in shambles. Fires burning, people running, those that were still alive were hiding in fear that the children would come for them next.

"You've got to leave!" he yelled. "The roof is burning!" Where the fire came from, he didn't know. Perhaps the children had set it themselves, but he feared their new mothers, the daughters of the Devil, were slithering amidst them all in the darkness, in their nakedness, waiting for the moment to burn it all to the ground.

"Come quickly!" he shouted again.

Reverend Winslow kicked a chair that was already knocked over beside the pulpit. "What are you waiting for? Let's go, let's go! Out with ye! Out into the night!"

But as the parents tried to move their stricken children outside, more than one of their bastardized brood rallied with the strength of a bear, seizing the moment to overtake their parents and tear flesh from their bones. Blood pooled on the meetinghouse floor.

He ran from the sight, back out into the hellscape that was the Roanoke Colony. He hadn't seen Eleanor, nor Virginia, or the boys- but he had seen Alice.

Or, what was left of her at least.

Galloping on all fours, in between the rows of houses on fire and black-eyed children feeding on their parents, he caught a glimpse of the skin beast as it ran among them.

God had surely forsaken them all.

Reverend Winslow burst from the meetinghouse, his dagger held high. Ananias watched as he ran in circles, screams surrounding them as the flames roared high into the night sky. The nearest child was bent over, feeding on his mother. Ananias's breath caught in his throat as he watched the reverend sneak up behind, raising his blade high and plunging it into the boy.

Ananias froze, his own blood rushing in his ears as he watched Reverend Winslow stab the child, again and again, throwing his head back and cackling. The reverend had surely lost his wits in this. "Ah HA! God! Are you happy, now? A sacrifice for our Lord! Cleanse the world of this evil! Save us!"

Yet, nothing changed.

The fires still raged, the children still fed, and the screams of their kinfolk still pierced both of their ears- a symphony of the end of times.

Ananias crouched behind a water trough, heart hammering in his chest as still he watched Reverend Winslow.

The reverend looked around, frantically, crying out in agony to the sky. He again sank his blade into the boy's flesh, tearing off a piece.

"Then will I walk stubbornly in mine anger against you," he cried, "and I will also chastise you seven times more according to your sins."

The reverend quoted scripture. Ananias could see the rage in his eyes. The fury. The hatred.

"And ye shall eat the flesh of your sons, and the flesh of your daughters shall ye devour!"

Ananias swallowed the bile that rose in his throat as the reverend raised the bit of flesh to his mouth, tearing at it with his teeth. He chewed it, gnashing his jaws against the forbidden communion, then swallowed.

Hell had come. Ananias turned, praying he could find more weapons to defend the ones that lived. They would run away from here, far away, and beg forgiveness and shelter from anyone who might have mercy. Manteo yet lived, or at least he was still alive before Ananias had stormed into the meetinghouse as a warning. Perhaps his people would take them in. That was his goal now, to get away, to survive.

Damn the New World. He wanted to go home. But first, he'd do what he could to rid the colony of the scourge that had plagued them for far too long. It was his fault they were here, after all. Eleanor had promised revenge against him. Her wrath had rallied these witches against them.

But she would not have her revenge so long as he drew breath.

He scanned the fiery, blood-slick chaos of their once quiet colony. His friends, brothers and sisters in Christ, lay scattered among the wreckage either dead or nearly there. Others nursed wounds, peering out from their hiding places for fear of another attack from the children.

Small shadows drifted around them, kicking up dust as they went. He could hear them growling, shuffling in the night. It was the children, stalking and preparing for their next kill as serpents slithering towards their prey, ready to sink their teeth.

"With me, kin!" he shouted, racing across the hellscape to reach the armoury. Surely they had weapons left. Spears. Arrows. Anything. Not many of their number remained, but those that did and were within earshot of his rallying cries limped forward to join him. The door of the armoury was open, yet little remained inside. He grabbed what he could, tossing their final defenses against these hellish beasts to any who could hold them.

"We stay together!" he shouted, hoping they could hear him over the roar of the flames. He hadn't seen Jon, or Agnes, and feared the worst for them. Agnes always had a kind heart for children. With Henry, Virginia, she'd even taken care of Alice's boys when he selfishly brought them into his home. Replacing his wife with their mother. What a fool he was. A sinful, wretched beast no better than they, consumed with his self-serving nature that led them to this place. The dead lay all around. Perished, because of him.

He shifted his gaze among the tearful faces that looked to him to lead. If Jon were here, he'd know exactly what to do. His son-in-law was brave and full to the brim with solutions. Jon was twice the man that he was. He must carry on without him.

"Stand together! If any of them come near, we end them on sight!" He motioned for the others to join him, closing in with their backs to each other, facing in all directions. He wanted to be strong, to have faith in this moment that God would carry them through to the end, but deep within his soul he feared it. A quick death would be a mercy instead of how he'd seen the others die. Their screams still haunted his thoughts, their trembling hands reaching for him as he moved past, praying, begging, crying out for help as they were ravaged by the children.

But it wasn't really death he feared– it was what came after. After all his sins and wrongdoings, his feeble trust, and the putting aside of God's will for his own desires, Ananias feared his fate was already decided. He would burn in the lake of fire, destined for tortures unknown for all of eternity. His judgement would be quick, much quicker than a merciful death, and surely God would cast him out without a second thought. Judgement had come, and he was ill-prepared for it.

A child came running, his once jovial grin twisted into a vicious sneer. He'd seen this boy, washing clothes with his mother, playing swords in the yard with his older brother, chasing after the chickens and laughing as they flocked. And now he came for them.

A woman screamed to his right as the boy drew near, creeping, crawling on the ground on his toes and fingertips. She raised her spear, one of Manteo's design, and with a pained shriek, jabbed her weapon straight through his chest. The child fell, violently twisting and shaking on the ground in the throes of what Ananias could only assume was a demon's death. For that was what these children had been turned into.

Yet even as he thought it, the child's face softened, all wickedness melting from his face– except for the blackened eyes. The child clutched his wound, blood spilling around his fingers as he stared at Ananias. Eyes wide, seeing the horrors all around, the child uttered a final word that tore at Aninias's heart.

"Why?"

He thought of Henry.

Another came, this one cut down with a swift slash from a man directly behind him. He heard the swish of the blade and winced at the thunk as it met with flesh. He didn't turn around, for fear that one would seize the opportunity to sneak up behind him.

Maybe they could do this, standing together, ending the threat of the children one by one. Their homes were destroyed, and they would surely leave this place and beg for safety among the natives of this land. Under the sorrow, the fear, the depths of despair devoid of all joy, the stirrings of hope fluttered within him.

They could do this. It was now a matter of outlasting the children.

Yet, as soon as he had thought it, larger shadows cast across the ground as their worst of fears surrounded them.

The witches had come to join their new children in the fray.

54
BLOWN APART

"Hello, husband." His clothes were bloodied. He must have encountered her children. Yes, yes. She sauntered towards him, adding a sway in her hips unlike she'd ever done when still his earthly wife. There was fun to be had here, screams and pain and an opportunity for torture, and she was of a mind to enjoy it– to relish in her revenge against him.

Ananaias stepped forward, leaving the pitiful settlers that remained behind him to fend for themselves. He probably didn't even know their names, but she did. She knew everyone in the village, and knew them all as they died.

Ananias shouted at her. "Eleanor, please! *Leave* this place. Let them be. You've made your point against me, yet these others didn't deserve it." He aimed his rifle at her, stepping slowly forward. "They've not wronged you, Eleanor. I swear, I'll do it. I'll shoot you mid-breast, so help me God."

She grinned. "God does not live here, Ananais. Not in the wilds. He never did."

Bang.

The searing sting of the bullet grazing her arm shocked her more than the fact that Ananias had done it. He'd pulled the trigger, trained at her, with all intentions to end her life.

She raised her arm, summoning the strength of the forest, pulling deep from the molten core of rage that boiled inside her at all times. She raised her hand, and with a single thought, slammed him through the air as if he'd been yanked backward by a rope. He broke through the wall of the nearest house, its thatched roof already ablaze. Hmph. The Harvie's home.

As she carefully stepped through the blown-apart wall after him, she had to dodge a flying object coming towards her.

"First, you shoot at me, and now you're throwing pots?" Her husband glared at her, the fires of hatred burning in his eyes. She laughed, "That's no warm welcome for your wife, Ananias."

He threw another, yet this one landed with unexpected force. The bastard. She shifted her eyes, searching for something, anything that she could use against him.

She spotted it. As Ananais lunged for her, she moved her hands again, better prepared for the burning pain that came with using this power of Croatoan, and sent the cabinet flying for him.

He crumpled, the weight of the cabinet knocking him to his knees, and yet he raised his eyes to meet hers once more. "Eleanor, please. Have mercy." He dodged her next attack.

Damn.

"You were a kind woman, once. A gentle woman." He dodged again, rolling away from her advances and clamouring to his feet, unsteady. He was quickly exhausting himself, which was in her favor.

Heat flashed in her cheeks as he reached for his rifle again. She hurled more of the broken wood and dishes at him, peppering him with blows against the whole of his body. Surely that would break some of his bones.

"I am neither kind..." she advanced towards him, "nor gentle, you selfish bastard!"

But Ananias was ready. He jabbed his rifle straight into her face, knocking her to the floor. He battered her limbs, the crack of bones and searing pain a welcomed sensation.

Yes, yes. Pain was something she was well-acquainted with now.

Burning pitch fell on the ground around them. How he could breathe among the acrid, black, plumes of smoke escaped her, but she would have to finish this soon or they would both succumb to the flames.

"We could have been happy together, Ananais. Like we were in the beginning." She rose, resetting her bones as her sisters had taught her. Again, she witnessed the fear in his eyes.

Yes, yes, little husband. Feast your eyes upon me. Drink it in.

"You cannot prevail against me." Raising her crooked fingers once more, she flung the rifle from his hands. He needn't have it anymore.

Ananais backed against the wall, eyes darting all around. He was looking for a way out, but there wasn't one, as she was too quick for him now. With this realisation he stared at her, a broken man, eyes filled with sorrow and hope departed, filled with the fear of death.

She crossed the room, clutching at the whole of his throat with her hand, squeezing until he gasped for breath. This was her chance. The final moment. She could finally bring about the revenge she craved.

"We still have children in this world, Eleanor," he choked out. "Agnes. Virginia." She loosened her grip. "And Agnes is newly with child!" The last of his muttered pleas surprised her, but no matter.

She scoffed, releasing him. "We? You mean I, husband." He narrowed his eyes, his mouth open with unspoken questions.

"Aye. They're not your children. Agnes might yet be yours, but Virginia surely isn't. She's the cobbler's from down the lane in England." It wasn't true, but before he died she wanted him to believe it, to feel a tiny piece of the pain she felt at *his* betrayals. "My heart never returned to you, Ananais. Not in earnest. Not after that first time."

There it was. The look she'd waited for from him.

Ananias looked at her, his face set in a pleading frown. "Even here among the wilds, my intentions were true in starting again."

Defeat.

With speed she wasn't prepared for, Ananais reached for a pitcher, throwing it high above her head. She cackled. "You missed."

But as the burning roof crashed upon her, searing flame contacting her flesh, consuming her whole, she knew he'd done it intentionally. Ananias escaped through the hole in the wall behind her, and, with her hair ablaze, she raced after him.

The chaos of their intentions still raged outside, her sisters chasing the last of the colonists as they attempted to flee. One of her sisters cried, "As you've taken from the forest and from those who came before you, we command you to replace them!"

Goody Archer froze mid step as her sister turned her into a tree. One of the younger men cried out as he was rooted in the ground, his legs hardening, transforming into bark, his arms stretching out as her sister changed them into branches.

They wanted so desperately to be a part of this new world, and now they'd have it. As planned, they transformed the colonists into the landscape, into boulders, into trees, destined to remain a part of the land forever.

In the clearing between the burning homes, Ananais ran from her in a bid to escape. She followed behind him, stopping only for a moment to dunk her head in the water trough to put out the flames with a sickening hiss. He turned, seeing her closing in upon him, reaching for anything he could use against her.

She spotted a body just to the side, raising her arms to lift it and fling it towards Ananais. He crashed to the ground underneath it.

Emme Winslow, the reverend's daughter.

"I can kill you with my very thoughts!" she screamed at him.

"Then do it! Do it, Eleanor. Kill me if it will end this madness!" His bloodied face streamed with tears now. "I'm sorry! I'm so sorry. I wronged you, betrayed you. God have my soul, I know I deserve it."

She paused, surprised that after all that had come to pass, this man had apologized. And in this moment, with her hopeless husband before her, she felt the stirrings of something other than rage within her. She hadn't thought it possible, and yet, inside her scorched soul she felt pity for him. Sorrow. How could it be that they'd come to this?

She thought of the first days. The time when they had courted in secret after meeting in church. Their wishes. Their plans. What a life they had desired to share together. And as their chance at a fresh start crumbled to ash around them, she suddenly yearned for it again. She parted her lips to respond, but before she could, a scream from behind met her ears.

"Aaaarrrgh!"

Sharp metal plunged into her back, ripping through her muscles. She reached behind, searing pain blinding her vision as she grasped her attacker on both sides of their skull and twisted. She didn't care to look at them. Instantly, the neck between her fingers cracked and broke. The body buckled within her grasp, the weight of it pulling her forward. She stared into the lifeless eyes of the one she had just killed.

No! How could this be? What had she done? The weight of the war she raged against them crashed upon her, the truth of her actions staring at her with a deadened gaze.

It was her daughter, Agnes Rose.

55

CARVING CROATOAN

ANANIAS DARE - AUGUST 1590

"*Give them a warning...*"

Even to his last, he must not allow the knowledge of their disappearance to crumble in ashes. Those that return, whenever they do, must know the fate of the Roanoke Colony.

Somehow, he would tell them.

He searched the surrounding woods, palms pressed together in prayer, blood trickling down about his wrists. Surely, with the weight of his sins, God had abandoned him, neglected them all in their darkest of nights. Yet, even in this final hour Ananias prayed for a sliver of mercy upon his poisoned soul.

God, help me. Give me a way.

The scrap of paper, ripped from the Word not three nights ago still lingered in his pocket— but he had no quill.

What to use. What to use. He felt his soaked trousers, desperate for an answer. He plunged his hand into the pocket concealed in his trousers and winced at the bite to his finger. Aye! He still had a knife, albeit small, often used for the skinning of rabbits and squirrels to provide for his family— but those days were gone. He'd forgotten it.

Blood then? He could scrawl a word of warning on the scrap and pin it to the tree. Such abominable thoughts these were, to besmirch the words guided by the hand of God, but he must warn the others of their trials. The governor needed to know.

And yet, those that followed would have a better chance of reading it if he carved a warning into the tree.

He gathered what little strength survived in his body and limped to the gatepost, the forefront entry into their desolate colony, the ruins of hope for a new generation, and set to carving.

God, giveth the time. Allow me to do this.

Shearing the bark proved a difficult task, the sticky sap mixing with his blood, causing his hand to slip on the knife's handle.

Damn this blade.

The effort pained his swollen fingers, but the crude letters were bold and legible once finished.

CROATOAN.

There was a chance this message would remain unseen. Their powers hide within this word. He must carve as many as he could muster, further from the fire's spread on the large oak under which his own family had rested on the Sabbath day when they first arrived. Memories washed over him. His son's playful steps. The new babe suckling at his wife's breast. Their daughter, laughing and basking in the sun's warmth upon her face.

The blade faltered this time, morality's weakness and pangs of sadness racking his soul. How far they had fallen from those days. He pushed through.

With the last mark of the first "O" finished, he glanced behind to view the colony.

When he turned around…her twisted face sneered at him from beside the tree.

He gasped, the knife slipping from his grasp to fall to the ground.

In this moment, staring into the eyes of hell itself, he stood still as stone. Hell hath no fury like the evil swirling in the black pits where once there had been a sparkling blue. He should run for safety, or fight back, but no power of God or man could move him from where he stood.

"Join me, Ananias," she purred.

"You killed our daughter! Our colony! How could I join you now?" He cried, tears mixing with the blood upon his face. "I'll never join you."

Eleanor placed her crooked hand upon his cheek, just like she used to do before, long before they travailed to this cursed new world.

"But together, we can bring her back. Unlock the gifts settled deep inside you, and help me raise her from the dead. We can do it, her mother and father. Together."

He trembled as her rancid breath blew into his face. Her eyes swirled as a night sky, speckled stars twinkling within them.

To their left, stepping out of the shadows and into the light cast by their burning colony, came the form of one he'd seen too many times since his death.

It was Henry, rotted flesh peeling from his bones, yet smiling up at him, holding onto the hand of another. It was their smallest babe, the first of the colonists born on Roanoke Island, staring up at him with blackened eyes, her mouth dripping in blood from those that she'd killed. Her third birthday would come tomorrow, a thought recalled from some distant portion of his mind.

"We can have our fresh start, Ananias. Here, in the woods, surrounded by love and powers untold, gifted to us by the forest."

How could she...how dare she speak of a fresh start.

As much as he wanted to, he could not look away from Virginia. He paused, wiping the tears from his eyes. Their love. Their children. Had all of their trials been for naught?

But if he considered what she suggested, truly joining as a family, if yet a bastardised one, they could be united. Together again, starting anew, as he'd yearned for when they crossed onto these shores.

But what of God?

Ananias tightened his fists, knowing the answer. God wouldn't have him anyway after the choices he'd made. The false saviour had allowed for every atrocity to transpire against his family. No, God would not welcome him to the pearly gates at the end of life. He was forsaken, either way.

He tipped his head, hardly a nod but an answer nonetheless, towards Eleanor. She smiled in response, and for the first time in too many months, he smiled at her in return. Perhaps it was time to embark upon a path few were brave enough to travel.

Or hurt enough.

On all fours, galloping towards them as if she were a dog, the skin beast, Alice, settled beside Henry as he patted her head.

Eleanor smiled again, more broadly this time, bending to collect his forgotten knife from the ground. "Hold out your arm," she whispered.

He obliged, looking away as she carved a word he'd come to know well into his flesh.

Croatoan.

She stepped back, motioning to the children as she backed away. "I've finished my part, but there is another whom you'll have to receive a gift from in order to join us." She nodded to the trees, where a large, dark presence stepped forward, with the torso of a man but the head of an antlered beast.

"This is Roshef." Eleanor smiled at Ananias as he worked to settle the tremble that enveloped his body. "He's delighted to meet you, husband." His wife and two children turned, heading back to the burning colony. The skin beast, Alice, trailed behind them.

Around him he heard chanting as the demon stepped forward.

56

THE RETURN

GOVERNOR JOHN WHITE - AUGUST 1590

"*It hath been three years since I've last laid my eyes upon this land which we intended to settle upon in earnest, breaking away from the ills of England and embarking upon a new path in the strange, new world. Politics and little support prevented my return for too long, and now, I fear for what we might find. It was dark upon arrival, after many a shaken night upon the sea, and we soon realised that in the winds we had overshot our landing intent by a half a mile, it seemed. We espied towards the North end of the island of Roanoke, a great smoke rising from betwixt the trees, in the very same location in which we'd left our planters three year ago. A good sign! Or so I thought. Towards the smoke, we rowed, and when close enough to landing let our grapnel fall near the shore. We sounded a great call, and a trumpet announcing our coming, yet none ran to meet us upon the shore. We played many a tune of English songs that our planters would find familiar, a signal that we were friendly and not of the Spanish scourge that pillaged along the shores of the wilds. Again, we heard no answer. Upon our landing on the shore, and the following investigation of the colony behind the palisades, what we discovered will therein not be recorded in the written word save for this penning of mine own. It was a ghastly sight, one fit to set my comrades into heaving sickness, with prayers to God of salvation cried out at the sight of it. Bodies, asunder. Crimson stains upon the ground. "Croatoan" was carved within a tree, yet had no meaning attached to it. We will not speak of it, nor describe the sights in detail to any other living man, for God had surely cast upon this settlement a terrible reckoning, a reckoning at Roanoke, at which we soon departed for fear of carrying the curse upon ourselves. May God have mercy on their souls."*

The End